Jess,

I hope my favourite Scotland readers enjoys the story as much as I did writing it.

# DEFECTOR
## IN OUR
# MIDST

*A THRILLER*

# TOM
# FITZGERALD

**MASCOT®**
**BOOKS**

*For Jeanette, Kelci, Madisyn, Hannah, Isaac, and Brock.*

## "Ulysses"
### Alfred, Lord Tennyson

'Tis not too late to seek a newer world.
Push off, and sitting well in order smite
The sounding furrows; for my purpose holds
To sail beyond the sunset, and the baths
Of all the western stars, until I die.
It may be that the gulfs will wash us down:
It may be we shall touch the Happy Isles,
And see the great Achilles, whom we knew
Though much is taken, much abides; and though
We are not now that strength which in old days
Moved earth and heaven; that which we are, we are;
One equal temper of heroic hearts,
Made weak by time and fate, but strong in will
To strive, to seek, to find, and not to yield.

Requests for permission to make copies of any part of the work should be submitted online at info@mascotbooks.com or mailed to Mascot Books, 560 Herndon Parkway #120, Herndon, VA 20170.

ISBN-10: 1620865408
ISBN-13: 9781620865408
CPSIA Code: PRB0514A

Library of Congress Control Number: 2013955284

Printed in the United States

**www.mascotbooks.com**

# DEFECTOR IN OUR MIDST

## A THRILLER

# Prologue

## St. Lucia, Caribbean Islands

If only he had been paying attention.

As it was with two young soldiers high in the Hawaiian mountains decades earlier, so it was with Chen Wu. If only someone had noticed what the radar equipment had clearly detected, Pearl Harbor may have been averted. And had Chen Wu been more attentive that day, the next catastrophe rolling its way toward the U.S. may have been prevented as well. But Chen Wu was not paying attention. He was checking his email messages on his phone. With each distracted step, his sandals slapped against his feet and moved his fate into the malevolent hands of his captor. If he hadn't given CJ, his four-year-old son, permission to run ahead with the room key, he might have noticed the door to the room already unlocked and partially open. If he hadn't been absorbed in checking his messages as he approached the doorway, he might have seen the smattering of blood on the pristine tile or the towels and beach toys scattered across the floor. Chen was oblivious to the scene of horror that awaited him inside his posh resort room.

He absentmindedly took the key from his son, who stood rooted in front of the door, and crossed the threshold, unaware that the fate of his life now belonged to someone else. As Chen stepped into his palatial suite, he froze, stilled by the shock of seeing his wife gagged and bound on the floor in front of him. Her hands were tied behind her back and tethered to ropes fastened around her ankles. His beautiful wife lay motionless and bleeding from the side of her face. As Chen instinctively turned to shove his son away from the danger, a sharp sensation stung the back of his neck. His vision blurred and his legs turned to Jell-O. The last thing he could remember was the sound of his son's voice as if it came from the end of a long tunnel.

"Daddy…"

The Chinese government had watched Chen's progress since elementary school. His last two years at MIT were spent expanding the boundaries of electromagnetism. The student had become the professor, and Chen became the preeminent expert in his field. Had there not been a downturn in U.S. defense spending, he would have been offered millions by a barrage of defense contractors. But it was not to be. It was the Chinese government who took the budding Einstein back home and put his immense knowledge to use in creating the world's most powerful electromagnetic weapon.

Chen's breakthrough discovery came while he and his team were in their laboratory, located in a discreet building in downtown Nanjing, China. After years of failures, they finally crossed the threshold of success. In the fifth year of the project, they constructed a device that looked similar to a small jet engine. They fired off the machine, and to their surprise, a massive bright-blue wave of neon light shot out from the device and caused almost half of the thirty-story building to lose power. Their laboratory instantly went dark. Electronic lighting systems were fried, heating and cooling systems were rendered inoperable, computers were destroyed, and every device with an electronic chip instantly became useless. Unprepared for their success, his team sat motionless, shocked after seeing the power of their new creation. They sat in the dark, staring at the blinking emergency lights until the reality of the moment finally sank in.

A few weeks later, they set the EMP weapon to its maximum power and fired it off. Chen and his team were astounded at the destruction and panic that ensued. Every traffic light within a square mile was wiped out. Cars came to a screeching halt, while subways and buses shut down and stranded thousands of passengers in their place. Patrons from the Zifeng Mall, one of the world's largest malls, flooded into the already overcrowded streets causing even more hysteria. The official explanation of the freakish power outage satisfied most of the public in downtown Nanjing that day, but to all those unfortunate enough to be within range of the electromagnetic pulse, no explanation was given as to why cell phones, watches, vehicles, or anything else with an electronic circuit no longer functioned. The thriving city of eight million people took months to recover, and both the government and media called it a "power failure."

Hakeem Ferron of Saudi Arabia was sitting in a restaurant across the street from Chen's lab on that fateful day. He had just concluded the contract renewal for his father's oil company with Chinese government officials. As he stood to leave the restaurant, the hairs on Hakeem's arm stood straight up, the air felt thick like it was filled with static electricity, and then suddenly all of the power in the building went out. He glanced out the restaurant's windows; it looked as if the entire street was frozen in time. Traffic came to a complete standstill while pedestrians stood in place and looked up and then in every direction, dazed and confused. He took a few steps farther and noticed all of the people staring at the blank screens on their cell phones. Those who were looking at their digital watches began to shake them as if to give them a jump start. All commotion and noise in the area had stopped. There was an eerie silence.

He looked for a cab that could take him to the train station to board the two-hour bullet train from Nanjing to the Shanghai airport. But all of the cars in the street had mysteriously stalled. He had to walk four blocks to get out of the mess left behind by the "power outage" to find a functional taxi. When he finally found a cab that was working, he slid into the back seat and glanced back at the scene. It was surreal. He had never seen or heard of such a spectacle as he had witnessed. On the train to Shanghai, he checked his phone for messages, but the phone was completely dead. He had charged his battery the previous night. Then it struck him; this was no power outage. He thought of all the stalled cars and all those people outside of the restaurant staring at their blank phones. It was at that moment that Hakeem determined he would find out the truth behind the phenomenon that had just occurred in Nanjing.

Hakeem had spent over a million dollars to obtain the information he was looking for. His investment paid off; he learned that a team of physicists had created a device capable of firing off an unseen electromagnetic pulse and had tested it from a building across the street from where he had eaten lunch that day. Eventually, he found out the name of the lead physicist, Chen Wu.

Chen was tightly bound to a chair. His wife and son lay unconscious on the floor in the adjacent room. Chen's captor, Hakeem Ferron, began to lightly slap his face with the back of his hand as he tried to coax him to wake.

"Dr. Wu, can you hear me?" There was no response, so Hakeem placed both of his hands on Chen's shoulders and started to shake him.

"Dr. Wu, you need to wake up."

Chen stirred. His head bobbed, and his face contorted as he attempted to open his eyes. Someone shook him until his eyes finally popped open.

"Dr. Wu, can you hear me?"

Chen looked around. He tried to stand, but heavy tape bound his arms and legs to the chair in which he sat. He turned to the man who had shaken him.

"Who are you? What have you done with my wife?" Chen asked in a slurred voice.

Hakeem stepped away from the chair to give Chen a clear view of his face as he replied. "Your family is unharmed and in a safe location."

Chen flexed against the tape, then said, "What the hell do you mean, 'safe location'? Where—"

"Settle down. We don't have much time. Your family's safety depends on your cooperation. If you do not come with us willingly, you may never see them again. You need to understand the severity of your situation, Dr. Wu."

Hakeem stepped around the back of Chen's chair, grabbed it with both hands, and spun him around. The sudden motion made Chen's already groggy head spin and his stomach lurch. Chen's wife and son lay face down and unconscious on the floor in the adjacent room, his wife bleeding from a gash on the side of her head. Another Arab man with a stolid expression stood over Chen's wife and son, aiming a silenced revolver at the head of the four-year-old boy. Chen's face paled.

Hakeem spoke again, softly. "Dr. Wu, I have a proposition for you. My sources informed me you were the lead physicist responsible for the discovery of a new electromagnetic pulse weapon."

"I don't know what you're talking about!" Chen blurted out.

Hakeem swiftly backhanded Chen across the face. His large, diamond-studded ring ripped a gash above Chen's cheekbone, and blood dripped down his face. "I don't have time for games! I was in a restaurant in Nanjing the day you fired off your electromagnetic pulse last year. You know exactly what I am talking about. Dr. Wu, you hold your family's fate in your own hands. Either cooperate with us, or I begin killing your family, starting with the boy. So what's it going to be?"

Chen sat frozen in silence. "Saji, shoot the boy!"

Saji raised the gun and aimed at the four-year-old's head.

"Wait, wait!" Chen yelled. "Okay, what do you want me to do? Please, just don't harm my family."

"Does this mean we have an agreement?"

"I don't even know what you want. What is it you're after?"

"The electromagnetics technology, of course. If you help us replicate the EMP weapon you built for your government, I will guarantee the safety of your family."

"What assurances will I have that my family will be safe?"

"Your wife and boy will sleep for another two hours. When they wake, we will be long gone. After they give up trying to find you, they will eventually head back to China, where my men will monitor their actions. If you help us build the EMP weapons, your family will remain unharmed. You will be allowed to briefly communicate with your wife once a month so you know we are keeping our end of the deal. If you stop working on the EMP weapon for any reason, or if the EMP weapons do not work, we will kill your family. Do you understand?"

Chen stared at his wife and son's motionless figures for several seconds, then looked back to Hakeem and nodded.

"Excellent." He turned and motioned to Saji. "Saji, cut him loose."

Heavy footsteps approached Chen from behind, then the tape

went slack.

"Stand," said Hakeem. "You may feel a little dizzy; if so, just sit back down."

Chen stood on his own but paused for a moment.

"Are you okay?"

"Fine." He groaned, then looked up. "I am a very important man in China. You will never get away with this. My government monitors my location at all times, and there is a security team here with me. You will never get me off the island."

Hakeem laughed and replied, "Oh, I am very aware your government is watching you. As for your security team, I am afraid they weren't quite as fortunate as you or your family. They are already at the bottom of the ocean. Dr. Wu, follow my men to the vehicle, and remember, your family's safety depends on your actions."

Chen followed the men down the hallway past the elevator to the stairwell exit. They walked down three flights of stairs and exited out of a metal side door. A cargo van sat with the sliding door already open. As Chen ducked his head to step into the cargo van, another needle stung his neck, and he collapsed onto the floor of the van. Hakeem slid the door shut, then hopped into the passenger's seat as the van rolled forward, glancing back at Chen. Before Chen's vision and hearing faded, he heard Hakeem speak to someone.

"The Americans are so unprepared for we are about to do to them. I have seen what this weapon can do, Saji. It's amazing."

---

"Mommy, wake up. Wake up."

Lin Wu recognized her son's voice. Then CJ's soft hand touched her forearm, and she opened her eyes. Blinking a few times, she lifted her head off the bed. Pain crushed against the back of her eyes. Through the bedroom window, lights illuminated the pier and the white froth of the evening waves along the beach. She looked at the clock: 7:42. Sitting up, she wrapped her arms around CJ.

"Mommy, I'm hungry."

*Why did I take such a long nap? Did Chen go somewhere without us?* The television blared in the other room. *What happened?*

Her memory flashed. A dark-haired man in her hotel room as she entered. A painful sting in the back of her neck.

*Where is Chen?*

She pulled herself up off the bed. "Chen?"

No answer. She walked to the family room to turn off the television, then looked into the kitchen and froze. An empty kitchen chair sat in the middle of the room with dried blood stains on the floor. Strands of grey duct tape dangled from the arms and legs of the chair.

"CJ," she whispered. "Where's Mommy's phone?"

# Chapter 1

## 15 months later, Ucluelet, Victoria Island, Canada

---

Myk sat on the edge of the bed, staring at the silhouette of Jen's body in the shadows of the predawn hours, at the movement of her breathing.

*They won't find out about you. I won't do anything to put your life in jeopardy.*

He had been awakened by the same consuming vision, one he had learned early on not to fight. Pavement was always the best antidote. But if he could find no pavement, then a dirt road or beach would do just fine. Myk slid out of bed, laced up his shoes, and left for a five-mile run along the damp forest road.

A hard run usually helped him clear his head, but not today. After he finished, he snuck through the door and sat in the chair across the room from Jen. His sweat subsided, but not his thoughts. The way her arms and legs lay contorted across the oversized resort pillows made him shudder, but he couldn't figure out why. Then it hit him: she was sleeping in the same position his first wife had been lying in when she died in his arms.

Jen rolled over and saw him staring. She brushed the covers aside and ran her fingers through her hair to pull it away from her face, then asked, "Are you okay?"

"I'm fine. I couldn't get back to sleep, so I went for a run."

"Spain again?"

He paused, then answered, "Yep."

His first wife had died on their honeymoon in Spain. He hadn't been able to share all the details with Jen yet, but she hadn't pushed. Someday she would need to know. But it wasn't just Spain that woke him this morning; the nagging secrets of his family history had his mind abuzz again.

"I can't believe I let you talk me into the zip lines today."

Myk knew she was trying to get him to think about something else. He cracked a smile and stood. "This will be interesting. I can't wait to hear you scream. Of course, that's if you don't chicken out first."

He chuckled as he walked by the bed. Jen lunged over the side and slapped his taut butt. "Go shower up, mister, so we can get this day started."

He turned and grinned. "Why don't you join me?"

Myk turned off the main highway and drove along the narrow dirt road scattered with pot-holes full of muddy water from the constant rains. When they reached the Rainforest Adventure Park, they made their way to the check-in station. The brochure had described the park as the highest suspension bridge and zip line park in the world. Each twisted cable zip line hung hundreds of feet off the ground, and where there wasn't a zip line, visitors had to negotiate wobbly, wooden plank suspension bridges to make it to the other side. The park resembled the Ewok village from Star Wars, the whole community of zip lines and suspension bridges meandering through the upper reaches of a dense rainforest full of eagles, bears, possums, snakes, and thousands of exotic, colorful birds.

The guide tilted his head to clear the low doorway and stepped forward with a clipboard full of waivers tucked under his arm. The tattered beanie-cap with the park's embroidered logo barely contained his thick head of blonde curly hair. He stroked his full beard and announced, "After the first zip line, you will not be able to turn back. If you still have doubts, now is the time to back out and you can receive a full refund." A teenage girl and an older gentleman stepped forward.

After the last-minute offer, the visitors boarded the gondola, which began its slow ascent through the forest and up to the first platform. The scenery reminded Myk of a small village tucked away in the dense jungle of Western Pakistan. As the gondola ascended, his mind drifted. Some had called his operation foolish, and some had said it was just plain luck, but Myk knew otherwise. For him, it had been a calculated risk. He had been on a covert operation to extract the CIA's most-wanted terrorist, Khatchi Abu-mon. Somehow, the enemy had been warned; both of the stealth version Black Hawk helicopters drew heavy fire and were forced to take hard landings. His troops were outmanned three to one, and the enemy had reinforcements on the way. Base command had ordered them to retreat into the forest. It's what the enemy would have expected too.

Myk had other plans. After being shot at for ten minutes, Myk realized the enemy was nowhere near the skill level of him and his troops. No amount of training can prepare a person for an assault by twenty expert American soldiers running at full speed with weapons firing from both hands. It didn't matter if they outnumbered Myk's troops. He knew they were untrained and that self-preservation and panic would immediately kick in. Myk and his men took cover in a small ravine ensconced with thick jungle overgrowth of damp ferns and moss connected between colossal trees. Myk clenched his fist and raised it above his head. His troops immediately turned their attention to him.

"When we start our all-out sprint toward them, you only have to hit one. The guy next to the dead man will turn and run once he sees his comrade fallen. Headshots only on the first target!"

And that's exactly what happened when Myk and his troops rushed the heavily guarded compound. The enemy panicked at the site of the Americans running top speed at them. To Myk and his troops, it felt like scattering turkeys in a pen; you just had to choose which one to shoot first. They captured Khatchi alive.

The slow-moving gondola ride arrived at the top of the mountain. The visitors disembarked onto a wooden platform attached to a massive tree over two hundred feet off the forest floor. As they harnessed themselves onto the zip line, a gentle wind whisked through the forest. Had they been on the ground, they probably wouldn't have even noticed the breeze. But up in the tops of the enormous trees, the massive timber swayed back and forth under their feet. Jen glared at Myk, but she was next in line to go, and had no time to gather her thoughts and back out.

Myk stepped up behind her, his six-foot-four body towering over Jen despite her own height. He wanted to be there in case she panicked, slowed down too much, and got stuck dangling in the middle of the zip line. He had heard stories of tourists sent to the hospital with twisted ankles and broken legs from gaining too much speed. But going too slow can strand the zip liner in the middle of the line, having to endure the embarrassment of the instructor stopping everything to rescue them.

Jen took the leap and zipped down the cable line at forty miles per hour. The metal rollers buzzed along the cable line, coupled with her screaming as she slid farther and farther away. When she landed on the other side, she screamed and jumped in the air, pumping her fists.

Myk grinned. *This was definitely worth it.*

Those gathered behind Myk gasped when he leapt backwards off the platform like a cliff diver performing a back dive. Rather than clasping the attachment for stability, he put his hands above him and sped down the zip line like Superman flying upside down. He had learned long ago how to achieve the maximum speed when he trained with the Israelis. As he slid into the landing on the other side, she met him with a face flushed red with adrenaline.

"Show off."

Other than a light mist of rain, their day in the zip line park only got better as they zipped from treetop to treetop. They were the last ones off the final platform. Before they stepped back onto the gondola, she kissed him, then put her lips to his ear. Her warm breath made his hair stand on end.

"I had the time of my life."

———————————— ///————————————

As he drove back to the resort, Myk's stomach growled. "How about trying that crab house we passed in Tofino?"

"I'm exhausted, but that sounds great." She placed her hand on top of his. "I can't believe how hungry I am. I'd like to wash the wilderness off of me first, though."

After a quick stop at the resort to get cleaned up, they arrived at an early 1900s two-story lighthouse that had been converted into a restaurant. It sat perched atop a small knoll overlooking the tiny harbor full of fishing boats and a disproportionate number of float planes bobbing along the docks. The undersized parking lot was full, forcing patrons to park along the side of the surrounding gravel roads.

As they entered, Myk and Jen found the restaurant bustling with laughter, conversation, and clanging dishes. The entire center of the restaurant opened all the way up to the second floor, with crowded tables, booths, and a second sports bar with big-screen televisions tuned to various sporting events. Enormous hand-hewn timbers stretched forty feet up to the tongue-and-groove wood-planked ceilings. On the walls hung giant elk and moose racks adorned with lighting that illuminated the old lighthouse, as well as grizzly bear skins and fly fishing rods—lest there were any confusion you were in the outermost region of the Great Northwest.

Myk and Jen slid into a booth made from the reclaimed cherry wood of a cotton mill in South Carolina that dated back to the Civil War. The booth was sanded and waxed so smooth it felt like sitting on soft, silky leather. From their location, the pair had a beautiful view of the Pacific Ocean; the horizon glowed with streaks of golden amber as the sun drifted below the ocean's edge. Myk peered out the window at the multitude of fishing boats and float planes tied to the docks.

"What a place." Jen shook her head and gazed around.

"I know. This must be the place to be."

Jen raised her eyebrows. "Actually, I think this is the only place to be around here."

A disruptive group of five people in their mid-twenties seated at a table across from Myk and Jen caught Myk's attention. The two women had multiple piercings, tattoos, and hair that came down to the middle of their backs, although the sides of their heads were shaved. Two muscular men wearing military-style black boots, leather jackets, and jeans accompanied the women.

Turning away from them, Myk took a deep breath and asked Jen, "Do you want to look over the menu, or should we just order the crab when the waitress gets here?"

She folded the menu and set it aside, shrugging. "The crab

sounds good to me. I want to get back to the resort and crash anyway."

"Hmm? Just crash, too tired for any . . . "

She raised her eyebrows and looked at him with a sensuous smile.

Myk glanced back at the five as they rose from their table. One girl with black hair had piercings in her eyebrows, ears, and bottom lip. Colorful tattoos covered her right arm and shoulder. The other woman had fluorescent red hair and piercings in her nose, ears, and tongue. She wasn't wearing a bra, which made piercings in other body parts obvious. The men, on the other hand, had short hair and no piercings.

Jen turned to look. "Rough crowd. I wonder who sleeps with whom."

Myk gave a polite chuckle but kept his thoughts to himself. He had run across neo-Nazi groups before and always asked them the same question: "There are only two types of people that would proudly tattoo their body with a Nazi symbol, degenerates or imbeciles. Which one are you?" The question always surprised and provoked them. A few times, it had even led to an altercation. Because of his family history, he wanted to make damn sure any neo-Nazi knew exactly how repugnant the symbols were. And if Jen hadn't been with him, he would have asked the same question to this group. Instead, he focused on Jen.

A slender waitress with long strawberry-blonde hair who could have passed as twenty year-old Julia Roberts approached. She looked at Myk and Jen with iridescent green eyes and a confident smile. "I'll be right back to take your order." She turned to clean off the table of the five who had just left. When she opened the black folder with the signed receipt and tip, a single dollar bill landed on the table. She shook her head and pocketed the dollar.

Myk rolled his eyes and turned to Jen. "Idiots."

"What?"

He opened his mouth, but the waitress turned back to them. "Are you two ready to order?"

She jotted down their order, and as she walked away, Jen asked, "Idiots?"

Myk looked through the window and down at the group in the parking lot mounting their motorcycles. "The neo-Nazi group screwed her on the tip."

"That's so irritating. You should give her something extra to make up for it." Jen craned her neck to look out the window, then turned back to Myk. "I think they looked more like bikers than neo-Nazis, though. Did you see the Harleys outside? One had a t-shirt that said 'Born to Ride.' Definitely bikers."

Myk knew they were neo-Nazis, but proving he was right was not that important to him. "You're probably right, I guess I didn't notice their bikes."

Jen tilted her head. "C'mon, Myk. I know the look on your face when you disagree. You can't do that. You are out of the country most of the year, so when you're here, you shouldn't feel obligated to always agree with me." She leaned forward. "I saw you eyeing that group. You knew something. I want to hear it."

He thought for a moment and then replied, "It's not uncommon to mistake them for bikers. But they were definitely neo-Nazis."

"That's it? You're going to have to do better than that to convince me, Mr. All-star CIA agent. After all, they were dressed in bikers' garb and riding Harleys, you know."

He knew she was egging him on, but there were a few subjects they just hadn't gotten around to talking about, and he could see where this conversation was going.

*Now is as good a time as any.*

"They were pretty inconspicuous, but each one had a small neo-Nazi tattoo and the name of a concentration camp on the sides of their necks. The tattoo on the scary-looking redhead jumped out at me."

"I guess I didn't really hone in on any of their tattoos."

"Well, that one caught my attention because it was the Ravensbruck concentration camp." She stared at him blankly. He could see the question in her look, so he continued. "Ravensbruck is the concentration camp my mother told me her parents were killed at."

Jen's eyebrows shot up. "I had no idea. Why haven't you shared this with me before?"

"I don't know. It always elicits so many questions, and I just don't have any answers."

"How in the world did your mother ever survive Ravensbruck?"

"She didn't." Jen gave him another puzzled look, so Myk continued, "She never made it to the concentration camp because her parents hid her from the Nazis. My mother wasn't the only one who was kept secret from Hitler's soldiers that day. She has a twin sister too."

"Wow. I'm so sorry to hear about your grandparents. That was pretty fortuitous they hid your mother and her sister."

Myk paused and thought for a moment about whether or not he wanted to go further down the rabbit hole. He was too embarrassed to tell her the twins hadn't spoken in decades. None of it made sense to him, so how could he possibly explain it to her?

The waitress appeared and poured more of the Riesling wine in their glasses. It gave him another moment to think. He took a sip, then continued, "Actually, my grandparents didn't die in the Ravensbruck camp either. It's just the story my mother told me growing up. Months before the Nazis arrived in Lidice, my grandparents worked out a contingency plan with my grandfather's business partner to care for the twins if something happened. They had helped one another on their farms. I've had to unearth what really happened on my own."

Myk gestured as he spoke. "After the funeral of the man who I thought was my father, my mother sat me down and revealed for the first time that my real father died while she was pregnant with me. From that point on, I questioned her on everything she had told me while growing up. She has a lot of secrets I'm uncovering. She won't open up, so it gets frustrating."

"Really? What kind of secrets?"

Myk's cell phone vibrated in his pocket. He set his wine glass down, pulled out the phone, and looked at the screen. Then he shook his head. "Damn."

"Who is it?"

"Langley." Myk put the phone to his ear while Jen watched the conversation. His brow furrowed after a moment, and he sighed as he hung up a few minutes later. "I've got good news and bad news; which do you want first?"

"Really? Okay, good news."

"We get to fly out of Vancouver instead of driving all the way back down to Seattle."

"And what's the bad news?"

"We have to leave early tomorrow morning. I have to get back to Langley; something came up."

It wasn't the first time their vacations had been cut short. It's what came with the territory when she married him in secret on a remote beach in Costa Rica. It was Myk's way of protecting her from the vengeful people he dealt with. Jen shook her head, and then shrugged.

"Not much you can do."

Jen broke the silence on the drive back to the resort, "How long this time?"

"I'm not sure, but it looks like I'll be in D.C. for a while, so I might have a chance to break free and see you."

"We'll see," she replied. She stared out of the window, then said, "That's interesting about your mother. Now I am really curious about her." After a pause, she asked, "How do you do that anyway? Every time we go somewhere, you have a knack for reading people. Like you did with the neo-Nazis tonight."

He thought for a minute and then answered, "Like most parents, I think my mom did what she thought was best. For as long as I can remember, she played a game with me when we went somewhere. Without exception. It started when I was a child and continued until I graduated from high school."

Myk glanced at Jen, then looked back to the road. "If we went into a store, whoever could remember the most details about the people or the surroundings in the store would win the game. When I was younger, she let me win the game, so I would try hard to get the reward, which was usually candy or something else. Pavlov's law, I guess. As I grew older, I became really adept at it. I was tested, and the results showed I had a partial photographic memory. Now I can't go anywhere without taking an inventory of everything around me."

A few seconds passed. Myk shook his head. "But if I hadn't been so inattentive, Dana might not have been killed in Spain."

"C'mon, Myk, there's nothing you—"

"I saw the guy with the backpack, Jen!" His voice rose. "I can't get his face out of my mind. If I hadn't been so stubborn and tuned out what my mom had gone to so much trouble to teach me, it would have been obvious."

He brought his hand down hard on the steering wheel, making Jen jump. They sat in silence for a few seconds.

"I could have gotten her off the platform before the explosion." After the explosion, Myk had seen the man's face on the news: Saji Aman. He didn't know how, and he didn't really care—but one day, he would kill Saji Aman.

# Chapter 2

## Windsor, Canada

---

It was in Saji's blood. He was the fourth generation now. Like his predecessors, Saji Aman was a terrorist. His great-grandfather had close ties with the Nazis and was credited for implementing the Nazi ideas he learned from Adolf Eichmann into radical Islam. Saji's father had followed suit, but his life was cut short when the Israelis caught him transporting explosives to Palestine for suicide bombers. He was blown to pieces when his car found itself in the crosshairs of an Israeli missile.

Women, children, it didn't matter. Saji spared no one. He had been the point man in the kidnapping of Chen Wu. He had planned the bombings in Madrid and London. He had massacred hundreds, and he was on his way to do it again. This time, he was after the blood of Americans, and with a little luck, American Jews.

Saji looked through his binoculars on the rooftop of his apartment complex, nestled into the upper banks of the Detroit River. When the lights beamed across the slow-flowing waters, a surge of adrenaline made him giddy. A yellow rubber life raft floated down the river in the darkness of the cool, early morning hours, and in it, the last three members of his team paddled across to the shores of Windsor, Canada. Shifting his binoculars, he focused on the city park located adjacent to the river where another team member signaled along the shoreline to the group in the life raft. Other than a teenage couple making out in the backseat of an old rusted-out sedan, they had the park to themselves.

Saji and two others were the first of his group of twenty that had arrived two weeks prior. A similar deployment routine occurred every few days: A group of Saji's men disembarked from the secret compartment of a secure container being shipped on the back of a massive cargo freighter. The group exited the container with an inflatable life raft and then took the raft down river in the darkness prior to sunrise, letting the current carry them to an awaiting team signaling along the shores of the city park in Windsor. So far, the operation had been executed flawlessly; sixteen of his men had already made it. This was the final group.

Each time a group arrived, Saji gave them strict orders to stay in their apartments until someone came for them to move to another location. Every two days, food was delivered late at night. They were not allowed to watch television, use phones, open the window coverings, or go outside. They had planned to come across the Mexico border, but Hakeem had come up with the much safer plan to enter the United States from Canada. The U.S. Border Patrol had always focused on its southern border but rarely discussed a threat from the northern border. The location also gave Saji and his men a shorter drive to New York. He would give the arriving team half a day to rest, then they would all leave for New York.

Saji could not tell if his pumping heart and flushed skin came from excitement or anger. Four years ago, U.S. Intelligence had targeted him and his brother because of their involvement in the Madrid and London bombings. The brothers had eluded the Americans for years, but despite Saji's warning about the enemy's technology, his brother grew lazy. Saji had stopped one afternoon to get supplies in a remote town along the Pakistani border. While across the street, he turned to see his brother, comrades, and their vehicle explode in a massive fireball. Their bodies turned inside out, their body parts mingled with the vehicle and its belongings, all strewn throughout the street.

The blast threw Saji ten feet, and it took a month for the ringing in his ears to fade, even longer to learn that the attack had come from an American drone. The memory sent a sharp pain rippling across Saji's chest, and his eyes stung. He lowered his binoculars.

*For you, brother.*

With Saji's entire team now back together, they crossed the Detroit River the next morning in the same rubber rafts in which they had arrived. It was Saji's first time on American soil, but Detroit struck him as a ghost town. The team had discovered miles of boarded-up houses and businesses. Groups of people with hooded sweatshirts sleeping by the curbside or in their cars, or gathered around blazing metal trash cans. Dilapidated buildings with broken windows, and houses that looked like they hadn't seen a fresh coat of paint in thirty years.

*What happened here? Maybe the place looks better during the day.* His team made its way to the designated meeting place in Green Springs, Ohio. The town was originally called Stemtown, after its founder Jacob Stem, but the name was later changed to Green Springs because of the color of the water emanating out of the spring. From Green Springs, the team would go separate ways to New York. Four people would ride in each of the five vehicles, all spaced twenty minutes apart on the highways. If the Highway Patrol pulled one vehicle over, Saji wanted to make sure it wouldn't jeopardize the others. Each vehicle would take a different route, even if it meant a few hours of extra driving time to reach the same destination. They took back roads and forgotten byways whenever possible; it would take them twice as long to get to New York, but they would rarely be seen near a major highway. Should any officers pull Saji or his men over, they would be killed on the spot.

# Chapter 3

## Langley, Virginia

CIA Director David Adelberg stared at the young woman across the table as she studied the grainy surveillance photo before her. Adelberg had been instrumental in toppling the Berlin Wall and ushering in the end of the Cold War, but somehow this Washington bureaucrat, Alison Dreher, got the best of him. This was a battle he could not win, so he waited on the tides of change to wash out her inexperience. He had been with the CIA for over forty years, while she hadn't even completed a year as Secretary of Homeland Security. Dreher had been yanked from her prestigious university professorship to head up the Department of Homeland Security. Director Adelberg was twice her age and forced to meet with her because of her position.

Dreher asked, "Why are the Israelis so concerned about an old man in a wheelchair?"

"Because they believe that frail old man in the wheel chair is a Nazi war criminal." He struggled not to come off as condescending, but he had been the key player in dismantling the Iron Curtain. It had started when he helped secretly fund the Solidarity Organization, which led to winning over ninety percent of the parliamentary vote in the 1989 election in Poland. The election sparked a flame that swept across Central and Eastern Europe and led to the end of communism there. Alison Dreher had still been in elementary school at the time and had no experience in matters of national security, another example of the current administration's push to fill high-level positions with intellectuals. She was flailing in the deep water, and Director Adelberg was growing tired of tossing out the life preserver.

As she frowned at the picture, Adelberg waited for the question he knew would come. After the long pause, she looked up from the photo and said, "I see." She paused, then asked, "An old Nazi is vital to the United States because . . . ?"

"Because they have evidence that a man with a history of killing Jews was meeting with a group of people who have made it known to the world, in no uncertain terms, that they would love to wipe Israel off the map. A pretty dangerous alliance, wouldn't you say?"

He peered at her over the top of his reading glasses. As usual, she contributed nothing to the briefing, but he continued to update her so she could move on to what she was good at: rubbing shoulders with the President and pretending her work would make the country safer. This suited Adelberg; it left him free to finalize a plan to defend the U.S. against an imminent attack.

Adelberg pointed to another picture. "One of the men identified in the photograph has direct connections to a terrorist we captured last year who was planning an attack against us."

"Do they have a name?"

"No name for the Nazi, or at least not one they were willing to share. But the leader of the group he met in Karachi, Pakistan, is Saji Aman. Does that name ring a bell?"

She paused and then responded, "No. Should it?"

*Hell yes, it should. You are the Secretary of Homeland Security!*

"No. I would have been surprised if it had. Saji Aman is the great-grandson of Haj Amin al-Husseini, who was booted out of Jordan in

1940 because they believed he was too radical. In November of 1941, Haj Amin al-Husseini met with Adolf Hitler. The Nazis granted him political asylum and paid him a monthly salary of 20,000 Reichsmark."

Dreher stared at Adelberg as he spoke. *Good, at least she's paying attention.* But part of him still expected the information to leak right back out of her brain after the meeting.

"He was supposed to organize radical Muslims in the Balkans and North Africa. Historical documents show he was taught by Adolf Eichmann about the Nazis' plan for the final solution of the Jews in Europe. There was a Jewish Dutchman, Ernst Verduin, who survived Auschwitz 3 and testified that he had seen al-Husseini with fifty men 'wearing strange clothes and golden belts' at the Auschwitz camp. The guards told Verduin that Haj Amin al-Husseini and his men were there to see the final solution being carried out so they could do the same thing to the Jews in Palestine."

"Why haven't I ever heard that? That's shocking."

*Because you're a twit in way over your head.*

He took a deep breath and replied, "Few have. Anyway, Saji Aman was involved in the Madrid train station bombings and the subway bombings in London."

Adelberg and Dreher pored over the list of personnel they were assembling for the joint operation between the CIA and the FBI. As Dreher looked over the list, she paused on a name and asked, "Myk McGrath; why does that name sound familiar?"

"Because of Khatchi Abu-mon."

"Ah, that's right. He's your agent who captured Khatchi in Pakistan last year. Is it true, everything that's been said about him?"

"Honestly, I've never seen anyone like Myk. The man is gifted. That's the only way to describe it."

She furrowed her brow. "Really?"

"Without a doubt."

"How did you find him?"

"We didn't. He found us. Tragedy, I guess. Do you remember the terrorist attack at the train stations in Spain?"

"Vaguely. I was in the private sector back then."

Again, Adelberg wanted to tell her she should have stayed in the private sector. Instead, he gave her the pertinent facts that someone in her position should have known verbatim.

"It took place during their morning rush hour. Ten bombs detonated on four separate trains that day, killing 191 people and wounding 1,800. If Myk hadn't gone back up the escalator to buy a snack, he would have died too. But he watched it explode right in front of him. His newlywed wife bled to death in his arms on the platform of the Atocha train station in Madrid."

Dreher covered her mouth as the director continued.

"For some reason, he blames himself. Her body was flown back to the States, and the day after her funeral, Myk was on a plane to Israel to join their army."

"Why the Israelis?"

"His mother is Jewish…"

Dreher interrupted, "Wait a minute. Myk McGrath is Jewish? How did he end up with a name like McGrath?"

"Myk's father died while his mother was pregnant with him and she married an Irish man. Anyway, it's actually not that uncommon for an American Jew to go to Israel and serve for a few years. Two years later, Myk was at the doorstep of the Marine Corps. His test scores and field operations agility tests were off the charts. They put him with the most elite and secretive special operations unit: Task Force 88, or as most people around here refer to them, 'the hunter-killer team.' They conducted operations in Iraq prior to the invasion and have done raids in Syria, Yemen, and the Horn of Africa. We're lucky to have him."

"Any explanation for his gifts?"

"I'm not sure." A small lie. Adelberg knew a great deal about Myk and his mother. "However, I know his mother put a gun in his hands at age five. Myk can shoot the wings off a fly."

Dreher snorted. "That's a bit eccentric, don't you think?"

"I don't know. Perhaps many of us are born with talents that remain unknown or undeveloped. In Myk's case, his mother found his gifts and helped hone them. Tiger Woods' father put a golf club in his hands at age two and helped him become one of the best golfers in the world. The father of Venus and Serena Williams put tennis racquets in their hands, made them play tirelessly day after day, and turned them into some of the best tennis players the world has known. Myk's mother, on the other hand, developed in him a very unique set of skills. He's the best I've ever seen—period."

Dreher shook her head.

Adelberg continued, "Myk won't talk about it, but his wife's death sparked something inside him; it's what drives him. He had won back-to-back NCAA wrestling titles and would have easily made the U.S. Olympic Wrestling Team. He seems to have little concern for his own life or safety, but he has a vendetta against those who kill innocent people."

"Is he okay?"

"I'm sure it still weighs on his mind. Sometimes killing as many terrorists as Myk has can play games with an agent's mind. Not Myk. Our best psychologists evaluated him, and he is in perfect mental health."

# Chapter 4

Myk would wait as long as it took, but every year brought him a little closer to Saji. He knew nothing about his next mission, and yet he had a feeling this would be the operation that would finally lead him to the terrorist that killed his first wife. He had come close the year before when he captured Saji's boss, Khatchi Abu-mon. Myk had no illusions of capturing Saji. He would kill him.

Myk turned down the volume to his favorite Coldplay song, "Spies," as he turned off Interstate 495 and onto George Washington Memorial Parkway, the tree-lined road that led to the Agency. For the longest time, Myk had dreamt of killing Saji with his bare hands, but many years had passed, and now it made no difference to him whether he killed Saji by gripping his head tightly and snapping his neck or by simply putting a single bullet through the center of his head.

He pulled up to the first security checkpoint in Langley, Virginia, in the early morning darkness and flashed his credentials to the security officer, who shone his halogen flashlight first at Myk's ID and then at his face. After a quick call, he told Myk to proceed. The two-foot-thick chrome cylinder posts lowered into the ground, allowing Myk's special edition black Ford Harley Davidson F-150 truck through.

He parked between two sedans, grabbed his duffel bag, and walked to the front lobby. He first visited the agency three years ago, but not much had changed. He handed his Beretta 92FS pistol to the security officers and watched it as it passed through the scanning device. Most in the agency preferred Glocks, but not Myk. He received his Beretta in the Israeli army, and he would never part ways with it.

A few minutes later, Myk stepped out of the elevator and into the gaze of an unsmiling receptionist with bags under her eyes. He flashed her a courteous smile and walked down the hall to an office with an open door. As he stepped in, Myk locked eyes with Director Adelberg, who interrupted his conversation with Deputy Director Brodie Bashford. Deputy Director Bashford was a few inches shorter than Myk with thick sandy-brown hair that partially covered his ears. Bashford had been a three-year starting quarterback at UCLA, but his real passion was an entirely different sport. When Myk had first met the man, Bashford struck him as bit laid back for someone in his position, but one step inside Brodie Bashford's office explained it all. Pictures of a younger Brodie Bashford with long hair holding his surfing championship trophies on the beaches of California adorned his office. Adelberg offered his hand.

"How was your trip?"

Myk ignored the question and gave Adelberg a firm handshake. "What's the situation?"

Adelberg handed three pictures to Myk. "The Israeli agency Mossad has been tracking an Egyptian named Saji Aman."

Myk's heart jumped at the mention of Saji's name. Adelberg continued, "He recently spent a lot of time in Tehran with two radical clerics at the top of everybody's watch list. The Israelis supplied us with the surveillance photos of Saji. Are you familiar with him?"

"I know a bit about him." Myk stared down at the photographs. "So what's the concern? That's routine stuff for those guys to meet with the clerics."

"The concern is who he met with after he convened with the clerics. Saji spent the next two weeks in Karachi with an old Nazi who disappeared off Mossad's radar screen over thirty years ago. Mossad intercepted a message between Saji and an unidentified contact here in D.C."

Myk handed back the photos as Adelberg continued. "We ramped up our threat level to its highest point after we connected Saji to the kidnapping of a Chinese physicist named Chen Wu over a year ago. Dr. Wu is still missing. The Chinese have been frantically searching for him because apparently Dr. Wu made some breakthrough discovery with electromagnetic pulse technology. If our assessment is correct, an EMP attack could wipe out the electrical power grid of entire cities, render our fighter jets or drones useless, and take out all communications."

His neck. The mental picture popped up in Myk's mind—not a bullet to the head. He would snap Saji's neck, after he beat him to a pulp.

Myk leaned in to get a better look at the documents on the table. "Damn. Do the Israelis still know where Saji is?"

"No. He disappeared. But I think Mossad isn't telling us something. I could sense they were nervous about it. When you captured Khatchi last year, you disrupted a terror plot involving both Saji and Khatchi. There is another leader too, a new player Saji has been communicating with, but we haven't identified him yet."

Myk fixed his bright, striking eyes directly on Adelberg's. "You guys should have let me extract the information from Khatchi when we had the chance. I guarantee we wouldn't be running around in the dark right now. Why do we have to treat these terrorists with such kid gloves anyway? He wouldn't have been worthy to be food for the buzzards if we left him in the desert to rot. Now he's on American soil and in our judicial system—that's pathetic!"

"Without a doubt, you're right." Adelberg replied. He sighed and shook his head. "Our hands were tied, Myk. We give a terrorist a bloody nose, and it's our agents who get treated like the criminals now. Trust me, it's a decision I will forever regret. I have a space for you to use for an hour until the rest of the agents arrive. We will start the briefing around six fifteen."

Myk bit his tongue and wondered at what point Adelberg had become so spineless. He asked, "What's it going to take, Director? It's coming, you know. One of these jihadists will figure out a way to massacre thousands. And time is not on our side anymore. Our enemy can't be found on a map, and he doesn't wear a uniform. We're not fighting a State, but individuals and radical Islamic ideas. Times Square, Fort Hood, Boston—we've been lucky the casualties have been low. It's only a matter of time—"

"I know, Myk. I know." Adelberg said in a somber tone. He handed Myk a file and placed his hand behind Myk's shoulder. "Come with me."

As they walked out of the office, Myk opened the folder and glanced at the name on the profile information, Faraq Majed. "What do we know about this guy?"

"He's smart as hell, but he's clean, Myk. Faraq was educated right here at Georgetown and then went to MIT. He worked in Europe for three years as an electronic physicist, and then his name dropped off the grid. No phone bills, no use of credit cards . . . nothing. Faraq's name just popped up on a flight arriving later this morning."

"Is there any solid intel that connects him to the missing Chinese physicist, Chen Wu?"

Adelberg pushed open the door leading to the stairwell and

waited for Myk to pass. "Nothing yet. This is all we've come up with in the last twenty-four hours."

Myk stopped on the stair landing and faced Adelberg. "So, Faraq goes off the grid about the same time Chen Wu disappears, and now he's on his way back to the U.S. loaded with whatever information they squeezed out of Chen Wu." Myk grinned as thoughts of Faraq leading him to Saji entered his mind.

They exited the stairwell as Adelberg replied, "That's not all. He was booked on the same flight as eighteen others we are putting under surveillance as soon as they land. We will brief the other agents in about an hour. In the meantime, see if you can dig up anything else on Faraq."

Adelberg showed Myk the computer station. "I hope you were able to enjoy what little time you had with Jen."

Myk grunted under his breath and pulled his chair up to the computer. The agency didn't know about his secret marriage to Jen; it went against every CIA protocol, but Myk had his own dictum by which he operated. From his perspective, the agency worked for him, not vice versa. His biggest reason for being employed by the CIA was so he could access their vast assets and tap into their intelligence resources.

Adelberg turned and walked back upstairs. As Myk rolled his chair closer to the monitor and keyed in his password, his cell phone vibrated. He checked the display but saw only zeros. An anonymous caller. He answered, "This is Myk."

"Agent McGrath, my name is Mordechai. I am calling to warn you." The deep, booming baritone voice carried an unmistakable heavy Israeli accent.

"Excuse me. Who in the hell are you?"

"You can call me Mordechai, but don't waste your time researching my name in your database because you won't find anything. I can only tell you I used to be a key player in the intelligence world. I wish I could give you more concrete information, but for now, I can tell you with complete certainty that you have a mole in your government. You should operate with a certain degree of cynicism and caution in your communication with those in your agency. Things may not be quite as they appear."

Myk's tone turned sharp. "Even if I did believe you, why would you tell me?"

"An appropriate question. I contacted you because I know I can trust you. You are one of the few people who might have a chance to stop whatever atrocity may be coming your way."

"You don't even know me."

"Not so. Actually, I have followed your development for many years. I knew your father and mother well—"

"Now I know you're lying; my father died in a car accident many years ago."

After a moment of silence, the caller asked, "Is that what your mother told you? That he died in an auto accident?"

A cold chill swept through Myk.

The caller continued, "Listen, I understand your skepticism. While it is true your father died in a car while he was in London, it definitely was not an accident. There's a lot about your parents you may not know."

Myk chuckled and shook his head. "I am well aware my mother has a wealth of secrets. She told me about my biological father at the funeral of the man I thought was my real father. She saved that little gem for my senior year in high school." Then Myk asked him a question dripping with cynicism, "Why don't you tell me something about *him*, since you seem to know so much about me?"

"I wish I could, but now is not the time. Perhaps later." He paused, then said, "Agent McGrath, trust no one. You are not dealing with typical terrorists who send in their minions to blow themselves up. I wish I had more information for you, but I don't. This is a level of sophistication I have rarely seen. After I disconnect the call, I will send you a text message with the number where you can contact me. If you text the number, I will call you back."

"Wait, how will I–"

The phone line went dead, and Myk's mind spun with ideas. He spent the next hour on the computer, and then went back upstairs for the briefing.

Myk grabbed his water bottle and sat at the massive conference room table. Every chair was filled. Adelberg walked to the front of the room as the lights dimmed, and an agent sitting behind a laptop fired up the video screen. Myk listened while he scrutinized everyone in the room for the mole, then looked down at his notes.

Adelberg cleared his throat. "We have credible intelligence from Mossad that links Saji Aman to a plot against the United States. He's also been linked to the disappearance of one of China's leading physicists. Thanks to some great work by Agent Luke Stanford, we know that a few weeks ago, a travel agency based out of Egypt booked exactly nineteen seats from Toronto, Canada, directly into Washington, D.C."

Agent Stanford was not part of the operational meeting or the mission, but Myk knew him well. Stanford's intel helped Myk capture Khatchi. But it was also Luke's miscalculation that almost botched the entire operation. Still, he was considered one of the agency's top targeters.

An agent asked, "Why don't we just arrest them when they get here and interrogate them?"

*It's got to be one of those young pups.* Sure enough, Myk looked across the table to the agent who asked the question. He didn't even look old enough to grow facial hair.

Adelberg answered, "Because right now, they are the only thing we have to go on that might help us stop an attack. If we arrest them, the trail would instantly go cold. That's why we've gathered you here. We are putting all of them under heavy surveillance to gather any information that might tip their hand. No return flights have been booked. Each of you will be assigned to follow one of these 'tourists' the minute they step off the plane."

Using his laser, Adelberg pointed to the information on the screen. "The only common link is they are all listed as members of the Muslim Brotherhood, except one—Faraq Majed. Agent Tom McMillan will give you a brief overview of the Muslim Brotherhood." Adelberg's phone lit up, and he looked down at it. "Excuse me, gentlemen. I have an urgent call I need to answer." He motioned at Myk to join him outside the briefing room.

After they stepped out, Myk asked, "What is it?"

Adelberg covered his phone with his hand and answered, "It's the Chinese. They found Chen Wu alive in Toronto."

"Damn. That's great news."

Adelberg took a few more steps away from the briefing room. "I'll gather any other information they have and fill you in. Why don't you lend them a hand in briefing the other agents."

"No problem." Myk stepped back into the room and glanced at the speaker, a short, middle-aged man named Agent Tom McMillan. Myk wondered if the man ever spent a day outside the office. The glow of the screen exacerbated McMillan's pasty skin and thinning brown hair he swooped over his head to hide his growing baldness. Myk doubted the man could run around the block without collapsing.

Agent McMillan walked to the front of the conference room and addressed the group. "To the best of our knowledge, the Muslim Brotherhood's origins can be traced back to Hasan al-Banna in 1928.

The Brotherhood is the parent organization of Hamas and Al-Qaeda. Since their inception, the Muslim Brotherhood has encouraged jihad against non-Muslim infidels, with a particular hatred against Israel and the United States. In the late 1940s, Egypt's Prime Minister Mahmoud Fahmi Nuqrashi thought the Muslim Brotherhood was gaining too much power and influence, so he forcibly dissolved it in 1948. The Brotherhood went underground, and a year later Nuqrashi was assassinated . . . "

Myk's mind drifted as McMillan droned on. Myk's mother had drilled the Muslim Brotherhood and its history into him on their visit to Egypt during his junior year of high school. By that time, he had figured out his vacations really weren't vacations per se, but more like summer school in a different country. Sure, he had traveled the world with her, but he spent all his time learning about the countries' governments and history and how close of an ally they were to the U.S. and Israel. The worst trips, hands down, were to Russia. Even as a boy, he had thought that something had sucked the happiness out of that country. At least when they went to Egypt, he got to see the pyramids.

He tuned back in to McMillan and remembered visiting the locations Agent McMillan was talking about. Myk knew all about the Muslim Brotherhood's connection to Osama Bin Laden and Khalid Shaikh Mohammed, the architect of 9/11, and how the Brotherhood controlled Hamas and Egypt and their attempts to gain foothold in Syria. He raised his hand.

"Yes, Agent McGrath."

Myk asked, "So are you suggesting the Muslim Brotherhood is behind this?"

McMillan replied, "Well, it's no coincidence the eighteen tourists flying in here are members of the Muslim Brotherhood."

"That's a bit obvious, don't you think?" At Myk's sarcastic

comment, a few heads turned toward him. "Besides, as far as I can remember, the Muslim Brotherhood might be a very influential group in the Muslim world, but they have never organized a terrorist attack. Has anyone considered that these guys might be decoys? If they've got their hands on an EMP, then it would make sense to have some decoys to keep us as far away as possible, wouldn't it?"

McMillan's mouth hung open for a few seconds, then he blinked and responded, "Perhaps. My job is to fill you in on the Brotherhood. Director Adelberg can answer any operational questions."

Myk wondered how many American lives might have been saved if more people in the intelligence community thought outside the box. It was a rare occurrence that the intelligence didn't exist, but no one ever connected the dots. That's why Myk clung to his independence. He didn't ever want to miss even the smallest clue that could lead to saving a life. It didn't matter if it was someone at a marathon in Boston or somebody else commuting to work on a subway—Myk always kept the lives of the innocent in his thoughts and close to his heart.

Agent McMillan pointed his laser to the pictures on the screen of a few key players in the Brotherhood, so Myk faded back out to his earlier conversation with the mysterious caller. Mordechai had said Myk's father died in a car while in London, but it had been no accident. If it hadn't been an accident, then someone had purposely killed his father, but why? Why would his mother keep that from him? Were they involved in something nefarious? Probably not, but Myk mulled over the information. It just didn't add up.

*London.*

He had visited London three times with his mother, and they stopped at the same quaint little bakery on Kensington Gore every time. His mom spent hours talking to the owner like they were best friends. The owner was about the same age as Myk's mother. He always grew bored and wanted to leave, but his mom told him to 'sit tight, Myk, just a few more minutes.' Every year during Hanukkah, a package with delicious baked goods arrived from the same bakery on Kensington Gore.

Myk decided he would delve into the connection between the bakery and his biological father when he had time. And if there was no link to his father, then maybe it had something to do with his mother's twin sister—whom he still had yet to meet. Maybe the woman in the bakery was her twin sister. There were so many unknowns.

Myk looked back up to the front of the room. Agent McMillan was finally wrapping up.

Director Adelberg returned to brief the agents on the connections to Saji and his meeting with the Nazi in Karachi. "A few minutes ago, I received a phone call solidifying the seriousness of the threat. I spoke with Gwan Chow, director of Guoanbu, the Chinese equivalent of our CIA. They recently rescued one of their top physicists, Chen Wu, who had been kidnapped fifteen months ago. Dr. Wu's wife received a phone call from the police in Toronto telling her the exact location of the warehouse where he was being held."

Adelberg took a drink of water and then continued, "Guoanbu had only partially debriefed Dr. Wu when they contacted us because of the urgency. According to the information given to Guoanbu, Dr. Wu helped his captors assemble four EMP devices. Before now, EMP, or electromagnetic pulse, was considered a decade out from becoming a real threat. However, the Chinese informed us that Chen Wu and his team of physicists made a historic breakthrough and developed a fully-functioning device capable of wiping out one square mile. For the most part, the EMP is harmless to human beings, but Dr. Wu's device will destroy any electronic circuit within a mile. An EMP weapon in the hands of a terrorist could wreak havoc on the infrastructure of our country. Chen Wu also described his captors in detail. One of them was Saji Aman. He said the name of the leader of this operation was Hakeem, a new player. No last name, and so far we have no information on him."

*I am coming for you, Saji!*

Myk surveyed the agents in the room. Their faces were expressionless. Several adjusted themselves in their chairs, while a few shook their heads. Adelberg paced the room.

"Guoanbu disclosed that Dr. Chen Wu was in relatively good health when they found him, which makes me question whom we are dealing with. Under normal circumstances, terrorists always kill their captors after they have no use for them. I contacted the Pentagon to find out whatever information they have on the EMP technology. This may be hard to believe, but technologically speaking, whoever has these EMPs will have the upper hand against us unless we can locate them before an attack begins."

A younger agent asked, "Director Adelberg, has there been any information uncovered that would give us a better indication of a timetable?"

*What an idiot! What the hell kind of a question is that?!*

Myk had voiced his annoyance with Jen about the motivations of some agents he worked with; he couldn't understand how they could treat their job as an occupation. For Myk, each terrorist killed saved countless innocent lives. Jen often reasoned with him, "Myk, every terrorist you cross paths with will pay a toll for the death of Dana. But the other agents don't have the same vengeance driving them as you do. You need to remember that.'"

After a pause, Adelberg replied, "Yes we have a timetable. It is imminent!"

Myk hung his head in embarrassment for the young agent and

let out an audible sigh.

Adelberg's voice rose a few octaves. "We have a group of nineteen alleged 'tourists' arriving in our country on perfectly legal travel visas. We have assigned two agents to each suspect flying in a few hours from now. In front of you is a briefing on the individual you will track. It is the most information we could come up with in this limited time. These guys aren't on anyone's watch list, so information was sparse. As details become available, we will securely forward them to you. Are there any questions?"

Hands shot up around the table. Adelberg spent the next thirty minutes fielding questions while Myk opened the folder and reviewed the information on Faraq again. It just didn't make sense. No patterns or connections. He got a strong feeling they were being played, but as long as it led to Saji, he would gladly play along.

# Chapter 5

## Toronto, Canada

———————————— /// ————————————

The clash between Faraq's heart and intellect had gone on for months. In the end, his intellect won out, and Faraq Majed finally accepted that he had been tricked. Conniving women using their beauty to snare rich and powerful men was nothing new, but Faraq had neither riches nor power. He did, however, have a P.H.D. in electromagnetism from Georgetown. But there was another reason the stunning Mineesha pulled up a bar stool and sat next to him that day fourteen months ago: Faraq was a Muslim. Mostly secular in his practices, but Muslim nonetheless.

When Hakeem kidnapped Chen Wu to construct the EMP weapons, he quickly learned that he was in way over his head. The electromagnetism technology was mind-numbing and completely incomprehensible to him. Hakeem then began an intense search for someone educated enough to assist Chen Wu in building the EMP weapons for him. In his search for a Muslim physicist, he found Faraq, who had been educated in the United States and graduated from Georgetown University and MIT. Faraq was working in Europe when Hakeem targeted him to help build the EMP weapons. Hakeem had done an extensive background check on Faraq to see how he might be able to lure Faraq into the fold without threatening the use of force. Faraq's father was a Muslim, but his mother was Jewish.

Hakeem's failsafe method for convincing a new recruit was a seductive and gorgeous woman, Mineesha. Hakeem discovered her as a young teenager working in a brothel in Cambodia. Mineesha knew exactly how to reel a man in, and Faraq had no idea what easy prey he had been. He never had a chance. By the time he had awakened from his three-month dream state with the most beautiful woman he had ever beheld, it was too late. A few months into the project, Faraq figured out that he was a pawn and tried to go home, but Hakeem refused. Faraq had become an integral part of building the weapons, so Hakeem made death threats against his family to force him to stay. He told Faraq that his father and mother would first be tortured and then killed, while his two younger sisters would be raped and then beheaded. Faraq was ensnared.

Faraq was told that after they extracted the information they needed from the Chinese physicist, Chen would be released to his family in China. Chen was allowed to speak to his family once a month. Since Faraq was the one responsible for implementing the information obtained from Dr. Wu, he had spent a lot of time with him over the past year. Faraq was impressed with Chen's vast knowledge, and he had grown to deeply respect the physicist.

After the four operational EMP weapons were completed and tested, Hakeem ordered Dr. Wu killed. Faraq had come up with a plan to help Chen escape. But how could he get out without making himself a martyr to an unholy and unjust cause, or even worse, put his family in harm's way? He was very frustrated that he had been so blinded by the temptress Mineesha, but he reasoned that at least he had figured out a way to save Dr. Wu. How to liberate himself was an entirely different matter.

Faraq told the men he would carry out Hakeem's orders while they packed the gear, then he would meet them at the vehicle. He took Chen Wu into the warehouse and quickly explained he had no intention of terminating his life. He told Chen he would fire several shots into the air, but one of the gunshots would need to graze his arm so Faraq could smear the blood on Chen's body in case anyone came back to check on him. Chen was to remain slumped over in the chair until Faraq and his men left. Faraq would leave a message with Chen's family explaining where Chen could be found.

Dr. Wu was overcome with joy and mystified relief. He thanked Faraq for sparing his life and asked, "What will you do now? When I resurface and they figure out I am alive, won't they kill you?"

"It's not a question of *if* they will kill me, but rather what method they will choose. I am sorry for what happened to you. If I could have gotten you released earlier, I would have. Please don't concern yourself with me; I'll figure something out."

"Thank you, Faraq, and good luck."

Faraq pulled out the plastic vial with earplugs and shoved a pair into his ears, then gave the spare to Chen. "The sound will still hurt your ears, but these will prevent it from making you deaf." After Chen pushed the earplugs into his ears, Faraq fired several shots in the air. The loud gun blasts were intensified by the concrete and metal surroundings of the empty warehouse. The bangs made both Faraq and Chen flinch, and Faraq winced at the earsplitting sound. He then placed the muzzle of the gun to the outside of Chen's shoulder. His heart rate increased, and he felt short of breath. He had never shot anyone before. He looked at Chen, who nodded and then turned away. Faraq squeezed the trigger.

The sound of the single blast pierced Faraq's ears and made both men jerk their heads away out of reflex. Faraq's ears rang, and his ear canals felt hot, sensitive. When he looked back to Chen, a half-inch gash dripped deep red blood—and a wave of dizziness washed over Faraq. He closed his blue eyes and took a slow breath, then took the ear plugs from Chen and put both pairs back in the case. Faraq suppressed the wave of nausea that rolled up behind his tongue and throat as he wiped the blood across Chen's upper body. Afterward, he pulled his cell phone out and called the police, giving them the address of the warehouse. As he left the building, Faraq glanced over his shoulder. Chen slumped over in the chair, where he would remain until the sounds of Faraq and his men faded.

---

Faraq made his way to the awaiting group of cargo vans that would transport him and his men to the Toronto International Airport. After he opened the passenger's door and stepped up into the front seat, Hakeem started the engine. As they drove out of the huge parking lot, Hakeem turned to Faraq.

"Any trouble?"

"None. I'll need a change of clothes before we get to the airport."

Hakeem looked at the blood on Faraq's clothes and hands. He nodded.

Faraq continued, "I dragged the corpse into the back closet and got some blood on me."

"You have done well, Faraq. We couldn't have pulled this off without you."

Faraq stared out the window.

"When you arrive in D.C., the Americans will track you and the others."

Faraq turned and asked, "What makes you so sure?"

"We've dropped them a few hints from an asset inside the American government."

"What?" Faraq's voice rose. "Why would you do such a thing?"

"It is an important part of the plan. While the serpent's eyes are focused on you and your men, another group will make their way into the U.S. at the same time as your team. Most of the members of the other team are on a watch list, so they cannot enter the country legally. This group will blind the serpent. If any of your men are detained, our sources tell us you will be held for less than a day. With our high-profile attorneys and a heavy dose of media coverage, the Americans will go out of their way to avoid being accused of profiling."

Faraq turned to Hakeem. "When Mineesha first introduced me, you told me we would only use the EMP device to free Khatchi."

"Faraq, what I do with the other EMP devices is my business. However, what I told you still stands true; you will go to Richmond to be part of our operation to liberate Khatchi. If you carry out what you are supposed to do, I will never bother you or your family again. You have my word."

Faraq turned and scowled out the window.

Hakeem continued. "I'll receive more information from my source in the CIA about when they will transport Khatchi to the Lewis F. Powell Courthouse. Khatchi was very disappointed his trial wasn't held at the federal court in Manhattan, though. He really wanted our spectacle on a larger stage than Richmond, Virginia."

Unsure of whether or not to believe Hakeem, Faraq just nodded as they pulled onto the main highway. As the van accelerated, Faraq stared at the road in front of him. The white lines blurred into one line as he reflected on how he had been cajoled into his predicament.

———————————— //// ————————————

As the plane at Dulles International Airport circled above Washington D.C., Faraq was running out of ideas. If he didn't come up with anything soon, he would have to sacrifice himself to keep his family safe from Hakeem. Faraq thought of Dr. Wu and hoped he had made his way back to his family. Reflecting back on his years at Georgetown University, he wondered how much had changed since the last time he had been in D.C.

A gentle tap on his shoulder startled him.

"Would you bring your seat back to an upright position? We are on our final approach," the flight attendant said.

When the plane touched down, Faraq's insides tightened. What awaited him on the other side of the doors? He located the other members of the team sitting throughout the plane and made eye contact with a few. They didn't appear as tense as he was, but perhaps they just concealed their nervousness better. After a loud ding, passengers began unbuckling their seat belts and opening the overhead bins. The flight was full and Faraq was seated near the back of the plane, so it took over ten minutes to get out.

As he walked into the noisy airport terminal, he looked around for his team, but they had already made their way to the U.S. Customs check point. He cleared Customs without any trouble. Hakeem had instructed them not to talk to one another unless it was an assigned partner, but since Faraq was not given a partner, he walked down to baggage claim and waited with the other passengers. After ten minutes, the luggage from their flight dropped down the chute. He tried to occupy his mind with what would happen in D.C., but he kept returning to figuring out how to get away from this group without causing harm to his family.

No one else in his group had received their luggage. He shifted from foot to foot as he waited. Other than the team he had traveled with, only two others from the same flight still waited for their luggage.

*What's happening? Do the Americans already suspect something?* Finally, a team member named Rieza grabbed his bag and left for a taxi. Then Faraq's suitcase appeared, and his tensed shoulders relaxed. He grabbed his luggage and headed for the transportation area. As he passed through the automatic sliding doors, he thought he saw a familiar face—one he had seen when he stepped into the terminal.

# Chapter 6

## Washington D.C.

As Myk McGrath sat inside the vast, opulent lobby of the JW Marriot, his leg fidgeted up and down while he impatiently waited for Faraq to exit the hotel. Myk scanned the file on his phone that Director Adelberg sent to him on his partner, Agent Jodi Black. Black had spent most of her career in drug enforcement, so she had seen firsthand how violent humanity can be. She had witnessed a number of beheadings and dismemberments from the drug cartels. During the previous decade, the Mexican drug cartels had been responsible for five times as many deaths as the U.S. military had suffered in Iraq and Afghanistan combined. Mexico just didn't get as much media coverage as the wars in the Middle East. On her last mission before coming over to the CIA, Black had tracked down the cartel member responsible for breaking into the mayor's house from Monterey, Mexico and killing his children right in front of him.

Myk scanned the lobby and then tapped his earpiece. "Jodi, what do you have?"

Black responded from the surveillance van parked across the street. "Nothing. Wait, he just came back into the room. He threw his suitcase on the bed. I think he's ready to leave."

Myk stood from the plush couch and walked toward the

registration counter. "If he gets a taxi, wait thirty seconds and pick me up outside the lobby. Otherwise, I'll follow him on foot."

"Got it. He just left the room, Myk. He should be headed down now."

---

While Faraq waited for the elevator, an American couple with two sons approached. When the elevator arrived, the children raced inside, and a small shoving match ensued as they tangled over who got to push the button first. Faraq moved to the back of the elevator and watched. As the elevator descended, the young boys jumped in the air and laughed hysterically as they landed.

The woman grabbed their hands, turned to Faraq, and said, "I'm sorry. They are fascinated with elevators."

He smiled. "No apologies necessary. They are just having fun."

The elevator door opened and the boys bolted out, dragging their mother behind. Faraq strolled into the lobby and gazed up at the massive, exquisitely crafted chandeliers. The entire center section of the lobby towered over sixty feet high. As he walked to the revolving circular door and stepped inside, he looked back and spotted the familiar face in the lobby, the face of the man at the airport.

Faraq glanced back again, and the man walked straight toward him, staring directly into his eyes. Cold fear jolted through him, and Faraq stepped into the large rotating doors and exited onto the sidewalk. Hakeem had told him he would be followed when he arrived. Suddenly, a solution to his dilemma dawned on him, and Faraq made a split second decision on what he would do.

Myk whispered into the microphone concealed in his collar, "I think I got his attention Jodi. He just bolted out the door. You should have a visual on him now."

"What'd you do that for? I thought Director Adelberg wanted us to lay low."

"I want Faraq to know who he's dealing with. I've got my own way of handling these guys. Just follow my lead."

"All right, Myk. I'm not going to second guess the guy who bagged Khatchi. Faraq just crossed the street. It looks like he's on his way to the bookstore on Pennsylvania."

Myk ignored Black's veiled compliment. "I've got him." He strode across the street, unhindered by traffic on this part of Pennsylvania Avenue, which narrowed as it dead ended into the White House in two blocks. When he reached the other side, Myk waited for Faraq to come out of the bookstore. He had dealt with hordes of terrorists, and there was no doubt in Myk's mind that Faraq was different. But what was he doing here, and how was he connected to the kidnapped Chinese physicist?

Through the glass, he watched Faraq pay for something and then exit the bookstore.

"Jodi, he's out now. He's carrying a bag and cutting across Freedom Plaza."

As Faraq walked quickly across Freedom Plaza, he pulled the book and map out of the bag and paused by a trash container long enough to ease his book bag into it. Then he entered the café.

"Myk, where's he headed?"

"He just entered the café on Twelfth Street. He pulled a few things out of the bag from the bookstore and tossed the book bag away. When he leaves the café, I'll grab the bag for the forensic team."

"Right."

"Jodi, have you talked to Director Adelberg?"

"I just spoke to him while Faraq was in the bookstore. He wanted an update. Apparently, our guy was the last of the nineteen to leave his hotel. Adelberg said all the other suspects are at different tourist sites scattered around D.C. So far, Faraq is the only one to break routine."

"I'm going to confront Faraq."

"Right now?"

Myk winced from Agent Black's volume. "No, not yet. The timing has to be right. I'll let you know when. I want him to be nervous. He's camped out at one of the booths in the café, drinking coffee and reading whatever he bought at the bookstore." Myk squinted, then frowned. "I left my binoculars in the van, so I can't see what he's reading. When he leaves, if he passes the van, I can grab my binoculars."

"Okay, they're right here on the dash. I'll have them ready for you."

---

Faraq sipped his cup of coffee and kept his follower in his peripheral vision. The coffee tasted of nutmeg but lacked the bold kick of caffeine; his heart already pounded under the American's stare.

The waitress stopped and asked, "How is the coffee, sir?"

"Just fine. Thank you. I noticed your name—Rajani. Are you from here?" He knew the answer to his question, but he just wanted to strike up a conversation.

"No, sir. I am from India."

"Is that so? I know a few people from India. What part of India are you from?"

"Have you heard of Panaji?"

"Of course. I stayed there last summer in a beautiful resort in the southern section of Panaji that overlooks the Arabian Sea. What brings you here to D.C.?"

"I am attending Georgetown. This is my third year."

"How about that. What are you studying?"

She smiled and replied, "I am pre-med."

"Good for you. I attended Georgetown years ago and have not been here since then."

"What brings you back?"

Faraq sipped his coffee and thought about Hakeem. "Actually, I am here on business for some friends. But I lost interest in their business and am trying to figure out a way back home."

"Oh, I am sorry to hear that. I hope things work out for you."

Faraq smiled and replied, "As do I." He scooted out of his booth and smiled. "Thank you for the coffee, and good luck with your studies."

She smiled and nodded, then walked away. He threw a generous tip on the table and walked out the door.

---

"Jodi. He's on the move again. He's deviated from the direction I thought he might take, so can you bring me the binoculars?"

"I'm on my way."

Myk passed the trash container, pulled a handkerchief from his pocket, and pulled out the book bag without contaminating the evidence.

"Jodi, I have the bag. I will give it to you when I get the binoculars on the next block."

The flat bag appeared empty, but Myk opened it anyway. A postcard lay at the bottom.

"It looks like he forgot an item from the bookstore."

"What is it?"

"Nothing really, just a postcard. We should get some good fingerprints. He's headed toward the National Mall. Wait for me on the south corner of Constitution."

"I'm already here."

He met up with Agent Black and gave her the bag with the postcard in it, then grabbed his binoculars. Putting distance between them, he walked on the opposite side of 14th a little more slowly than Faraq. As Faraq waited for the light to change at Constitution Avenue, Myk paused at the Ronald Reagan building and waited until Faraq arrived at the National Mall, then cut across the grass and headed toward the Washington Monument.

"Where's he going, Myk?"

"According to the paperwork in his luggage, we thought he would visit the Holocaust Museum. He started in that direction, but he just cut across the grass and is walking toward the Washington Monument."

"You know, Myk, if Faraq shaved his beard, he might just pass as your brother."

Myk scoffed. "A younger and much *smaller* brother! No terrorists in my family."

She laughed. "Jodi, this guy seems to be an anomaly. He's the only one who hasn't followed the itinerary found in his luggage." As Myk sat on a bench, he peered through his binoculars and monitored Faraq as he approached the Washington Monument.

---

Faraq walked across the grass to the concrete pathway leading up to the historic structure. He looked out across the vast green lawn at the White House off in the distance. As he neared the monument, he looked straight up at the great, towering obelisk.

From a distance, the monument appeared bright white, especially at night when the multitude of floodlights lit it up. But up close, the stone wasn't nearly as white as it appeared in the postcards he had seen in the bookstore. In the daylight, the mammoth stones were actually all different shades of white, with small cracks and chips.

Turning, Faraq looked back across the mall and paused to admire the trees ablaze in autumn colors. He walked to the other side of the monument to see the Lincoln Memorial and noticed a structure at the base of the reflecting pool that led up to the memorial. He pointed and asked a nearby guide, "What is the structure down there with all of the water features?"

"That's the World War II Memorial."

"Thank you. I haven't lived here for some time."

He walked across the large, open grass area toward the memorial. The first thing Faraq noticed was the large gathering of people standing at various points around the memorial. A group of elementary school students walked back up the stone stairs. There was a team of tall, athletic-looking women with matching warm up suits. The logo read Ohio State. Everyone walked slowly and kept their voices low, almost a reverent whisper.

As Faraq walked down to the lower level, he gazed at the water spilling out from the magnificent water features, the sound reverberating off the polished granite walls. He came across an older man in a wheelchair pushed by his elderly wife. The old man pointed up at one of the inscriptions on the granite-faced wall and said something to his wife. His wrinkled hand shook and bobbed as he struggled to hold his arm in the air.

Looking across to the other side, Faraq noticed another elderly man and his wife sitting on the carved concrete bench. They gazed at the water pouring over the top of the polished marble, and the elderly man's head was stooped, perhaps as he reflected on days gone by, his eyes moist and red. Faraq's own thoughts drifted to his family, and as he gazed at the old man, sympathy tugged hard at his chest. He, too, sat on one of the stone benches alongside a pool of water and observed as people passed by, some pausing to read the inscriptions carved into the granite walls.

*"Western infidels." I think not. What other country has fought and conquered so many and yet taken nothing for it, not even the people or land it defeated?*

He sighed and propped his elbows on his knees, clasping his hands. After a few minutes in thought, he put his head in his hands. He had to break free of the web Hakeem had spun around him.

---

Myk spoke into his radio, "Jodi, he's headed your direction."

"Okay, Myk. I'm in position."

"He's walking over the Kutz Bridge on his way to the National Holocaust Museum. I need you to enter the museum now. I will tell you when he gets to the entrance."

Agent Black locked the van and entered the museum. "Myk, I don't understand what these guys think they can pull off. This place is pretty secure, and the other sites are secured just as well."

"It's a diversion, Jodi. Faraq knows something about the EMP weapons. He's the key. I just haven't figured out what he's doing here yet. He's walking up to the entrance. Did you pick him up?"

"I've got him. This place is like a maze in here. Are you coming in?"

"No. I've got something else planned. Tell me when he's ready to leave."

Myk walked back across the street and found a place under a massive oak tree aglow with the rays of sunshine that illuminated the yellow and auburn leaves. He sat in the shade and monitored both exits.

After sitting outside of the museum for a few hours, Myk's phone vibrated. He touched his earpiece and made the connection.

"Myk, this is Brodie. Can you hear me?"

"Yes, go ahead, Brodie."

Unlike Adelberg, who was near the end of his career, Deputy Director Brodie Bashford was young and energetic. The only complaint, if you could even call it that, was the man never ceased to smile. Some in the agency even joked that he had a monthly appointment to get his teeth whitened.

Bashford asked, "What's Faraq's status?"

"He's still in the Holocaust Museum. He's been acting like a normal tourist the entire day, even taking pictures, but he seems to do his own thing. What's happening at the sites with the other suspects?"

"They are behaving like model citizens and following their agenda. But I had a great conference call with the Canadian Security Intelligence Agency this morning."

"Oh really?"

"They picked up some chatter from a mosque in Windsor, Canada, across the river from Detroit. Twenty of the mosque's newest members had a six-month lease on some apartments fronting the Detroit River. It's been less than a month, and the members vacated all four apartments. The mosque's imam made two trips to Pakistan and one to Saudi Arabia in the past six months. We matched the imam's picture to a surveillance photograph two months ago from a meeting he had with Saji Aman in Karachi."

Myk sat up straight and clenched his fists.

Bashford continued, "Director Adelberg believes this is the sleeper cell, but they've vanished. We checked all video footage from the tunnel under the river and cameras at the Imperial Bridge in Detroit but came up empty. The Detroit Police recovered five empty rubber rafts along the river."

"Those are the real players, Brodie. These guys in D.C. are just pawns."

"It sure looks that way."

"What about the traffic cameras on the highways or the gas stations?" Myk asked.

"We are checking those as we speak, but nothing so far. They must be taking the back roads. There's a whole network of those who would be sympathetic to their cause and provide cover for them. Hopefully something will surface soon."

"I am going to have a face-to-face with Faraq when he exits the museum. I want to get a read on him."

Bashford hesitated for a moment and then replied, "It's worth taking a chance, Myk. Let me know how it goes."

While he waited for Faraq and Agent Black to leave the museum, Myk texted the number the anonymous caller Mordechai gave him, then waited for the return call. Two minutes later, his phone vibrated. Myk answered on the first ring. "This is Myk."

"Agent McGrath, I wasn't expecting to hear from you so soon. What's happening?"

"A sleeper cell entered across the Canadian border, and I am babysitting a man I am certain has never injured another human being in his life."

"How do you know this?"

"Call it intuition, whatever. We think they will use an advanced EMP weapon we have no defenses for, and I am running out of time. Do you have any more information?"

"I am afraid not. We seem to have the same intel as you do."

Myk replied, "Nothing on the mole you warned me about?"

"Agent McGrath, you have a decrepit old Nazi dealing with an unknown new player in the terrorist world who happens to have a devastating weapon the world has yet to see. What do your instincts tell you? I know your mother taught you well."

"How in the hell do you know so much about me and my mother anyway? One thing is for damn sure; my mother has never been shy about voicing her displeasure for Director Adelberg. But I don't see him as the mole. It just doesn't fit. I think it's someone else."

"Your mother has good reason not to trust Director Adelberg. I don't trust him either, but I agree with you. As far as your question about how I know so much about your mother, I'm afraid that will have to wait for another day."

Myk replied, "Fine. I am wasting my time here in D.C. Every fiber of my being says it's a diversion."

"I am sorry I can't be of any further assistance to you, Agent McGrath."

Myk disconnected the call. As he slid his phone back into his pocket, Agent Black's panicked voice came piping through on his earpiece. "Myk. I lost him! Faraq just stood up and bolted toward the museum exit."

"Damn it! How could that happen?"

"I'm sorry. I got stuck behind a big group of slow senior citizens. He's already downstairs."

Myk jumped up from the park bench and sprinted across the street. Leaping over the curb, he jogged to the exit on the left side of the museum's massive glass exterior. As he picked up his pace and walked around a blind corner of the huge concrete pillar supporting the museum, Faraq exited the building. Faraq looked down at his watch as Myk approached him, and before he could look back up, Myk stepped directly into his path. Faraq ran straight into the solid mass of muscle and toppled to the hard sidewalk, flattened like a beach house in a hurricane. He looked up at Myk McGrath and said, "I'm sorry. I must not have been looking where I was going."

Myk stooped over and picked up the program that had fallen out of Faraq's hand, then extended his hand to help him up. "No problem. I came around the corner fast."

Myk wanted to get a feel for him. He clasped hands with Faraq and moved slow and deliberately while he studied Faraq's face and made eye contact with him.

Faraq brushed himself off and said, "Sorry about that."

Every childhood training session came screaming back to Myk. His mom had dragged him everywhere from the bank to the grocery store, teaching him to read people and the "gives" and "tics" that exposed who they were. He became so adept at reading salespeople that they would turn to his mother. Myk always landed the best deal. And he'd certainly used the skill to his advantage when it came to dating girls in his teenage years. He didn't doubt the training his mom had engrained in him. But as Myk assessed Faraq, he got goose bumps. This man looked anxious, but not guilty. Something did not feel right.

After he thanked Myk for helping him up, Faraq walked the opposite direction, looked back, and then headed down 14th Street until he stopped at a street vendor to grab a quick snack. Myk's mind was filled with thoughts from the past as he walked slowly back to the van. Agent Black arrived a few minutes later, out of breath from running. She saw Myk staring into oblivion.

"Myk, is everything okay?"

"Yep, we're good. I told you I wanted to have an encounter with him."

"What happened? You look like you've just seen a ghost."

Myk replayed the words of the anonymous caller in his mind. *Things may not be as they appear. Trust no one.*

Agent Black asked, "Are you sure you're okay?"

Myk looked up at the massive glass structure of the Holocaust Museum. "I don't know. There's something about this place."

"Sorry, I'm not sure I follow you."

"It's nothing. Don't worry about it."

She squinted at Myk. "C'mon, what is it?"

Myk rubbed his hand across his unshaven face. "Faraq wasn't looking, so I leaned into him and popped him to the ground. I'm pretty good at getting a read on people, but I wasn't expecting what I got."

"What's that?"

"I know there must be a connection between Faraq and Chen Wu, but I think there's a disconnect between Faraq and the rest of the group he came to D.C. with."

"Really?"

"Yeah. There's something else that happened to me at this same museum. Last year, I was shocked to find my grandparents' names displayed on one of the walls up on the second floor."

Agent Black looked up at the museum. "Whoa! Are you serious? Your grandparents were Holocaust victims?"

"They were, but I had been raised my whole life thinking they had died in the Ravensbruck Concentration Camp until I saw their names in the museum. They lived in the small community of Lidice, Czechoslovakia. Hitler had the entire town demolished and removed from all the German maps."

"That's awful. Why Lidice of all places?"

"One of Hitler's SS officers . . . " Myk paused while he tried to remember the name. "I think it was Heydrich. Anyway, he was assassinated outside Prague, so Hitler decided to take out his vengeance on Lidice. He had the town leveled to the ground with bulldozers, flattened all the farms, filled in the lakes, and had the streams diverted."

"Wow. How in the world did your mother survive?"

"Actually, my mother and her twin sister survived, while the entire town of Lidice was massacred on the side of a barn. My grandfather's business partner hid the twins from the Germans. My grandfather and his business partner helped one another on their farms. That's who raised my mother and her sister."

"Is that why you didn't want to follow Faraq into the museum?"

"No, I wanted to confront him without anybody else around. Anyway, it's hard to explain. You would think this would be something I knew about while growing up at home, but I've had to find out the truth about my grandparents death and their village on my own."

"Okay, that's a bit odd." After a moment, Agent Black looked down the street at Faraq, who ate from a small box of popcorn in his hand. "He's on the move again. Do you want me to follow him?"

Myk turned around. "No. I've got it."

It was nearing the end of the day, and most of the sites around the Capitol had closed. Myk had waited for Faraq to leave the Lincoln Memorial for the last hour, and now Faraq sat on the bench facing the reflection pool. As Myk watched, Faraq meticulously folded his newspaper and left it lying on the bench. He looked around but didn't see Myk this time, and as he left, Myk spoke into his microphone.

"Jodi, he's on the move again. He left his paper sitting on the bench. I'll check the bench to see if he left anything else behind and then follow him. Can you see him from your position?"

"Yes, he's pretty easy to spot. He's crossing Seventeenth and cutting across the grass at the Washington Monument."

"Okay."

Myk picked up the paper and looked underneath to see if he left anything else. Faraq had left the newspaper open to the third page with an obscure article about the Department of Justice's trial of an accomplice to the Madrid bombings. Myk skimmed the short article, knowing there was a connection but unable to connect the dots. He tucked the paper under his arm and turned to see if he still had a visual on Faraq, then stood and walked along the reflecting pool's path toward the World War II Memorial. A rather large contingent of tourists still sat around the water features enjoying the solitude.

"Jodi, I lost my visual on him. Which way did he go?"

"You just missed him. He reached the top of the grass hill leading to the Washington Monument, and he's walking back down the other side toward the White House. It looks like he's going back to his room. What did you find on the bench?"

"Just the paper he was reading. There is a connection; I just haven't made it yet."

"What do you mean 'connection'?"

"I'm not sure. I need to look at that postcard he left behind."

He jogged across the street and up the grassy hill. When he reached the top, he spotted Faraq leaning against the large wrought iron fence surrounding the White House grounds.

"I have a visual on him, Jodi. I can take it from here. He's standing at the fence just staring out at the White House. They must have something going on at the White House tonight."

"Why's that?"

"There are four huge, white event tents set up on the back lawn and a band warming up. Anyway, have you heard from Brodie?"

"He said the other suspects are back in their rooms. He contacted the FBI and the D.C. SWAT teams for their gathering tomorrow morning."

"Okay, I will let you know when he's on his way back to the hotel, assuming that's where he's going. If he stays near the fence much longer, White House security will come around and ask him to move on."

Myk remained up on the small hill of the Washington Monument keeping his eye on Faraq. The sun had just gone down, and the western sky was glowing in a stunning palette of orange and lilac ribbons on the horizon. The lights in D.C. sparkled around the city, and alluring autumn colors of gold and bronze lit the surrounding Capitol area. He stood at the intersection of axes—the National Mall represented the north and south axis, from the U.S. Capitol to the Lincoln Memorial; the east and west axis ran between the White House and the Thomas Jefferson Memorial. The Washington Monument and Myk McGrath stood at the center of it all.

# Chapter 7

Myk and Agent Black monitored Faraq's room and updated Central Command every hour. Myk's phone vibrated.

"Hey, Brodie. What's the news?"

"We just got a big hit on the sleeper cell that went missing in Canada. We have a positive I.D. from a gas station video camera in upper Pennsylvania; it's Saji Aman. I don't know if you had a chance to read through the information given to everyone, but Saji's great grandfather was intertwined with the Nazis and was even identified at several concentration camps."

Myk set his binoculars on the dash. *The day of reckoning is coming for that bastard. I'll take him apart piece by piece.*

"Did they get the license plate number?"

"No, they didn't have any video cameras at the gas pumps. They only had cameras in their convenience store; that's where we got Saji's picture."

"Brodie, we've got a handle on the nineteen here in D.C. If they attempted anything suspicious, they wouldn't get twenty feet without a federal agent on top of them; I think they're decoys."

"It looks that way, Myk. And we still don't have any answers for an EMP attack. If we don't get to them first, entire cities could become disaster zones. I'm less concerned about this group in D.C.;

the other twenty that snuck across the Canadian border make me nervous."

"Have you contacted the President? When will you evacuate some of our leaders?"

"We've put everyone on high alert. Director Adelberg is at the White House right now going over the contingency security travel plans. We are keeping a close watch on all the roads coming into the D.C. area, and we're bringing in a few more agents to help us track the group here in D.C. before they all meet this morning. By the way, Jodi told me about your face-to-face encounter with Faraq at the Holocaust Museum."

"Yeah, it was strange. I looked him in the eyes, Brodie. I got a weird vibe from him. He was a bit intimidated by me, but other than that, the guy was calm. Even though he flew in with the same group, I can't shake the feeling that somehow he's not a part of it."

"Hmm . . . really? We just received another call from the Chinese government. Chen Wu identified Faraq as the one who spared his life and called the authorities."

Myk paused. "Faraq won't blow himself up, or anyone else for that matter. I gave him the opportunity to reach out when I put him to the pavement this afternoon, but he didn't take it."

"We'll see if anything turns up at their gathering in a few hours."

Myk checked his watch. It was 2:07 a.m. He looked through his binoculars back up at Faraq's dark room again.

*Faraq, what are you doing here?*

# Buffalo, New York

As Saji drove through Buffalo and crossed into Lancaster in the darkness of the early morning hours, he glanced into the back seat.

"Brothers, we are here. We will be nearing the flight school in a few minutes."

Shamir and Simon straightened up from their slumber, rubbed their eyes and looked out the window. "Where is it?"

"It will be coming up in two miles on the right side of the vehicle." A few minutes later, Saji pointed. "There, right there. That is the hotel where they have stored our weapons."

The two men in the back looked out the side and rear windows as they passed a rather plain-looking motel, the parking lot scattered with older model American vehicles—a few with rusted out wheel wells. As he drove, Saji's mind flooded with thoughts. He had planned this operation with Hakeem and Khatchi for so many years he wasn't sure if the time would ever arrive. Then the old German Nazi contacted him and offered his sources inside the CIA in exchange for killing more Jews. Saji had visited so many countries over the past few years: Iran, Russia, China, and Saudi Arabia. It was all a fog now. He had no place to call home.

He looked at the GPS as the pleasant female voice spoke from the Garmin GPS, "Final destination. Jeff Miller Flight Training School."

"Shamir, here it is. Coming up on the right. See the sign? 'Jeff Miller Flight Training School.' We will circle around so you can have another look at it."

Saji drove beyond the school another mile, then made a U-turn. He eased off the gas pedal as they drove back by the flight school which was difficult to see because of the darkness. A few minutes later, he pulled into the motel parking lot looking for a white Ford Taurus. He spotted a car with its parking lights turned on that was parked on the other side of the fenced-in pool. He drove around the back of the pool and parked next to the Taurus. Everyone in the car tensed. An older man with streaks of gray in his beard got out of the vehicle and approached with a peaceful smile. When he made eye contact, Saji nodded and then lowered the window. The man reached into his pocket and pulled out an envelope.

"I presume you are Saji Aman."

The man's high, feminine voice startled Saji. He cleared his throat. "Yes, I am."

"A mutual friend would like you to have this."

The man handed Saji an envelope with three motel keys and said, "You will find everything as directed under the beds and in the showers of your rooms. The rooms have been stocked with food. This will be our last contact with you unless there is an emergency. We will leave someone to watch the rooms until you depart later this morning. Just look for this white Taurus in the parking lot, and someone will be able to help you, should you need it."

"Thank you. We will be fine."

"Yes, of course."

The man poked his head in the window and looked into the back seat at Shamir and Simon. Then he closed his eyes and clasped his hands. "Praise be to Allah."

He walked back to the Taurus, got in, rolled up the tinted windows, and drove away.

Saji opened the envelope and dispersed the motel keys with their large, red plastic room numbers; the dilapidated motel hadn't converted to the magnetic key cards yet. The men found their rooms adjacent to one another at the rear corner of the complex. Based on the number of cars in the parking lot, Saji assumed the place was less than half full.

As he turned the handle of the motel room door, Saji glanced behind him and gazed into the darkness of the cool and crisp morning air. No one. He entered the room and locked the door. The room had an old and musty smell partially masked by the pine air freshener. Saji surveyed the bathroom to make sure he was alone, then got down on his knees and checked under both double beds. His heart leapt—automatic guns, silencers, body armor. He went back to the bathroom and opened the door to the shower stall. Two oversized black suitcases sat in it.

Saji unzipped them, then sat on the closed toilet and stared at the piles of explosives. He checked his watch and then did the math; Abdul and his team had taken the longer route and would arrive within the hour. He left the bathroom and sat on the side of the bed, then decided to rest before getting on the road again.

A light knock at the door woke Saji. He checked his watch; forty minutes had gone by. He could hardly believe it. He got up and peered through the closed shades, then opened the door and pulled Abdul inside. As the door shut, Saji embraced him.

"Can you believe it, Abdul? It's finally here. We have waited years for this. This morning, we will strike a mighty blow to the beast for Allah."

Abdul grinned. "I know, I know. Did you drive by the flight school? How many planes could you see?"

"It was too dark to see, but don't worry, my brother. There will be many planes in the hangars."

"How are the others?"

"Simon and Shamir are fine, but Meham felt a little carsick; he will be fine with some food and rest. Shamir has the room next to yours."

"Of course."

"Abdul, I wish you could continue on with me when we shock the Americans and liberate Khatchi with the EMP weapon's magnificent power. We will gain instant respect and become a mighty force for Allah, and we will forever remember your ultimate sacrifice."

Saji kissed him on the cheek. "Praise be to Allah." He walked out the door and got back into his vehicle, and he and the others began the final leg of their journey to New York and then on to Richmond, Virginia.

# Washington, D.C.

The portly man stared at his reflection in the mirror while he straightened the knot in his tie. He tucked his slick black hair behind his tiny ears, one pierced with a diamond earring. He spoke in his trademark high-pitched nasal voice as he stared at himself.

"The Americans have no idea what's coming."

Jaffa Banzel then walked across his office to adjust the large photograph of the Grand Mosque in Mecca and the hundreds of thousands gathered there. The photograph was highlighted with three halogen art pendant lights and framed by intricate hand-carved wood from India. It reminded him of the journey he took when he was just eighteen.

He sat in his leather chair and pondered about the phone call he was about to make. He looked at the phone, then spun his chair around and glanced out the window at the Washington Monument which was illuminated against the dark sky. He wondered how he ever became both a well-known attorney around the Capitol and the president of the Muslim Brotherhood while maintaining his previous alliance in the same law firm as Attorney General Derek Helter. Only CIA Director David Adelberg had noticed.

After a few minutes, Jaffa spun his chair around, took a deep breath, and dialed the number.

"Hakeem, this is Jaffa."

"Jaffa, how good to hear from you. What news do you have?"

"Wonderful news. I received a call last night and confirmed the route they will take to escort Khatchi to the Federal Court in Richmond, Virginia. I have been instructed to be in the courtroom by three o'clock in the afternoon to await his arrival."

"Indeed, this is wonderful news. Is everything ready with the package?"

"Yes. There was a slight delay at the Port Authority, but we explained that since they did not allow us fireworks for our celebration of the mosque permit approval, we will use this equipment for a state-of-the-art laser show. They allowed us to pick it up after a day. Everything is assembled and in place."

"Jaffa, you have done well. Our time has come. In a few hours, we will ignite a flame of worldwide support for our cause."

# Chapter 8

The only way to stop an avalanche is to keep it from ever getting started. And any hope of thwarting Hakeem's plan depended on stopping it before it began.

Myk sat in the lobby of the JW Marriott at 5 A.M. drinking coffee. The CIA had intercepted a message that all nineteen suspects would gather at the same location early in the morning, but they didn't know where.

"Jodi, has he left the room yet?" he asked over his wireless microphone.

"Yes. The lights just went off. He should be on his way down."

"Okay. Have any others left yet?"

"I just spoke with Brodie. Khaled and Abdul left their hotels first. Brodie and one of the SWAT teams followed them so they could set up their surveillance equipment before the other suspects arrive. Brodie said they took their luggage with them. Whatever they're up to, it doesn't look like they plan to come back."

"I just saw Faraq get off the elevator. He's got his suitcase with him, too. Keep an eye out for him. As soon as he gets in his cab, pull the van forward, and I'll come out."

Faraq strode by Myk and out the rotating lobby doors. As soon as Faraq left the building, Myk followed.

Agent Black piped in, "He just got in the cab. I'm pulling forward now."

"Great. Stay out on the street. Don't pull under the hotel porte-cochere; you might get caught behind all the taxis."

"Right. Can you see our van? I'm just pulling in."

Myk stepped out from behind a massive column wrapped in imported hand-carved stone and jumped in the passenger seat of the van. "Which cab is his?"

"That's his taxi four cars in front of us. Brodie said seven of the others have arrived at an empty retail building on Connecticut and N Street. Brodie has agents set up on the second floor of the building directly across the street. Within the next thirty minutes, they will have all the audio and video equipment producing a live feed so we can all see and hear what's going on inside the building. They are waiting on Langley to download the file for the building blueprints."

Myk stared at the congestion from the rush hour morning commuters. "I can't believe the traffic in this city! There's no way I could live in this every day. I don't know how these locals stand it. It'll take us ten minutes to drive one mile; I could walk it faster than we're moving."

After twenty minutes in traffic, Myk and Agent Black finally approached the building.

"Brodie, this is Myk. We're a few blocks away. What do you want us to do with the van?"

Bashford responded, "All the parking spots on the street were full, so we sent local officers to the surrounding businesses and shops to locate the vehicle owners so they can move their cars. We have a spot across the street directly in front of the building where they are meeting. You should have a good visual from there."

"We'll be there in a minute."

"The SWAT teams are on standby just around the corner. They

will do the heavy lifting if something goes down."

"Got it."

Myk and Agent Black pulled their surveillance van into an already jam-packed street lined with maple trees and sweeping arched streetlights spaced every thirty feet. Most of the redesigned buildings looked like old bungalows with reclaimed red brick and washed out mortar joints. Many shops had colorful awnings fastened to the building with decorative hand-forged wrought iron. Several other taxis with their fluorescent-green "Save the planet by using hybrid cars" dropped off suspects in front of the building. A final taxi carrying the last passenger arrived ten minutes later. All nineteen suspects met in a storefront building with floor-to-ceiling glass windows across its entire front, a typical retail store not yet painted with unfinished drywall and concrete floors without any tile or carpet installed.

Myk tapped his fingers in rhythmic motion on the dash as his leg fidgeted up and down. He felt like he might combust. From the moment he and Agent Black parked the van, his internal alarms blared. He did not control the operation. Deputy Director Brodie Bashford was located in the building directly behind him, but Myk was not comfortable with someone else calling the shots. Some in the agency envied his gifts and wanted to bring him down by hanging his glaring problem with authority around his neck like an oversized albatross, but he rocketed beyond his peers so quickly that it got swept under the carpet.

After five minutes, another taxi arrived, and an Arab man wearing a silk Shalwar Kameez with colorful ribbons of gold and russet running its length got out and walked toward the entrance. Myk assumed by the look of the man that he was an imam. After entering the building, the man shut the large metal folding scissor security gate in front of the building, then locked it with a padlock and chain.

Myk spoke into his radio. "Brodie, who's the guy who just entered?"

"The local FBI officer identified him as an imam from Baltimore. He arrived at the Baltimore mosque a few months ago. He's the real deal, strict obedience to Sharia Law and everything."

"Got it. Something's not right, Brodie. Did someone sweep the area? With so much law enforcement in a confined space, it would be like shooting fish in a barrel."

"We are sweeping the area as we speak, Myk."

For the next twenty minutes, the imam spoke to the nineteen suspects. Then someone came from a back room and handed out prayer rugs to the group.

Myk turned to Agent Black, "Really? Their sunrise prayer?"

She laughed. He looked back into the building at all nineteen suspects down on their knees facing west toward Mecca reciting the morning prayer.

Myk screamed into his radio, "Brodie, are you fucking kidding me! We have half the entire security of D.C. over here monitoring these guys, and they're getting together for their morning prayers! This is just brilliant. Damn it." He curled his fingers to dig into his scalp, then opened the van door. "I'm telling you they have us on defense. We are on our heels, and they are about to push us over. Let me rush the building."

Bashford replied, "Sit tight, Myk. Let it play out."

Myk shut the door and pulled the binoculars back up to take another look. After fifteen minutes, the group in the building finished their prayers, and the imam spoke. The surveillance team on the second floor across the street picked up every word with their sophisticated, state-of-the-art surveillance equipment, to which Myk and Black had a direct link. After a few minutes, the imam's speech turned into a farewell speech in which he told the group about the blessings of ultimate sacrifice and how their place would be made sure in Paradise.

Every instinct drilled into Myk since he was a child took over. "It's staged, Brodie! We're being set up. Are you catching this? He's getting these guys ready for a suicide mission."

"We already have the local officers evacuating civilians in the area."

Myk looked back across the street to the nineteen suspects now standing. After a few minutes, two new men appeared from one of the rooms in the back, both Arab men with dark stubble on their faces and pushing a massive wooden crate on wheels. Myk felt the strong inclination to take both of them down, but he couldn't without provocation.

"Brodie, what the hell is in the huge crate? Do you guys have a better angle from up there?"

"I don't know. We see the same thing you are; it's a big wooden crate. Whatever it is, it must be heavy because those guys are straining to push it."

The two men steered the crate toward the front of the building facing directly toward the street. One lifted the wooden top off the crate and let it fall to the floor. All four sides of the crate collapsed, exposing what looked like a huge jet engine attached to a massive power-generating machine. All nineteen suspects disappeared into a back room.

Myk opened his van door and radioed Brodie. "Fuck this! I'm crashing their party! What the hell is that thing anyway?"

"Stay put, Myk! I just gave the green light to the SWAT teams; they'll be here any second. That thing looks exactly like the sketch the Chinese gave us of the EMP weapon!"

# Chapter 9

As Myk listened to his radio, Bashford ordered the SWAT teams and bomb squads to seize the building. Ten seconds later, two SWAT team cargo trucks screamed down Connecticut Street from opposite sides of the building. As soon as they turned the corner, Myk looked back into the building. All nineteen suspects had vanished into the back room.

Before the last man left the room, a heavy static swept through the air around Myk, and the hairs on his arms stood up. He glanced at Agent Black's head, and her hair rose a few inches. Half a second later, a massive, blinding neon-blue cloud of light that looked like the rings around Saturn exploded from the EMP weapon. All the power went out, and the two SWAT cargo vans came to a screeching halt in the middle of the street. Every piece of surveillance equipment, cell phone, or any other electronic device died.

Myk turned and asked, "Holy shit Jodi, did you see that blue flash?"

"What the hell was that? Did you feel the wave of energy? It was like standing next to the bass speaker at a concert."

Myk reached for the radio. "Brodie, do you copy? Brodie . . . "

Dead silence. But before Myk could exit the van and rush the building, a massive explosion at the other end of the street broke the silence. A huge fireball erupted at the end of the block, and flames emanated from the explosion. Myk jumped out of the van. Helicopter propellers stuck out from a mangled heap engulfed in flames that illuminated the FBI logo on the wreckage. The helicopter had lost its power and fell from the sky like a wounded bird.

Myk ran across the street to the SWAT team's truck. "Get the security gate ripped off this damn place! We have to get inside! We have dozens of terrorists holed up inside here."

The SWAT teams opened fire on the security gate, then a few men came forward and yanked on the gate. The SWAT team leader looked to his commander. "We can't get it off."

"Blow it off!"

Two more SWAT members placed explosives at the hinges of the security gate.

"Everyone take cover!"

Myk and Agent Black ran back across the street and ducked behind their van. The explosion caused shattered glass to rain on Myk's surveillance van. Both SWAT teams filed out of their vehicles. He glanced back into the building; a terrorist came back out of the room, wearing a suicide vest. Myk jumped out from behind the van and waved his arms at the SWAT teams, screaming at the top of his lungs, "Take cover! It's a trap! Stop!"

But he was too late. Two SWAT team officers entered the building as the terrorist reached down and detonated his C-4 lined suicide vest. Myk leaped behind the van. A muffled explosion ripped through the air. Myk got up off the pavement and brushed off the debris; his ears felt like they were stuffed with swimmer's plugs. Thick smoke billowed out of the building as he walked closer to the carnage. He counted seven bleeding officers—two dead—and various body parts from the terrorist. He approached the SWAT commander, who was having a tourniquet applied to his leg because of the shards of glass from the explosion.

"Commander, station your men around the perimeter! If any more of those bastards take one step out of that back room, shoot them in the head. I'm going in. I need to grab a flashlight from your truck."

The commander looked up at Myk. His face was covered in a mixture of blood, sweat and debris. "Agent McGrath, that's suicide. Give us a few minutes to regroup, and we'll have another team storm the building and take them out."

Myk grabbed the flashlight from the SWAT cargo van. "I'm not waiting for anyone! If you've got someone who wants to join me, they are more than welcome, but I'm going in."

The SWAT commander barked out, "Bennett and Rodriguez, follow Agent McGrath and provide whatever backup he needs."

The two men leaped out of the cargo van and followed Myk into the smoke-filled building. He pointed to the back room and motioned for Rodriguez and Bennett to cover him. With his weapon drawn, he rushed the door and gave it a swift boot. The door flew open, and he crept into the room. He aimed the flashlight in all directions and saw nothing but a vacant, smoky room. Then he remembered Mordechai's comment: *This group is too sophisticated just to blow themselves up.* Nothing added up. For the first time in his life, Myk drew a blank. Had he actually been outfoxed?

For the next ten minutes, he searched the building room by room and found no one. As he came back out to the front of the building, much of the smoke had dissipated and he could see body parts from the suicide bomber lying around. He found Bashford waiting outside.

Bashford stopped his conversation with the SWAT commander and approached Myk. "What did you find?"

"They're gone, Brodie! The place is empty!"

"That's bullshit! They can't just disappear; unless that EMP weapon can somehow make people vanish too!"

Bashford turned to the SWAT commander. "Have your teams sweep the building and see what they can find." Then he turned back to Myk. "Nothing at all?"

"Nope, just an empty building. Brodie, the last time I felt like this was when the bombs went off while Dana was still on the train station platform in Madrid. I'd love to crack some terrorist's head right about now."

"We'll get back to Central Command and put a plan together. We have to, before they hit us again. They couldn't have gone far."

After another ten minutes of the SWAT team sweeping the building, the commander approached Bashford. "We've got nothing so far. We've swept it twice. The place is empty."

"There has to be something," Myk said. "The smoke cleared; let's check the room they last entered again."

He went back into the room and pointed his flashlight up. The SWAT team had already removed many ceiling panels as they looked for a possible escape. "There are no back doors to this place, right?"

The SWAT commander answered, "The only exit is out the front."

"Well, that's not exactly true, is it? We've got nineteen terrorists that vanished into thin air. Get some halogen floods in here. This is the last room I saw them enter. Let's light this place up."

A few SWAT team members brought the floodlights into the room. As Myk pointed them at all angles of the room, they exposed a small crease of a shadow on the floor. He stepped over to the area and jumped up and down.

"It's hollow! I need some equipment over here, now! Tear this floor up; we may have found their exit."

After several attempts with pry bars and guns, the floor remained intact. The few small holes they managed to create revealed a passageway underneath the floor.

Myk turned to the SWAT commander. "We need explosives. Blow that damn floor off; we've got to find these guys before they get too far." He asked Bashford, "Did you say you had blueprints?"

"We had the electronic file of the building blueprints, but the EMP weapon fried everything. We'll have to wait until we get back to Central Command."

While Myk and Bashford spoke in the hallway, the SWAT team blew the hatch off the floor, exposing a massive underground tunnel sealed shut when the nineteen had escaped. Almost thirty minutes had elapsed since the EMP weapon had gone off.

Myk turned to Agent Black. "We had a few radios in the back of the van. If they were turned off, they might still work. I'll follow the tunnel and see where it leads. Also, see if you can find any cell phones that may have been left off."

She came back with the radios and handed them to Myk while he examined the tunnel with the halogen lights. He held up some thick cable lines. "Brodie, here are the pulleys they must have used to lower the EMP weapon down into the tunnel. What is this place, anyway? It's big enough to drive a small car through."

"One of the FBI agents, whose father is a bit of a local historian, just informed me this building sits on top of what used to be the U.S. Vice President's residence over a century ago. They originally built the tunnel as a secret escape route for the Vice President in case of an attack."

Myk replied, "That's just brilliant! The wrong guys escaped! I'm pretty sure this wasn't quite the intended use of the original designers."

He lowered himself to the bottom of the tunnel and looked up at Agent Black. "Jodi, see if the van starts. If not, find a vehicle that works. Weave your way through the dead vehicles and pick me up wherever this tunnel terminates. I will radio you and let you know where it comes up."

He jogged down the tunnel, following the movement of the multitude of flashlights from the other agents fifty yards ahead. Old weathered brick lined the tunnel. *Whoever built this built it to last.* After about a mile, he reached the other agents as they climbed the exit ladder toward the sound of traffic overhead. When he reached the top, he looked up at the George Washington statue.

The tunnel ended at Washington Circle, a circular intersection where Pennsylvania Avenue and New Hampshire Avenue converged into a roundabout with the statue of Washington in the center. Almost an hour had elapsed since the EMP weapon had been fired off.

Myk spoke into his radio, "Jodi, we're at Washington Circle. There's no sign of anyone. These guys are long gone. Is Brodie still around?"

"No. A helicopter came and got most of his team a few minutes ago. I'm on my way right now. Myk, this place is a disaster zone."

# New York City

While Faraq and the rest of Hakeem's team escaped from the secret tunnel in Washington D.C., Hasan and two assistants drove a large van with an EMP weapon mounted in its rear cargo. Khalid and two others followed him in another van with an EMP weapon. At six-thirty in the morning, Hasan and Khalid drove their vans together to the first target. They arrived at the first location and simultaneously fired both EMP weapons at the Astoria Power Station in Queens, New York. The men gazed with wide eyes as massive sparks, like a raging monsoon lightning storm, shot off in the morning sky. They waited a few moments to make sure there were no delayed effects of the electromagnetic pulse before they started the engine to their cargo vans.

After destroying their first target, Hasan moved on to the Narrows Station, while Khalid went to the Fore River Power Generating Station. At the Narrows Station, Hasan's assistants jumped out of the van and opened the double doors in the rear. Hasan fired up the weapon and then engaged the pulse button. The weapon produced a dazzling array of glowing lights when it discharged. Hasan was instructed to leave immediately, but he couldn't help but stop and stare at what was happening at the generating station. It looked like the glowing lights of the Aurora Borealis had collided with the rings of Saturn for a ballet of Tchaikovsky's Swan Lake. Spectacular ribbons of sapphire and auburn weaved and twisted in the crisp morning air. He had never seen anything like it and attributed the wonder of the blinding blue waves of light to the power of Allah.

Each time they left a power station, they passed emergency vehicles traveling in the opposite direction. By eight o'clock in the morning, the EMP weapons had permanently destroyed over seventy percent of the electric power to New York City. The four power generating stations had been rendered useless and irreparable. It would likely take over six months to rebuild the power plants by importing entirely new equipment. The EMP weapon would also wipe out seventy percent of the water supply coming into New York City by destroying power to the pumping stations. Most importantly, the three main targets would have no source of power: Wall Street, JFK, and the New York Air Traffic Control Center. Hakeem knew that taking out those facilities would send a massive shock wave through an already fragile U.S. economy and put the country into full panic mode.

# Richmond, Virginia

At the hotel's presidential suite in Richmond, Virginia, Hakeem sat down at his computer and logged onto a live feed of the air traffic control center from the JFK tower. Anyone with access to the internet could log in and watch the monitor as it showed little symbols of airplanes and their locations flying above New York.

Hakeem monitored the site for a little more than an hour when the screen went blank. Khalid and Hasan had taken out the air traffic control. Beaming, Hakeem logged off his computer turned on his eighty-four-inch plasma television to CNN. They had already reported on a few power failures in New York City in the early morning. Hakeem looked at his watch.

"It has begun."

# Chapter 10

## Muslim Brotherhood Headquarters, Washington D.C.

Faraq and the others had foiled those masters of intelligence, the Central Intelligence Agency, at their own game, eluding some of the world's best security forces on their own turf and setting the stage for a bigger plan. After exiting the tunnel, they had climbed into the back of the awaiting carrier and driven to the other side of the city in the back of disguised FedEx vans. They parked in the private parking garage under the Muslim Brotherhood's national headquarters.

As Faraq got out of the FedEx van, he turned and asked, "Rashid, you can't be thinking of being a part of this, are you? I know you're a peaceful man."

"Faraq, were you not listening to the imam or Hakeem's instructions before we left? No one will hurt any more people; we're just going to scare the Americans and get the media's attention for Hakeem's cause. Hakeem said we will spend a few years in jail, but my family will be paid millions of dollars for simply scaring the Americans. There's no harm in that. It would take me ten lifetimes to earn that kind of money. A few years in an American jail are worth it."

Before Faraq told Rashid he had good reason not to trust Hakeem, self-preservation took over. When he'd heard the suicide bomb go off while he escaped through the tunnel, he worried about what Hakeem intended for the other eighteen. He had witnessed the power of the EMP weapon and knew there was no defense against it. "Yes, Rashid, I suppose you're right. If you think you can trust Hakeem, then a few years in jail is worth financial freedom for a lifetime."

Jaffa entered the underground garage and embraced everyone as he met them.

"Brothers of Islam, this morning we lit the fuse of a mighty explosion of Islam against the West. By the end of the day, the Americans will tear themselves apart from the inside out. Our brothers in this country and around the world will unite in a revolution against the infidels."

Faraq looked at the man's face. The man practically cried tears of joy. Faraq turned to Rashid again. "I hope everything works out as you hope. I must leave in the other van now to Richmond, Virginia."

He entered the FedEx van. The garage door reopened, and Faraq left for the courthouse.

# Langley, Virginia

Myk returned to the CIA's Central Command Center as a steady stream of vehicles entered the parking lot. A long line had already formed at the security screening check point, and every available agent had been called in. Eighteen suspected terrorists were on the loose in the Nation's Capital.

When Myk stepped off the elevator, the entire floor buzzed with voices. He looked through the glass partition walls to the massive video screens. More than two dozen monitors displayed a live feed from many of the cameras throughout the D.C. area. Adelberg and Bashford stood in the glass-enclosed mini conference room connected to the newly renovated Command Center. Adelberg was discussing with Bashford about reports just coming in from New York City about power failures. He motioned for Myk to join them.

When Myk approached, he asked Adelberg, "Did you guys pick up anything from the security cameras near the tunnel's exit?"

"No. They definitely knew what they were doing. Three hours before the meeting, the cameras went out. We are running the license plates of every car in the area just prior to the cameras going down, but we've got nothing so far."

Myk shook his head. "Director, a suicide bomber in the middle of D.C. can be quite shocking, but I think it's a diversion. Do we have any more information on Saji and his team?"

"Nothing new, Myk. Right now, we are calling in every available agent. We set up some added security measures for the arrival of Khatchi Abu-Mon at the courthouse in Richmond later today, but I've decided to call some back to D.C. to give us the extra manpower we'll need here. We sent snipers and bomb squads to set up at all the sites the suspects visited yesterday, and we evacuated the President and his cabinet members last night. All congressional meetings at the Capitol have been cancelled. Obviously, this is something we've never dealt with before."

Myk gasped. "Shit! Did you say the Khat Man is arriving at the Richmond Courthouse today?"

"Yes. Why?"

"Damn it!" Myk shook his head, then hesitated. He remembered Mordechai's warning to trust no one. But he could trust Adelberg and Bashford. "I'll be right back." He turned and bolted out of the office, stopping to ask Agent Black, "Jodi, did you bring the bookstore bag and newspaper to forensics yet?"

"No. They're still in the box next to the headphones in the back of the van. Why?"

"I'll explain in a minute."

He sprinted out the door, passed the elevator, and flew down the stairwell, skipping four steps at a time with his long legs. He had almost made the connection when he picked up the paper Faraq had left behind, but he'd become distracted. Now it seemed so obvious. He jerked the van door open and looked for the container. Grabbing the bookstore bag Faraq had thrown away, he looked inside and found the postcard: the historical Lewis F. Powell United States Courthouse—the same courthouse to which the Khat Man was being transported.

*How could you be so blind, Myk?!*

He pulled the newspaper out that Faraq had left on the bench at the Lincoln Memorial turned to the third page and folded precisely to show the small article about Khatchi Abu-Mon's arrival for his trial. Myk scanned the article again.

*I should have put a bullet through Khat Man's head when I had a chance.*

He locked up the van and ran back to the Command Center. When he stepped out of the elevator, Adelberg was having an animated discussion with the D.C. Chief of Police. Myk looked up at the multitude of live video monitors and wondered where the terrorists would have gone after exiting the secret tunnel.

Adelberg looked over. "Myk, what do you have?"

"I think Faraq tried to reach out to me by leaving a few linking clues, but I didn't piece it together until now. After speaking with Brodie, everyone agrees Faraq was the only one who broke protocol and mixed up his routine, right?"

"Yes. Brodie mentioned that to me."

"Okay, so yesterday when he left the hotel, he turned around and spotted me. He may have been checking to make sure I was following him. He went to a bookstore, then walked across the street to eat breakfast at a café. Before he entered, he pulled his items out of the bookstore bag and tossed it into the trash. I grabbed his bag from the trash container and found a postcard inside. I think that was his first attempt trying to send a message."

Myk handed the postcard to Adelberg. "Look, it's a postcard of the Lewis F. Powell Jr. United States Courthouse."

"Did you share any of this with Brodie?"

"Not really; I just told him we picked up some stuff he left behind that would give us fingerprints if we needed them later."

"Okay. Go on."

"Take a look." He handed Adelberg the newspaper and pointed to the article. "Faraq left this at his last spot of the day. He folded it on the bench exactly as I just handed it to you. The article talks about the Department of Justice's wet dream of getting another one of these scumbags into their U.S. District Court. Faraq was leaving breadcrumbs." He paused for a moment. "I think he's trying to defect."

"You could be right, Myk, but why would he do that?"

Myk thought for a moment and then explained, "Well, it could be a ruse. They might be trying to get us to divert our assets away from D.C., but my gut tells me this guy might be trying to find a way out and he's sending out an S.O.S." He gestured as he explained. "Think about it: If he turns himself in, he knows that the next time he sees his family's faces, they won't be attached to their bodies. Whoever is behind this operation could have the members of any defector's family tortured or killed. I got a strange feeling when we ran into each other and made eye contact."

Adelberg replied, "Go down to Richmond. He'll recognize you, and you're the one he's trying to reach out to. From what he's left behind, he wants you at Khatchi's trial. Take Agent Black with you. But before you two leave, go downstairs to the weapons munitions clerk and load up with everything you can fit in the helicopter. I'll call the clerk and let them know you're coming. The chopper will be ready to go."

"Director Adelberg, one more thing."

"Sure. What is it, Myk?"

"Something is just not adding up for me. These guys obviously did their research and knew about the old V.P. tunnel, right?"

"Yes, of course."

"Okay. Since they knew we would be there watching them, they could have had that whole block set up with car bombs and suicide bombers. We could have walked right into an ambush. They've had this planned for a long time and could have killed a multitude of agents and officers this morning, but they only killed two. Not to be disrespectful to the officers who lost their lives today, but it doesn't make sense. They would normally want to kill as many people as possible, especially government agents. Why go to all that trouble this morning and only kill two?"

Adelberg nodded. "Myk, I asked myself the same question. This bunch appears a bit more cerebral than most we've dealt with. Hopefully, you can find Faraq at the courthouse in Richmond. Perhaps he has some answers for us before anything else happens."

# Chapter 11

## Lancaster, New York

---

Shamir had been resting on the bed for the past hour waiting for the designated time to begin his attack. He didn't want to disturb Simon who was sleeping soundly on the queen bed next to him. Shamir's hands were behind his head with his fingers tightly interlocked as he stared up at the dilapidated ceiling of the run-down hotel and contemplated his last day on earth.

Simon finally stirred in the bed next to him. Shamir whispered, "Simon, are you awake, brother?"

Simon rolled over and looked at the clock. "How long have you been awake, Shamir?"

"An hour or so. I just keep rehearsing over and over in my mind our mission today. I hope our brothers in New York destroyed the air traffic control, or it will be a very short flight."

"Have faith, Shamir. Allah will provide a way for us to strike down the infidels and bend them to His ways."

"See if the others are awake. The flight school will be opening soon; we need to load up the vans."

Shamir helped load the explosives and assault rifles into the back of the van behind the hotel. Afterward, he checked his watch; they were a few minutes early, but it was best to keep moving forward. After the group recited their prayers, they threw the room keys on the bed and shut the doors behind them. Shamir started the engine and turned to the men seated in the back.

"Any last minute questions?" No response.

"Okay. Remember, if you see any police cars on our drive to the flight school, let me know. We have to get the planes off the ground without any trouble. Abdul, as soon as we pass through the gates in the parking lot, grab our chains and locks and get those gates rolled shut and locked, understand?"

"Yes, Shamir."

Then he turned to Simon. "As soon as you hear my shots inside the building, you and Ali take out the control tower. Ali, remember, you have fifteen seconds to detonate your explosives in the tower, or we risk communications being sent out to the authorities."

"Of course, Shamir. We have gone through this a thousand times this past year."

"I know. We are approaching the school, brothers. Praise Allah." The van rolled into the parking lot. The flight school was located several miles outside of town and had its own private runway. As the van slowed, Abdul jumped out and ran back to the gates to chain and lock them shut. Shamir parked next to the flight school's front entrance, then leaped from the van and burst through the front doors, pointing his assault rifle ahead. On his left sat an older couple whom Shamir shot with his silenced weapon before they could turn around. An overweight man with a white button-down shirt that didn't quite reach the bottom of his massive stomach ran out from the hallway behind the front counter. Shamir shot the man in the chest. The man's white shirt turned crimson as he crashed forward, almost breaking the front counter.

A voice emerged from the other side of the counter. "Don't shoot! I am a Muslim!"

Shamir swiveled his head and the assault rifle to the right to see a young man standing behind the counter with his hands raised over his head. Shamir hesitated as he pointed his weapon at the young man. "What is your name?"

The man shook so badly he could hardly get the words out of his mouth. "My, my, na-name is Malik Lateef. I just started working here a few weeks ago. I am from India. I am getting my engineering degree at the University in Buffalo."

Shamir noted Malik's heavy Indian accent. "And you are a Muslim?"

"Yes. I attend Mohammed's Mosque on Walden Avenue in Buffalo."

Shamir decided to take advantage of this unexpected stroke of good fortune. "Where do they keep the keys for the airplanes?"

"Most are in the back office on the right side of the hallway, and some are in a lock box in the maintenance and service hangar. Please. Please don't shoot me!"

"Thank you, Malik. I'll see you in Paradise in a few hours."

Malik attempted to duck and cover his head with his arms, but Shamir squeezed the trigger and shot him through the head.

Shamir found the lock box with the keys for the planes. As he jogged down the hallway toward the back office, several rounds of gunshots came from outside. When he entered the office, he found the lock box hanging on the wall behind the desk and shot it open. The keys were organized and coded to match the planes and hangar numbers. He grabbed a piece of paper and a pen from the desk and wrote down the corresponding plane and key numbers before emptying the keys into a canvas bag.

A huge explosion went off outside, making the pictures on the wall rock back and forth. Shamir looked out the window; smoke billowed from the top of the air traffic tower. On the ground below, Simon gunned down two aircraft mechanics trying to run for cover around the back of a hangar, while Abdul drove the van around the office building and into one of the hangars. Shamir checked his watch, grabbed the canvas bag full of keys, and exited out the back door to join the others.

Simon shouted, "Shamir, what took so long? Is everything okay?"

"Yes. I had one unexpected complication, but I resolved it. Here are the keys."

He dumped the contents of his canvas bag onto the black asphalt. "We've had a bit of good fortune, brothers. The keys are organized and coded much better than we anticipated which should make pairing the keys with the planes much easier."

Over the next ten minutes, the six men searched for newer models full of fuel, then found the corresponding keys. Five men loaded three planes with bags of explosives while Abdul found the forklift to load the heavy tanks of fuel into the planes. After he loaded the second plane with a huge fuel tank, Shamir looked at his watch.

"It's time to leave! Let's go!"

Shamir taxied his plane past the smoking tower and pushed the throttle to full speed for take-off. The plane accelerated and, after a few moments, rose into the air. Simon and Abdul followed as Shamir banked his plane to the left, noted the coordinates of the instruments, and pointed the plane toward New York City.

Shamir was impressed by how smoothly the plane operated. The planes they had trained on the past two years were very old and had to be worked on weekly. He maintained a very low but safe altitude. Simon flew on Shamir's left, and Abdul flew on his left at a higher altitude. Shamir looked ahead and wondered if Paradise would be everything he had been taught it would be.

# New York City

It was supposed to be a private wedding with only parents and siblings in attendance. They would put out a press release the following day along with postings on Facebook and Twitter accompanied by a few pictures of the private event. But the groom's agent just couldn't resist the temptation of even more exposure for his client, who the public already adored. A slight hint of the wedding was dropped to the right reporter and a few bloggers, and that was all it took. The couple finally acquiesced to a public wedding, and a clamoring fan base turned the private affair into a media frenzy. It had been a slow year for Hollywood; no major stars going to drug rehab, no big divorces, no stars losing control in a drunken stupor, so all of the attention gravitated toward the wedding of the decade.

The groom, Adam Goldberg, was one of the most sought-after actors in Hollywood. He had cut his teeth as a comedic actor. He quickly burst onto the scene by selling out every one of his comedy shows; his sharp, self-deprecating humor about his life as the child of a Rabbi had audiences in stitches night after night. His transition to Hollywood was seamless. After two Oscar nominations, Goldberg had become a household name.

The bride, Rebekah Cohen, was adored by everyone. She was the daughter of an Israeli diplomat to the U.S. and the prime time anchor of a major cable news network. By the end of her second year, she had moved the network's ratings for her hour from third to first. Her contract was quickly renegotiated. She was sharp, witty, articulate, and her looks stopped men in their tracks and turned the heads of most women. She had graced the front cover of three major magazines.

Having given up all hope of a secluded wedding, the occasion had gone polar opposite. There wasn't a synagogue with enough capacity to host the event. New York's largest synagogue had been reserved and a deal had been brokered with the Mayor of New York to shut down two city blocks and erect massive video screens to accommodate the overflowing crowds. The video screens were powered by their own generators. It was a security nightmare. Every precaution had been taken; or so they thought.

---

The three stolen planes loaded with explosives fast approached New York City. Shamir turned to his companion in the back. "We are minutes away from impact. Are the detonators active and ready?"

"Yes, Shamir."

He looked out his window. Abdul and Simon veered their planes off to the left on a direct path to the large gathering at the wedding of the Jewish stars. Shamir banked his plane right and lowered his altitude, heading to the financial district.

As Abdul aimed his plane toward the synagogue, the screaming crowd scattered like a herd of gazelles from a charging lion. A massive fireball burst into the air as Abdul's plane struck the synagogue holding the wedding. Moments later, Simon's plane exploded as it hit the large frenzied crowd gathered outside that had been watching the wedding on the massive video screens. Debris showered down from the explosion, and smoke filled the air. Shamir looked up at his target, the New York Stock Exchange building. The last thing he saw before he closed his eyes was an enormous American flag draped on the front of the building.

# Chapter 12

## Richmond, Virginia

///

Hakeem sat down in his oversized leather couch in a penthouse suite overlooking Richmond's bustling downtown area and sipped his freshly brewed coffee, watching the breaking news pour into CNN. He had flown from Toronto, Canada into Richmond on his private jet to be in the U.S. while much of his plan unfolded. According to CNN, almost half of New York City was without power, and JFK had been completely shut down. With JFK blacked out, all air traffic throughout the United States would be tied into knots. JFK and the surrounding area had lost all power, and two jets had crashed on the tarmac. One jet crashed before landing, and the other had crashed at the same time as it lifted off the ground for take-off.

CNN was reporting another unexplained phenomenon: All the jets on the tarmac had lost power and sat stranded at various locations throughout the airport. A CNN reporter was interviewing a professor from New York University who explained that the massive power outages at the four generating stations in New York City were somehow connected to the electrical problems at JFK.

Hakeem laughed and set his coffee down on the large marble table so he could clap. As he listened to the news, he turned to Mineesha. "Did you see what the reporter said? Two jets crashed! I never thought there might be planes in the air when the EMP weapon fired."

Mineesha smiled and got up off the couch. On her way into the kitchen, she asked, "Does this mean my days of seducing gullible men to your cause are over?"

Not even bothering to take his eyes off the television, Hakeem replied, "Of course, my love. The operation is a complete success because of you."

His cell phone lit up and vibrated. "Hello," answered Hakeem.

"Hakeem," said the caller in a thick German accent. The elusive Nazi. "I presume you are watching the news."

"Of course."

"I must compliment you on how well your men have performed thus far."

Hakeem grinned. "Isn't it wonderful? The Americans have no idea what's coming."

"Yes. I have waited a long time for my revenge against the Jews. I take it you received the money from my wire transfer?"

"Yes. Are you sure the times and locations for the operation's next phase are correct?"

"I just spoke to my contact inside the CIA. The snare has been set, and everything has gone as planned. Were there any problems with the Iranians?"

"None so far. We abducted six Iranian guards working close to the border last week. When we use the EMP weapon against the Israeli anti-missile defense, Israel will be completely vulnerable. We'll leave the bodies of Iranians behind and frame them for the EMP attack."

Hakeem could hear the old Nazi's smile through his voice. "My God, that's beautiful. Israel will have no choice but to counter attack

Iran, and their defense system will be completely wiped out by the EMP."

"We have waited a lifetime to see Israel's demise."

"Well done, Hakeem."

"Not so quick. First we have to get the world's attention on the U.S. Once the conflict ramps up against the Americans, Israel will be left to fend for itself."

"Excellent. What's the news from Saji?"

"He has his assets in place in Richmond. If all goes well, Saji and Khatchi will be on my jet with me by the end of the day."

"Very good. I will monitor the news. I might contact you tomorrow." Hakeem disconnected the call, then switched channels and listened to another report of the New York crisis, which announced that Wall Street would not open on its normal schedule. Hakeem whispered to himself, "Wall Street may never open again."

He switched back to CNN. Reports filtered in about millions of cell phones and other electronic devices being wiped out. Communication, transportation, and power generating sites were completely dead. Many subways lost power, trapping people in the dark tunnels under the city. Schools and businesses lacked power, and hospitals operated on backup generators. In one interview, a city official said, "If power isn't restored before it gets dark, the city might experience its worse looting since the rolling blackouts and Hurricane Sandy hit."

Hakeem sipped his coffee and pointed his finger at the large plasma television. "Let the looting begin. Your city will feed on itself and self-destruct!" Hakeem looked at his diamond-encrusted 18k Patek Phillippe watch and smiled as he flipped through the channels.

Finally, a station was reporting flames coming from the widely-publicized wedding in New York City. Hakeem stood up and threw his hands above his head as if he had just scored the winning goal. He sat back down, turned up the volume, and listened to the female reporter from CNN.

"We have reports that several small planes have struck New York City. Behind me, you can see the panic taking place at the highly anticipated wedding of Adam Goldberg and Rebekah Cohen. It is believed that another plane has struck the New York Stock Exchange building."

Hakeem switched channels again and mumbled to himself, "The great jihad has begun."

---

Myk arrived in Richmond via helicopter and arranged an early check-in at a hotel across the street from the courthouse of Khatchi's trial. He threw his duffle bag on the bed and skimmed through Faraq's file one more time, starting where he had left off during the short helicopter flight from D.C. He searched for anything in Faraq's background that might provide another clue.

After skimming through the remainder of the file, he threw it on the desk, grabbed the remote, and turned on the television. Almost every station was reporting the same breaking news. New York City had lost most of its power, the airports were a disaster zone, and a small plane had crashed into the New York Stock Exchange. However, most coverage focused on the two planes that had crashed into the Goldberg and Cohen wedding, and reporters already forecasted hundreds of casualties. The large gathering of media was releasing an abundance of video footage to the public.

As Myk stared at the live-feed video of smoke and fire rising from the buildings in New York, the memories of his last day with Dana in Madrid came flooding back. The station played a cell phone video recording that showed the small planes smashing into the synagogue and the subsequent explosions. The memory's sinking sensation turned into an electric current of anger that shot through Myk; he stood and threw the remote control as hard as he could. It hit the wall and exploded, spraying shattered pieces throughout the room.

Grabbing his room key, Myk stormed out of his room and across the hall to Agent Black's room. He pounded on her door. When she opened it, he shoved her out of the way and headed straight for the television, turning it on.

He practically yelled, "Have you seen this? They've got one of those damn EMP devices like the one we experienced this morning. They used it on the power generating stations around New York City this morning, and those dumbasses don't even know what hit them! The idiot reporters interviewed some college professor who tried to explain the power loss."

Agent Black's eyes remained glued to the television.

Myk turned away from the screen and looked at Agent Black. "After they fried the power generating stations, they went to the New York Air Traffic Control Center and the JFK tower and used the EMP device to destroy almost all air traffic control for the eastern seaboard. Listen to the damn reporters and the people they interview; they're clueless! Do you have any idea of the rioting and looting that will take place if they don't get on top of this? New York City without most of its power and water—are you kidding me?"

He walked to the window and took a few deep breaths as he tried to gather his thoughts. Myk paced back and forth when Agent Black asked, "Have you heard from Brodie or Adelberg on any of this?"

"Hell no. If you thought the Agency had its hands full trying to find out how nineteen jihadists vanished, then they are really drowning in demoralization now!"

She looked back at the news report and turned the volume up on a report streaming live from the JFK airport. Two jets had crashed on landing and take-off from the airport, and live video showed the emergency crews treating many survivors.

"Sources close to the crashes were amazed that the survival rate might be as high as eighty percent."

Agent Black turned to Myk. "Whoever was behind this knew what they were doing."

"Damn right. I was in Madrid when the bombs went off and slaughtered the innocent people just going about their normal business on the trains that day. These animals can't be reasoned with, bargained with, or even respected; they just want to kill us. The so-called 'intellectuals' in our government just don't get it. I guess they must be smarter than the rest of us knuckle-dragging hicks." Myk glanced up at Agent Black, who had sat on the edge of the bed. He continued. "Well, you can see how well that works, can't you?! These damn jihadists only understand one thing: who has the biggest stick! Dunk 'em in water or put your gun barrel down their throat; that's something they understand! If not, kill them before they kill more innocent civilians, or at least until they crawl back into the cave they came out of!"

She stood, and as she passed by him, she placed her hand on his chest, "Go get your things, and let's find Faraq. If he really is sending out an S.O.S., then maybe we'll get a break today and find him."

He turned and headed back out the door.

"You're right. I can't control what's happening in D.C. or New York, but we can do something here in Richmond. I'll see you in the lobby in a few."

Myk went back to his room and looked at his cell phone where it lay plugged into the charger on the desk. He considered calling the secretive caller who had warned him of the mole, but there was too much to do. He needed to find Faraq.

# Chapter 13

## Washington D.C.

Sixteen-year-old Kam sat on a bench at the West Potomac Park, a large grassy area that fronted the Potomac River and separated the Lincoln Memorial from the Jefferson Memorial. Kam faced the Potomac River and waited for the Tourmobile to make its stop. Hakeem had assumed that since it was early, the Tourmobile would not be crowded with tourists, as it likely would be later on in the day, and the driver would let Kam on board with his oversized remote airplane.

Kam's father, Jaffa Banzel, walked along the pathway of the Potomac River while he kept an eye on Kam and watched for the arrival of the Tourmobile. Jaffa had been very busy earlier in the morning trying to make accommodations at his Muslim Brotherhood headquarters for the eighteen missing "tourists" the CIA was scouring the city for. If the Tourmobile driver allowed Kam on board, then Jaffa would call his other son, eighteen-year-old Masoud, who was waiting at the Washington Monument with the remote that controlled his brother's plane.

The Tourmobile made its way across the bridge. Kam grabbed the plane and waited at the bus stop for the bus to arrive. The Tourmobiles were open-air tour buses with an open viewing deck on the top, painted red to resemble the double-decker buses in

London. The Tourmobiles made a continuous loop around all the sites between Arlington Cemetery and the U.S. Capitol. The Tourmobile arrived and came to a stop.

Kam stepped forward with his huge remote plane and said, "Good morning." He handed the driver his pass.

The driver pointed to his plane and said, "Good morning, young man. Whatcha got there?"

"It's a model plane. I am headed to the National Air and Space Museum. I won an award for this plane, and the Smithsonian is taking pictures with me and my plane next to some of the other planes on display at the museum."

"Congratulations. As you can see, we are pretty empty; otherwise, you probably wouldn't be able to fit. Go ahead and find a seat."

"Thanks."

Kam smiled and boarded. He made his way to the back of the bus and up the stairs to the viewing deck on top. It was difficult for him to maneuver the large plane up the stairs. Fortunately, the driver waited for him to get to the top before proceeding to the next stop.

As soon as the Tourmobile moved forward, Jaffa called Masoud, who was waiting at the Washington Monument. "Kam is on board and heading your way." He disconnected the call and ran back across the street, through the large open grass area of the Potomac Park, and over to the Franklin Delano Roosevelt Memorial. He retrieved his video camera and waited. From his elevated view, he could zoom in and get an unobstructed view of the remote plane.

As soon as Jaffa ended the call, a van carrying an EMP weapon turned off of 23rd street and onto Constitution Avenue, which ran between the Washington Monument and the back of the White House. Masoud was waiting. The Tourmobile carrying Kam and the plane was over a mile away and out of range of the EMP weapon.

The traffic was surprisingly light along Constitution Avenue. The van stopped when it reached the fenced-in, grassy open area leading to the back of the White House. The driver pulled the van all the way up on the sidewalk so the back faced directly at the White House. He turned off the engine to protect the electrical system of the van from being damaged by the EMP weapon. Two other passengers in the van quickly jumped out and opened the back cargo doors, exposing a full view of the White House in the distance. As soon as the van doors flung open, another man fired off the EMP weapon. A massive, bright blue-neon pulse wave shot out of the weapon. Within seconds, the men closed the cargo doors, then waited another thirty seconds before starting the van to make sure no lingering effects could possibly affect the van. Whatever traffic was on the road before the weapon went off was now completely stalled within a five-block radius of their location. The van made its way back down Constitution Avenue, weaving in and out of the stalled cars stranded on the roads.

Three minutes after the EMP device destroyed White House Security, the Tourmobile carrying Kam and the remote plane turned off Henry Bacon Drive and onto Constitution Avenue. Kam's brother, Masoud, spotted the Tourmobile and was waiting atop the elevated knoll of the Washington Monument for Kam to pass in front of him. Masoud would have a perfect view of the Tourmobile and the White House directly in front of him from his position. He would need an unobstructed view to operate the airplane with his remote.

Masoud was an expert in the operation of remote planes. Just two months earlier, he had competed in the Top Gun Competition for remote airplanes in Lakeland, Florida, the largest competition of its kind in the world. Masoud had done very well, considering he was the youngest legitimate competitor at eighteen years of age. He was the three-time junior champion in the remote plane competitions, so he had been anxious to finally compete for the first time with adults at the Top Gun Competition.

Masoud spotted the red double-decker Tourmobile coming down Constitution Avenue. This was the most critical moment for their success; normally the plane would have a running start along the ground before taking off, much like a normal plane. But the plane was too big and heavy for his brother Kam to possibly throw off the top of the Tourmobile, so they devised a plan and welded a handle on each side of the plane for Kam to hold onto while Masoud powered it up. When the plane achieved enough power to fly on its own, Kam would let go of the plane and it would fly off. They had practiced many times during the past six months.

The Tourmobile crossed 17th Street, and Kam hoisted the heavy plane filled with explosives over his head. Masoud saw Kam lift the plane and immediately increased the speed on the engines with his remote. Kam struggled to hold onto the plane because Masoud had pushed the remote to full-throttle. He braced his legs against the railings at the edge of the deck and held onto the plane for dear life, trying not to let go of it too early.

Finally, the White House came into his view, and he released the plane. He had been using all his weight to brace against the plane's powerful engines. When he let go of the plane, it was like releasing the tension on a sling shot, and he landed flat on his back. It shot out of his release and took off racing toward the White House. All of the pedestrians and motorists with dead cars in the street were so preoccupied trying to figure out the loss of electric power that no one noticed the small remote plane filled with explosives heading toward the White House.

It had already been determined that the chances of the President, or anyone else for that matter, being in the White House at this stage of the operation would be extremely unlikely. Therefore, it was critical that Masoud be very precise in where the plane struck the White House. The two optimal targets were the President's residence upstairs or his office. It was decided that having the plane hit the President's office would have the optimal effect.

Masoud focused on his plane buzzing toward the President's White House office. He firmly gripped his remote control in both hands, sat down on the grass, and tried to hide the remote from the tourists behind him at the Washington Monument. Compared to the competition he had just competed in, this would be a relatively mundane maneuver; it was almost a straight shot. The plane buzzed along toward the target.

Suddenly, when it got within one hundred yards of the White House, Masoud heard a multitude of gunshots being fired. He quickly maneuvered the buttons on his remote, and the plane danced up and down and to the right and left. It zigzagged on its way to the target, virtually impossible for anyone to shoot down. As the plane got closer to impact, the shots being fired increased tenfold. Three seconds later, the plane smashed through the window of the President's Office and exploded into a loud fireball.

Jaffa had been recording the entire episode on his video camera. It was doubtful that any deaths would occur because of the attack, but the imagery of such a worldwide icon of American power being struck by the jihadist would produce a symbolic image of victory that would last for decades. Hakeem's plan was to instill fear so that his vision of a grand jihad would take root. The men recording the attack let the video continue for the next several minutes, making sure they recorded the shocked reaction of all those who witnessed the smoke and fire emanating from the White House.

After helping launch the plane, Kam hopped off the back of the Tourmobile at its next scheduled stop on Pennsylvania Avenue. His brother, Masoud, left his jacket covering the remote control lying in the grass and walked to the awaiting vehicle on 15th Street. Two minutes later, the vehicle transporting Masoud and Kam crossed the George Mason Memorial Bridge, the opposite direction of oncoming emergency vehicles.

# Chapter 14

## Richmond, Virginia

After grabbing his things, Myk went downstairs to wait for Agent Black. Only a few people sat at the tables and chairs that had been set up as an eating area. Almost everyone was crowded around the wall-mounted television in the corner, expressionless as they watched the live reports coming in from New York. Agent Black stepped off the elevator and approached him.

"So what's the plan?"

"I just spoke with Director Adelberg. He downloaded the route they're using to get Khatchi to the courthouse onto my device. Hopefully, Faraq is waiting somewhere along the route. We have to find Faraq, or that EMP weapon will have us operating blind again. If they wait until he gets too close to the courthouse, it will be a lot harder for them to snatch Khatchi, if that's what they're up to."

"If Faraq needs a way out that still protects his family, wouldn't it make sense if he tried to fake his death?"

"I agree but—" He looked up at the television. Several people came in from the lobby to get a closer look. CNN was just breaking news that several witnesses had seen a large explosion occur at the White House.

Myk shouted, "Someone turn the volume up!"

The live shots from CNN showed smoke and fire billowing from the back of the White House. Myk shook his head. "Just when you thought it couldn't get any worse. If you thought the Islamic extremist had taken fresh courage before, just see what happens when this video hits the Al-Jazeera network. There'll be no stopping the stream of radicals signing up for jihad."

"Good thing they got the President out," Agent Black said.

"It doesn't matter. Do you have any idea how effective that video of the White House burning will be to the Jihadists for the next decade? I've got to call Director Adelberg before we go out."

But Myk doubted the director would have time to talk. He dialed Bashford's number instead, stepping away from the crowd around the television while he waited for an answer.

"Bashford speaking."

"Hey, it's Myk. I know you guys are slammed, but before Jodi and I go on our hunt for Faraq, I was hoping to get a quick update from you on what's happened."

"You're right. I don't have much time, Myk. Since you left in the helicopter this morning, they attacked New York and the White House. They used the EMP weapon again and knocked out every security device and all the anti-missile systems we had at the White House grounds. You won't believe this one, though; witnesses said a remote control airplane flew into the White House. If there were any silver lining, it would be that we identified the vehicle carrying the EMP weapon."

"What was it?"

"They pulled up on Constitution Avenue in a FedEx van and fired off the electromagnetic pulse, then left. It took less than a minute. All the security cameras in the surrounding area went black after the pulse went off. I doubt it will help, but you and Jodi should look for a FedEx van."

"Okay. Got it. Anything else?"

"No, we've got eyes in the sky over Richmond watching the motorcade."

"Anything on the eighteen who disappeared yet?"

"Not yet. We have snipers and agents at every location, but David is still fighting with the suits, trying to get all the sites shut down."

"You've got to be kidding me; they still haven't shut down the Capitol?!"

"Trust me. He's furious. But everything happened so quickly. He expects the green light to close the tourist sites at any moment."

Myk shook his head. "As much as I would like to be in D.C. or New York, I think Faraq will be the key to finding out who's behind this if we're going to prevent any more attacks. I just hope we find him before it's too late."

"I hope you're right, Myk. That's why you're in Richmond. I'll keep you updated with the latest intel."

# Chapter 15

## CIA Central Command

—————————————— //// ——————————————

Every seat in the CIA's Central Command was filled. Every agent was in direct contact with the field officers setting up at the same sites the nineteen had cased out the previous day. Wall-to-wall video screens and monitors displayed the live images from surveillance cameras throughout D.C. Over twenty video screens were mounted throughout the room, each one displaying a different image. The larger screens focused on the more prominent sites, giving constant updates. Supervisors roamed the room. The place looked like NASA moments from a space shuttle launch.

Adelberg and Bashford stood in the small, glass-enclosed conference room adjacent to the command center, both talking on the phone. Hundreds of CIA agents, FBI agents, and local officers and detectives had scattered throughout the city, searching for the FedEx van or any sign of the suspects who had vanished. A few at Central Command watched the video screens and security cameras to see if any videos suddenly blacked out. Agents and snipers perched in position for any possible suicide bombers.

Adelberg hung up the phone with the Saudi Arabia General Intelligence Director. Bashford leaned closer. "So what did he say? I could tell it wasn't good news."

"Not good news at all, Brodie. He ran background checks again on all nineteen of the passengers we were following. They all checked out again. He confirmed a few days before the passengers arrived that they were doctors, lawyers, professors, and businessmen. After this morning's incident, I demanded that he explain why one of his 'mainstream' Saudi men had blown himself up and killed two of our officers this morning. He was very abrupt and said he would investigate and get back with me quickly."

Adelberg sat down. "Apparently, the Saudi Director immediately ordered raids on the homes and businesses of our suspects with addresses in Saudi Arabia, and he called his Egyptian counterpart and asked him to do the same. He now has some apologizing to do to a few shocked Saudi citizens because almost all the names he checked out were actually at their homes and not here in the U.S. None made the flight except Faraq Majed."

Bashford asked, "Then who in the hell are the other eighteen running around D.C.?"

"He interviewed those who were supposed to make the flight, and they all had the same story: The travel agency that had booked the flights contacted them and told them entrance to the U.S. had been temporarily denied, then gave them a full refund. The travel agency substituted the cancelled flights with eighteen different people with fake passports."

"So I guess these nineteen aren't the average Arab citizens we thought they were."

"Quite the contrary."

Bashford asked, "Why would they get together in such a public place? They would have known that we would be watching them and that they could inflict a tremendous amount of damage. They chose to meet in a very visible place."

"You're right. They knew we would be there; that's why they had the EMP weapon and the escape tunnel planned. I just haven't figured out why."

"They wanted us to see the EMP weapon. But why? Just to taunt us? I doubt it."

"No, I doubt that too."

An agent peeked his head in the door and handed Adelberg a surveillance photograph. "Sir, we have something urgent developing at three sites that needs your immediate attention."

They hurried out to the large command center. The agent pointed his red laser light at two larger video screens on the wall. "Three taxis just parked across the street from three different sites: the Lincoln Memorial, the U.S. Holocaust Memorial, and the Jefferson Memorial. No one has gotten out, and the drivers refuse to take any new passengers. Excuse me; hold on, sir."

The agent touched his earpiece, listened, then ended the conversation and turned to the agent in charge of coordinating the live video on the multitude of screens. "Bring up the Capitol and the U.S. Supreme Court on the big screens."

Within seconds, the live video feed of the two sites displayed on the larger screens at the front of the room. The agent turned to Adelberg and spoke quickly, his voice tense. "Sorry, sir. We now have six taxis sitting in front of six different sites. Agent Jeff Kirk, our sniper at the Lincoln Memorial, positively identified the passenger in the back of the taxi at the Lincoln Memorial. It's Amil, the same one who scouted this site. He is wearing a vest similar to the one the suicide bomber was wearing this morning!"

Adelberg asked, "Agent Wiezer, does Kirk have a clean shot? Where's the bomb squad?"

Agent Wiezer pointed to the screen with his laser at the bomb squad and the position of the CIA sniper. "Agent Kirk said he doesn't have a clean shot from his position yet and that there is a lot of pedestrian and tourist foot traffic around the taxi."

"Damn it! I told that bastard AG Helter we needed these sites shut down."

Six more taxis pulled up and parked bumper-to-bumper behind the other taxis. Adelberg's eyes widened. "Identify the six taxis that just pulled up."

Thirty seconds later, Agent Wiezer turned to Adelberg. "Director Adelberg, I have confirmation that the passengers of all twelve taxis are the ones that went missing this morning. We have all twelve taxis up on the video screens."

Agent Wiezer pointed up at the video screens and then spoke to the agent coordinating the live feeds. "I need these six sites bunched together on the front screens so we can watch them simultaneously without having to look around the room."

The live images showed aerial views of the taxis parked outside the six sites, as well as the tourists moving in and around them. Agent Wiezer turned around again. "Director Adelberg, we have confirmation that the suspects are holding the taxi drivers at gunpoint. We may have a hostage situation. What do you want the agents to do?"

Adelberg turned to Bashford and Agent Wiezer. "Connect me to the snipers and the other agents in the field. Brodie, contact the agent on the sites, clear out the pedestrians, and order the sites shut down immediately; I don't give a damn if we haven't received authorization yet."

Agent Wiezer replied, "Director Adelberg, you are now connected to our snipers."

"Okay."

Bashford got on his phone to order the closure and evacuation of the sites.

Adelberg stared at the six video screens in front of him. "This is Director David Adelberg. You have orders to shoot to kill as soon as you have a clear shot. We want to minimize any civilian—"

All twelve taxi cab doors opened, and the twelve men sprinted out of the cabs yelling, *"Allah Akbar!"*

Adelberg yelled into his phone, "Shoot! Shoot them now!"

The entire command center stood staring at the screens, everyone tensed up, waiting for one of the suicide bombers to blow themselves up.

The man in the rear taxi at the Lincoln Memorial was already in the crosshairs of Agent Kirk's scope. He took three steps before Kirk put two rounds through his head. Pieces of the man's skull and brains sprayed forward as he dropped in the street in front of an elderly couple; the gray-haired woman recoiled at the carnage lying two feet from her blood-splattered shoes.

Agent Kirk swung around to find his next target, who was already across the street. Kirk squeezed the trigger, but as he fired, a bus drove in front of his shot, and he missed his target. The back windows of the bus shattered out, spraying glass everywhere. Kirk looked up to see if any passengers were hit and was relieved to see that the back of the bus was empty. He looked through his scope and found his target halfway up the marble steps to the Lincoln Memorial. Kirk was ready to take his next shot when a tourist darted in the way. Just two more steps and the man would reach the top of the steps. Finally, he had a clear shot. He squeezed the trigger and shot the man in the back of the neck, severing his spine. The man's legs crumpled beneath him, and blood spurted from the back of his neck, spilling down the white marble steps of the Lincoln Memorial. Adelberg jerked his head to another screen showing a broader view of the mayhem happening. Four FBI agents and the bomb squad ran onto the scene to secure the suicide vests. The FBI agents yelled and frantically waved their arms at the crowd to clear out. Tourists and pedestrians scattered like feathers in the wind. One man lay dead in the street, stopping traffic in both directions. The second man lay face down with his head angled toward the bottom of the steps, his arms and legs in a mangled heap. The blood had already reached the bottom of the steps.

Adelberg shifted his focus to the large monitor displaying the U.S. Capitol. Both taxis had moved forward one block, taking the sniper out of position. The terrorists bolted from their cabs running full speed toward the Capitol Reflecting Pool. The FBI agents on the scene sprinted toward the terrorists who were weaving their way through tourists as a shield against the pursuing agents. The agents fired several shots in the air and yelled at the bystanders to take cover. The pedestrians immediately dove to the ground. FBI agents converged on the fleeing terrorists from opposite sides of the Capitol Reflecting Pool as the two men raced across the small grassy area screaming in Arabic.

Three agents closed in on the closest man, stopped, and emptied the chambers of their guns into him. The air around him erupted into a cloud of misty red from the bullets penetrating his flesh. His momentum carried him forward two more steps, then he toppled into the water of the Capitol Reflecting Pool. Deep ruby swirls clouded the water. The few nearby tourists ran or dropped to the ground.

The other terrorist made it to the back side of the reflecting pool and rounded the corner of the Ulysses S. Grant Memorial in a full sprint; he didn't see the two FBI agents waiting for him on the other side of the Memorial. The agents extended their arms and held their Glocks with two hands as the terrorist came around the corner. Both agents chose head shots. The smiling face of the terrorist vanished when the four bullets hit his face at the same time. The force of the gunshots to his face, combined with his running at full speed, caused his body to lift off the ground. His legs flung out horizontally into the air, and he landed flat on his back. After a few seconds of twitching and convulsing, the faceless corpse lay dead on the concrete at the base of the Ulysses S. Grant Memorial.

Director Adelberg quickly looked across to the scene unfolding at the Thomas Jefferson Memorial. The cabs sped forward and barreled down East Basin Drive, which wraps around the Jefferson Memorial. Both cabs rammed over the curb going 60 mph across the large, grassy area surrounding the memorial. The agents in the black GMC Yukons pursued; grass and mud flew out from their tires like a Monster Truck competition. Both vehicles hopped the curb and followed the taxis across the grassy area.

When the FBI agents shot at the fleeing vehicles, the two cabs immediately swerved off the grass and accelerated up the crowded pedestrian path along the water's edge toward the Jefferson Memorial. Pedestrians screamed as they jumped out of the way. The cabs turned into the circular path surrounding the Jefferson Memorial, then slowed long enough for the terrorists to leap out of them. By the time the Yukons squealed around the corner, the terrorists had sprinted up to the top of the stairs that led up to the huge statue of Jefferson.

As the agents jumped out of their vehicles and bounded up the stairs, Adelberg tensed, anticipating two large explosions. When the eight agents reached the top, the two terrorists jumped up and down and spun in circles, chanting Arabic. All eight agents fired, and the large domed ceiling combined with the hard stone and concrete made the sounds of the gunshots deafening. Both terrorists collapsed and landed on top of each other on the travertine floor, just five feet from the base of Thomas Jefferson's statue.

As men and women in the Command Center gasped, Adelberg scanned the monitors and fixed his eyes onto the one at the Washington Monument. The sniper had shot two terrorists; one lay in a twisted pile on the floor of the taxi and the other on the curb in a mixture of blood and muddy water with the debris and leaves of the gutter.

# Chapter 16

Director Adelberg and the entire Central Command room sighed in unison after watching the precision of the joint FBI and CIA operation. The agents in the Command Center gazed at the pandemonium taking place at the various sites as they frantically communicated to the field agents and bomb squads. The snipers had killed four terrorists within seconds of stepping away from the cabs, and although the other eight died in a more dramatic fashion, the CIA and FBI believed they had averted a disaster. The carnage lay scattered between the six high-profile historical sites in D.C.

Adelberg shook his head as he turned to Bashford. "Something's not right, Brodie."

"How's that?"

"No suicide vests blew up. I'm not buying it; after all the careful planning, there's no way they would—"

"What are you talking about, David? It's a good thing no bombs were detonated."

"Not necessarily. Not if they sent them out there as pawns!" Bashford turned away to take a call from the bomb squads.

When he finished the call, he turned back to Adelberg. "David, it looks like you were right; they may have been pawns. We've got a problem. Actually, we've got a serious problem."

"Let's hear it."

"I just got word from the first two bomb squads, and they can't find anything."

"What do you mean, 'anything'?"

"I mean there were no damn explosives on the twelve we just shot. Nothing! Not even a trace of C-4."

"Shit." Adelberg's frown dissolved into a blank expression as he replied, "We played right into their hands. They set us up with the suicide bomber this morning and then pranced the other twelve right out in broad daylight, knowing we would take them out." He turned and clenched his jaw, then shouted, "Damn it!"

"What other choice did we have?"

"We should have followed up on Myk's inkling. What's done is done. We'll analyze it later when we have time. The only thing we can do now is prevent them from making the next move. Now their hand is played. We've got to beat them to the punch. Brodie, have a team scan the video from the sites where the twelve were just killed—"

"What are we looking for?"

"Tell them to replay the videos and watch for anyone who doesn't look like a panicked or flustered tourist. If they look closely, I think they'll find someone with a camcorder or cell phone recording the shootings. If I'm right, they might be the other six we're looking for. They will go public with this thing and try to incite global chaos. I'll get in touch with the White House Press Secretary. If we can get ahead of this thing, we might be able to stop it dead in its tracks. Otherwise, God help us. To anyone who doesn't know what really happened here, the perception alone will paint a pretty damning picture."

The team in the command center reviewed the footage for about twenty-five minutes before they found the suspects. The computer database matched the weight, height, and faces of six individuals in the footage to the six missing from the EMP attack that morning.

After the team confirmed a positive match, Adelberg turned to Bashford. "I'll inform the White House that we've got a frenzied public relations nightmare about to erupt. If they don't get on top of this immediately and get the truth out first—and en masse—we will have full-scale rioting. They need to contact every network and get the President in front of a camera within the next thirty minutes. If we don't get our version out first, there's no way they'll ever get this genie back in the bottle. We'll need to mobilize the riot prevention teams, or we'll have more than a public relations problem; we'll have a lot of dead Americans."

# Chapter 17

## Muslim Brotherhood Headquarters, Washington D.C.

Jaffa Banzel reviewed the video recordings of the shootings at the DC sites with a professional editor at his Muslim Brotherhood headquarters in Washington, D.C. From the doorway, his sons Kam and Masoud inched closer to Jaffa and the editor, who hunched over four large-screen computer monitors. With every scream and burst of gunfire from the speakers, the two adults laughed and clapped. Jaffa's sons grimaced and exchanged glances at the sight of their father rejoicing over the murder of their fellow brothers. Then, the boys peeked over to watch the footage on which the editor worked.

Unlike the aerial shots from the surveillance cameras on site, the handheld camcorders taken by Hakeem's men recorded the massacre in high definition, zooming in as gunshots took out faces and skulls in bursts of blood, skull fragments, and gray matter. When one close-up captured a bullet taking a man's teeth and one eye with it, Kam and Masoud ran to the bathroom and vomited, one in the toilet and the other in the sink. The editor had almost finished splicing and editing when Jaffa got up, walked into another room, and dialed a number.

"Hakeem, this is Jaffa. I just finished with the video editor. In another twenty minutes, he will post the video to YouTube. You should have your file for the Al Jazeera network shortly."

A hoarse laugh erupted from the earpiece. "You have done well, Jaffa. Tell Kam and Masoud their work with the remote plane hitting the White House this morning will forever be etched in history as our victory over the infidels. It was truly inspiring."

"Hakeem, I have been watching the news. Why are they not showing the video of the plane hitting the White House? I sent the video file to you hours ago."

"Because I haven't released it yet."

"What?! Is something wrong?"

"No. As I told you before, when the world sees this footage, it will have a tremendous effect. But we must wait for today's other events to unfold. The timing of its release is just as important as the video itself. All in good time, Jaffa. Be patient."

# Chapter 18

## Richmond, Virginia

There was a sparse group in Washington that was extremely anxious for the case against Khatchi to succeed. Director Adelberg regretted turning Khat Man over to AG Derek Helter the minute Helter announced he was taking Khatchi out of the prison at Guantanamo Bay and transferring him to the mainland. Khatchi's hearing would be their second attempt to bring to trial a high-profile terrorist. It was met with much opposition and public outrage because a terrorist was being extended the rights to the American judicial system as if he were a U.S. citizen.

The first trial had been a disaster. Zacarias Moussaoui was arrested in Minnesota on immigration charges. His trial was held in the same courthouse as Khatchi. The jury had felt that the evidence linking Zacarias Moussaoui to the other nineteen terrorists on 9/11 was inconclusive. In a bizarre twist, Moussaoui declined representation and decided to represent himself. The trial was an utter disaster, so now the small group in Washington were pinning their hopes on the trial of the Khat Man, hell-bent on extending the civil rights of U.S. citizens to terrorists.

Myk and Agent Black spent several hours searching for Faraq and a van with the EMP weapon. When they failed to find it, they parked in a large city park a few blocks away from the historic courthouse, where they waited for Khatchi's security motorcade to turn onto Main Street and travel the final few blocks to the courthouse.

"The motorcade is just a few minutes away," Myk said. "There might be an EMP weapon out there somewhere, so we had better turn the engine to the van off."

"Good idea. We should shut everything else off as well."

He turned off the engine, went around to the rear cargo doors, and powered down the equipment in the back. When he looked down the street toward the courthouse, a large Goodyear Tires semi pulled in and parked along Fourth Avenue. The large canopy of old trees that filled the park provided the much-needed shade from the bright sun. By the look and size of the trees, Myk figured most of the trees throughout the park must have been over a century old, or even older if planted at the same time as the courthouse.

The old courthouse had played a significant role in the Civil War. When the Confederate States formed a Congress and seceded from the Union, they chose Richmond as their new Capital. The new president of the Confederate States, Jefferson Davis, used the courthouse as a home to his newly established government. When the Confederate Army evacuated Richmond in 1865, they torched everything. Oddly enough, one of the only buildings to survive the fires was the courthouse to which the motorcade carrying Khat Man now traveled. A year after the Civil War ended, a Grand Jury of the United States District Court found Jefferson Davis guilty of treason at this same courthouse. Fortunately, a forgiving country and President Andrew Johnson granted him amnesty, and he never had to go to trial.

Myk got back inside the van. "I powered down the gear in the back. The motorcade should come down the street any minute now." The park in which they were located was four blocks long and scattered with statues of American historical figures. The massive root structure of the old trees presented constant maintenance problems to the city officials because the roots caused the sidewalks to buckle and heave. Still, the city could easily replace the sidewalks, but not the trees. Many of the old trees had probably seen Confederate soldiers camping underneath their young branches. They had seen a nation divided and then put back together. These same trees were about to witness another chapter of violence in American history.

Three police motorcycles rounded the corner on Main Street, followed by three black Suburbans; one of them contained Khatchi Abu-mon. Myk decided that once the motorcade passed the park, he would follow on foot for the remaining three blocks to the secure location in the underground parking structure next to the courthouse. He noticed some movement in his driver's side mirror: another Goodyear Tire semi. He checked the semi's previous location, and his internal warnings signs went off.

Two separate Goodyear Tire semis parked at opposite corners near the park. The motorcade now reached the park's midway point and almost directly in front of Myk's line of view. He reached to turn on the handheld satellite radio so he could warn the agents in Khatchi's motorcade of the imminent danger, but before he could power up the device, the hairs on his arms and head stood up. The thick presence of static electricity went through him, the same sensation he had felt this morning before the EMP fired off.

The two Goodyear Tire semis exploded in simultaneous, massive eruptions of fire and thick, black smoke. The blast's reverberations shook him from his position in the van. A few seconds later, a bright, neon blue electromagnetic pulse wave shot out from the vacant deli shop across the street. Shards of glass sprayed into the street like a huge blast of water from a fire hose.

Agent Black and Myk reached for their weapons. The vehicles in the motorcade had become sitting ducks. The helicopters moved in from the distance; they had learned their lesson from the earlier attack and stayed out of the EMP weapon's range. Unfortunately, thick clouds of smoke billowed into the air from the gigantic tire fire. Within minutes, the smoke would black out the whole area to the drones, helicopters, and satellites, and the stranded motorcade would receive no air support.

As agents from the motorcade took a defensive position behind the Suburbans, bursts of automatic weapons erupted from the deli and the third floor of the building across the street, pinning the agents. They returned fire, but from where Myk glanced out of the van, three agents already lay in the street. He could barely see beyond the smoke.

While Myk jumped out of the van, he glanced up at the movements in the tops of the gigantic trees. At first glimpse, he estimated at least fifteen terrorists seventy feet up in the old trees, dressed in camouflage perfectly matching their surroundings. He reached for his weapon, but by the time he stretched out his hand to pull the trigger, the targets disappeared behind the thick, black pillows of smoke. He saw movement and fired six rapid rounds at his target in the trees, and three bodies toppled end over end until the lifeless corpses smashed into the hard ground. An immediate response of return fire came from across the street. Myk took cover behind the van.

A few seconds later, unusually loud, cannon-like shots boomed from the treetops. He looked up to see thin cables appear from the smoke-filled air. Titanium anchors at the end of the cables secured into the buildings across the street, and the terrorists zipped out of the trees. Myk looked up and aimed at the radicals descending along the zip lines. He drew heavy fire again as the sky filled with smoke.

It was like a scene from *The Wizard of Oz*, with flying monkeys swooping down through the trees.

*What the hell?*

The terrorists buzzed along the zip lines, plunging through the smoke. He shot off seven rapid rounds, hitting four more targets—a near impossible task, since visibility had been reduced twenty feet. Then he took cover.

Gunshots from automatic weapons erupted all around. The historic courthouse in Richmond had turned into a war zone again. After three minutes of nonstop bursts of fire, a brief pause allowed Myk to break from the cover of his van into a death sprint toward the motorcade. Visibility was now less than ten feet, the air so thick with smoke he could hardly breathe. He had captured Khatchi over a year ago in a daring raid along the Pakistan border, and he could not let them get the man responsible for the death of thousands, even if it meant his own demise.

The motorcade that had been about sixty yards in front of Myk's van had disappeared behind the dense blanket of smoke. He thought for a second about the wisdom of dashing into the unknown without grabbing the masks he had in the van, but the thought vanished as he realized time was of the essence. He slowed as he neared the proximity of the motorcade, barely perceiving the outlines of the black Suburbans.

When he arrived at the motorcade, bodies lay strewn about the street. A familiar face suddenly appeared from behind the thick smoke. Before he could raise his gun, a sharp pain shot from the back of his neck down his spinal cord. He tried to shoot, but his body wouldn't respond. His legs gave out, and his eyesight blacked out. The last thing he heard before he collapsed was the Khat Man.

"Agent Myk McGrath. So we meet again."

# Somewhere over the Atlantic Ocean

Myk woke with a splitting headache. As he regained consciousness, his blurred vision cleared. The first thing he noticed was the roar of jet engines and the bounce of turbulence. A gag dug into the sides of his mouth, and rough rope bound his hands to a seat in the back of a plane. He turned his head and looked out of the small window beside him down onto the ocean.

Judging from the sun's position in the sky, Myk figured they couldn't be flying trans-Atlantic. That narrowed down the possible destinations to one of the Caribbean islands or parts of Mexico; South America would be a stretch for a jet this size. From the looks of the plush interior and the insignia stitched into the leather seats, Myk guessed it must have been a private jet belonging to one of the Saudi families.

He remembered Khatchi Abu-mon appearing from the midst of the smoke-filled streets. Khatchi probably had planned something excruciating for his death, or he would have left Myk dead in the streets of Richmond. When Myk had captured him, Khatchi had spit huge gulps of phlegm on anyone within range before the other officers gagged him. While in captivity, Khatchi had defecated on himself just to make his captors clean up the slimy stench. After two weeks of that routine, they finally made him wear an adult diaper.

After a few minutes, Myk's mind cleared. Four people unbuckled themselves from their seats in the front of the jet and walked back toward him. There was no mistaking three of them; one was Khatchi and the others were Faraq and Saji. He didn't recognize the overweight, bearded Arab man. Three of the six leather seats faced the other three, and Myk was strapped into the seat facing forward. Faraq and the fat Arab man sat down in two of the leather seats facing him while Khatchi and Saji stood above Myk and removed his gag.

"Agent McGrath," Khatchi said. "Your involvement in our plot turned out to be an unexpected bonus."

"Piss off, you piece of shit! How's life without your diaper?" Myk snapped.

Khatchi landed two swift blows to his face and an extremely hard punch to his abdomen. Myk caught his breath almost immediately and kept his eyes on Khatchi as the terrorist stepped away. "That was nothing, Agent McGrath. In a few hours, you'll wish you were back here in the comforts of this plane getting punched out."

"You're right; that was nothing. Unbind me, and let's see your real manliness. That's how you cowards operate, isn't it? You kill the defenseless and innocent. You better kill me now, Khatchi, or you'll be the one wishing you were back on this plane!"

"It is Allah's will that we kill you immoral infidels. You are a godless nation, and you spread your filthy living standards on humanity."

Myk flexed against the cords that bound him. "Bullshit, you kill your own innocent and unwilling people in your quest to purify the world. You animals still stone your own women. How pathetic. Look around you, Khatchi; our American way of individual responsibility and freedoms elevate mankind, while your archaic ways leave your people living in mud huts and your women with no freedom to think for themselves. "

Khatchi smiled and gave a soft but forced laugh. "You Americans and your whorish women are a blight to this world. You can ramble all you want, Agent McGrath. You may have had your moment of fame with your lucky capture of me last year, but I will be the last one standing while you die a headless man for the whole world to see."

"I should have killed your sorry ass when I had the chance."

Khatchi laughed again. "You can thank your government for that!"

Myk turned to Faraq, who sat across from him. Faraq remained expressionless. Myk yelled, "What's your excuse, you wannabe scientist? Couldn't make it on your own, so you had to kidnap someone smarter than you and steal his ideas? Oh, and by the way, there'll be no seventy-two virgins waiting for you, pal. Your girlfriend Mineesha is a whore for recruiting."

Faraq shifted in his chair. Myk continued, "That's right; they used her to lure in four others. You've been screwing a whore. There's no Paradise for screwing whores, dumbass!"

Faraq got up and walked back up to the front of the plane.

Myk turned to the Arab man he didn't recognize. "Who are you? You're pretty fat and ugly for a stewardess, but I'll take a Diet Coke and a bag of peanuts, princess!"

Hakeem leaned forward in his chair and replied, "Are you Americans always so cocky before your death? Agent McGrath, your country is on the cusp of tearing itself apart. After we destroy your country and get the EMP weapons back to the Middle East, your drones will be completely useless."

"Who the hell are you?"

"My name is Hakeem Ferron, and you can thank me for bending your country to the will of Allah."

Myk chuckled. "And you can thank me when those seventy-two virgins don't join you in hell after I kill your sorry ass." He lunged forward, but the restraints held him in check. He squinted as he stared at Hakeem. "You have no idea about the concept of American pride. Your plan will crumple and fold like a plastic bottle in a bonfire. It's the one thing you mindless fucks never account for when you attack us. We run into burning buildings and dive on live bombs for each other. And when we're attacked, we band together."

"Wishful thinking, Agent McGrath. Even if your country does come together, it will be too late to rescue Israel. By that time, Israel will be wiped off the map."

For the first time in his life, Myk did something he had never done before . . . he questioned his own judgment. His instincts had never been wrong, and yet he had followed Faraq straight to his own demise. He turned and stared out the window, confused and frustrated.

# Chapter 19

## CIA Central Command

---

Agent Luke Stanford, one of the CIA's foremost targeters, was feverishly working at his computer downstairs. Stanford had discovered the nineteen "tourists" in the first place. He had just run across something on the internet. After several failed attempts to contact Director Adelberg in the Command Center upstairs, Agent Stanford ran up the stairwell to present what he had just uncovered. Director Adelberg focused so much on his discussion with Bashford and several agents that he did not notice his phone vibrating. Agent Stanford burst through the Command Center door. "Sir, we just came across a video on the internet that displays the twelve killed. It's pretty bad. They labeled it 'The Muslim Massacre in D.C.,' and it's already gone viral. It was posted forty minutes ago and already has almost half a million hits, most from the posting in an Arabic language. The English language version is starting to take off."

Adelberg shook his head and put his hand to his forehead, then looked up and nodded. "Damn, I thought it would take them more time to get this posted." He turned to Agent Stanford. "Good work, Luke. Let's see what you found."

Agents escorted Stanford to a nearby computer station. After a frenzied blur of fingers on the keyboard, a full screen view of the YouTube video popped up. Bashford peered over his shoulder. "I want this computer station put up on the big screen."

Fifteen seconds later, the YouTube video appeared on the big screen in front of the Command Center. Agent Stanford pushed play, and the fifteen-minute video started. This was not an amateur YouTube video. Hakeem had anticipated a slow reaction from the White House, and that's exactly what they got.

Some of the most influential events in American history had catastrophic consequences simply because of inaction. General George G. Meade's failure to attack Robert E. Lee allowed Lee to retreat and subsequently prolonged the Civil War, costing the country hundreds of thousands of lives. Soldiers sitting atop the mountains of Hawaii detected something on their newfound radar equipment and radioed their superiors, whose inaction allowed the Japanese to fly undeterred into Pearl Harbor. The only chance to prevent the hell about to break loose was for the White House to call a pre-emptive, worldwide emergency news conference—which Adelberg had explicitly told them to do.

While everyone in the Command Center watched the You Tube video, Bashford said, "I need an Arabic interpreter up here immediately. What the hell is this guy saying?"

Seconds later, Agent Salim Kaafer stood next to Bashford, interpreting the broadcast. The video showed high-definition footage and close-up shots of the killings. They had pre-recorded one of the most radical and influential clerics in Saudi Arabia, Reiza Vanni.

"He is calling all brothers to arms," Agent Kaafer said. "He says the American government has grown tired of Islam and is looking for any excuse to kill or jail Islamic loyalists in America."

The cleric's rhetoric played in the background of the gruesome footage as the video displayed the violence and then cut back to the cleric. Agent Kaafer translated throughout the video.

"He calls for all brothers to smite the beast in defense of Allah . . . and to strike back in solidarity for the slaughter of the twelve innocent Muslim tourists murdered by . . ." He paused and glanced at Adelberg.

Adelberg nodded.

Agent Kaafer continued. ". . . the Jewish CIA Director."

The Command Center grew quiet. Nine minutes into the video, Adelberg said to Agent Stanford, "Get your team working on the source of this video and find who posted it."

"We already have, sir. It originated out of Saudi Arabia. We don't have an exact location yet, but we're working on it."

Adelberg and Bashford walked to the private conference room and called the White House. Adelberg's knuckles tightened around the phone until they turned white. When Stu Collier, the Press Secretary, picked up, Adelberg screamed into the phone.

"What the fuck is your problem, Stu? I told you in no uncertain terms to get the President in front of a camera or all hell would break loose. The cat's out of the bag now. What in God's name were you waiting for?"

"I was told to sit on it until I heard back from you," Collier replied.

"Did you not understand the severity of the situation when I first called? Are you a complete moron? Who in the hell told you to sit on it?"

"Someone from your office, sir. He called and told us to sit tight."

"You idiot! What in the hell are you talking about?!"

"I received a call from a Douglas Phillips out of your CIA office. He gave us the proper codes, so I assumed it was legit."

"Shit!" Adelberg's face paled at the mention of the name Douglas Phillips. He covered the phone as he took a deep breath and stared up at the ceiling. Then he put the phone back up to his ear and listened to Collier.

"What's wrong, sir?"

Adelberg replied in a somber tone, "Get the President in front of the cameras immediately, and don't do anything else unless you hear directly from me. Is that clear, Stu?"

"Yes, sir."

Adelberg hung up, slammed his fists on the desk, and ranted under his breath. His fists shook. Bashford turned to glance at him.

"David...what's wrong?"

Adelberg shook his head. "Someone from our office called with the proper codes and told the Press Secretary to delay the broadcast momentarily."

"Who the—"

"The caller identified himself as Douglas Phillips." He paused and gazed at Bashford as he took a deep breath. "Douglas Phillips is the name we gave to a Nazi defector we put into our witness protection program decades ago. Only a few people know that name. We've got a mole in our agency, Brodie. Someone on the inside is helping to coordinate these attacks."

Within minutes, footage spilled across the Command Center monitors showing the anarchy developing in New York and the attack on Khatchi's motorcade. Only the tallest trees and buildings poked through the heavy smoke in Richmond, and gunfire flashes illuminated small patches beneath the smoke.

Power generator stations with the capacity to match the ones destroyed in New York could not be replaced overnight; it would take several months to build them and then get them up and running—and that was the optimistic estimate. The outage left thirteen million people in New York without electricity and water.

A door behind Adelberg burst open, and Agent Stanford darted across the center to his team leader. He sat down at a computer station, and as he typed, windows appeared on the big screen. Glancing at Agent Stanford and then the big screen, Adelberg walked to the center of the room with Agent Kaafer and watched the screen. Agent Stanford brought up a high-definition YouTube video and played it.

In the video, two Jewish Rabbis burned a Koran on the front steps of a synagogue, then spat upon it. Then the video cut to the planes crashing into the wedding of the Jewish stars at the same synagogue.

Agent Kaafer interpreted for Adelberg. "The cleric says earlier today, the United States killed innocent Muslim tourists, and it was recorded on video for the whole world to witness. In response to the killing, cleric Reiza Vanni asks all Muslims to defend themselves, to take up arms and strike back. He praises the brave brothers who struck back at the infidels with a masterful attack on the White House and on the wedding of the Jewish movie stars."

Then it showed the remote airplane gliding across the White House lawn and exploding when it hit the White House. The actual footage of the White House getting attacked sent a bolt of dread through Adelberg's gut. The rest of the agents sat in silence as the YouTube video played. Dialogue was cued over the footage.

His own eyes wide and fixed on the screen, Agent Kaafer continued, "He is trying to persuade his fellow brothers everywhere to strike back like they did with the attack on the White House. He says this should inspire others to follow the example and lash out against the vulnerable infidels and those Jews who have disrespected the Koran."

Bashford said, "I wonder how they made that Koran burning video on the synagogue steps without getting caught. Now we know why they waited so long to release the video of the remote plane hitting the White House. They made it look like the White House got attacked in response to the cleric's call to violence in order to motivate others to do the same."

Adelberg shook his head. "Facts are funny things. CNN showed the White House burning before the shootings. I guess people will believe what they want to believe." Then he turned to Agent Stanford. "Luke, I've seen enough. Thank you for your work. See if you and your team can find out where the videos come from. Before you leave, put the Richmond site back on the center screen."

"Yes, sir. Is there anything else I can do?"

"No, just see if we can find the source. We're running out of time."

# Chapter 20

## Cancun, Mexico

As Myk awoke, his entire body ached. He ran his tongue across his swollen, gashed lips, then tried to open his eyes. He could see through one, but his right eye throbbed, swollen shut. He vaguely remembered Khatchi and Saji beating him mercilessly and yelling at him to wake up, but he couldn't, so they battered him anyway. Then, the distant sounds of ocean waves and squealing sea gulls and even the salty ocean air reached him. A rope bound his wrists behind what felt like a chair, and his saliva dampened the gag. He scanned the room with his one eye and discovered a camcorder on a tripod ten feet in front of him. He turned his head enough to see the black sheet pinned to the wall behind him. And on the table beside the camcorder lay a machete.

His stomach tightened. He had seen it a dozen times from videos in Iraq.

Footsteps approached from the adjacent room. As Myk debated whether or not to feign unconsciousness, a familiar face with dark hair appeared in the soft arch of the doorway. Faraq Majed leaned against the archway and stared at Myk. After a few minutes, Faraq grabbed a chair from the other room and dragged it across the floor. When he came within five feet of Myk, he placed the chair down and sat.

Myk lunged for him. His chair hopped a foot off the ground, but the rope kept his body pinned. Still, Faraq jumped, then moved his chair back. After studying Myk for a moment, Faraq cleared his throat.

"Agent McGrath, I need you to sit still for just a moment and listen. First, have the drugs worn off enough so you can comprehend what I am saying?"

Myk thought for a second, and then nodded. He could stall for time and get his arm loose.

"Agent McGrath, I will attempt to explain why you're in Mexico at the tip of the Yucatan Peninsula, in front of a camera provided to record your death by beheading."

Myk straightened himself in his seat and worked on one arm. "As you are aware, my name is Faraq Majed. I know you and the woman agent were assigned to follow me. I left you the postcard at the café and the newspaper on the bench to lead you to Richmond. If I had not intentionally left a trail for you, you wouldn't be here. I apologize that you find yourself in such a predicament and that Khatchi almost beat you to death, but I have been searching for a way to escape, and I am afraid luring you to Richmond was the best thing I could come up with."

Myk stopped working his arm and peered through his eye at Faraq.

Faraq shifted in his chair. "I have made every effort to keep my hands unstained by innocent people's blood. I was supposed to kill Dr. Chen Wu after he was forced to help Hakeem replicate his EMP weapon. But I am sure your agency found Dr. Wu healthy and alive. You are aware of that, are you not, Agent McGrath?"

Myk raised his eyebrows and nodded. The CIA couldn't understand why Dr. Wu had been spared, and Faraq could not have known this information unless he was the one responsible for freeing Dr. Wu. The sinking sensation in his chest lightened.

"Agent McGrath, your statement on the plane was hurtful, but true. I couldn't say anything in front of Khatchi or Hakeem. I was foolish to get involved with Mineesha. By the time I had my first doubts, I could not escape without putting my family in grave danger. The longer I stayed, the more I realized how fanatical these people are. They would have killed my family without a second thought. I can't decide if they are zealots who simply don't understand the true nature of the God they claim to worship, or if they are just thugs."

Faraq looked out through the sliding glass door towards the ocean. "I am an educated and peaceful man. I am an innocent bystander swept up in their wave of hate. I had no idea you captured Khatchi, and perhaps you will get the last laugh after all. I am not a violent man, Agent McGrath, but I am smart enough to realize I would not last thirty seconds in the same room with you."

*No shit.*

Beneath the soaked gag, the corner of Myk's mouth curled in a smirk.

"That is why I need your word you will not attempt anything if I remove the gag. I have never killed anyone, and I am not here to kill you, but if you attempt anything, I will leave you tied to the chair in the hands of the Mexican authorities. If you decide to cooperate, I will supply you with all the information you need about the people responsible for the attacks in New York, Washington D.C., and Richmond. Do we have an understanding?"

Myk nodded, making the gag's cloth flap.

"Do we have a deal, Agent McGrath?"

Myk nodded again.

Faraq walked towards Myk, then stepped behind him and untied the gag. As he walked back to his chair and sat back down, Myk asked, "Where's Khatchi and Saji?"

"Hakeem flew back to his estate in Saudi Arabia, and Khatchi and Saji are on the yacht."

"Why didn't they kill me?"

"They almost did, Agent McGrath, but they wanted you awake so you could see what they would do to you. I knew the only way to keep you alive was to sedate you enough so that you couldn't wake up. They had no idea I had administered a tremendous amount of drugs to you."

Myk tried to open his other eye so he could see Faraq a little better. "So what happened?"

"They got their pound of flesh out of you and grew tired of beating on you and waiting for you to wake up, so they left me behind to chop off your head with a machete and record it."

Myk's head pounded, and his face felt like it was on fire. "Faraq, I am grateful that you will spare my life, but have you thought this through? This makes no sense. Why? You and your family will only be in more danger if they know you set me free. Eventually, they will find you and kill your whole family."

Faraq replied, "You are right. That is why it is imperative they never find out I set you free. They expect me to deliver the recording of your beheading, which is exactly what you will help me produce."

Myk cocked his head and frowned. "What did you—?"

Faraq put his hand up in the air. "I will give them a recording of a beheading." He then held a small DVD disc in the air. "It just won't be *your* head on the recording."

"What the hell are you talking about?"

"This disc contains the recordings of many beheadings in Iraq and other places over the past several years. I analyzed the recordings and came up with a plan to splice and edit some of them with video footage of your face today. I contacted friends I can trust back in Europe, and they have a professional editor standing by. They understand that my family and I are in danger."

Faraq leaned forward, maintaining eye contact with Myk. "I spoke to the video editor, Agent McGrath. He gave me specific instructions to follow and said if I followed his directions, he could put together a video that would look exactly like your beheading."

Myk tried to process everything he was just told, then said, "Sorry, I am still a little groggy from whatever drugs you shot in me. You're saying we will shoot a video to make it look like my beheading, and you have an editor who can put your previous recordings together with what we record today. And then the editor will make it look like I actually have been beheaded. This is your plan to get you off the hook with the Khat Man. Did I get that right?"

"Yes. But there is one fairly important caveat."

"And what would that be?"

"Well, obviously I will need your cooperation. To make it convincing, we will need a bit of acting on your part."

Myk laughed, which made his battered face hurt, but sent shivers of giddiness down his arms. "To be perfectly honest, I was thinking of a way to break these bonds so I could snap your neck. But now, I must admit, I am relieved I get to live to see another day. But you should know that in all my school years, I made it a point to stay away from the theatrical classes or anything close. I was an accomplished collegiate athlete, but I am void of any acting skills."

Faraq asked, "Does this mean you will do it?"

"Of course. Hell yes. You just tell me what your video editor wants us to do."

Faraq clasped his hands and bowed his head in a moment of reflection.

"Just one thing though, Faraq."

"What is that?"

"Assuming your friends can put together a convincing video showing my beheading, how will you explain yourself when I show up on the radar screen sometime in the future? I don't think Khatchi and his friends will look too kindly on that. The minute they find out I am alive will be your death warrant, along with your friends and family."

"Yes, you are right. But that is assuming Khatchi is still alive when you resurface. But if Khatchi is dead . . . I won't have much to worry about, will I?"

Myk's eyes widened, and adrenaline shot into his bloodstream as he imagined confronting Khatchi.

"Agent McGrath, this is a bit strange talking to each other at opposite sides of the room. I hope you understand, but a man such as yourself and your reputation, you make me a bit nervous. May I approach?"

"Of course, what are you asking me for? I'm the one strapped to this chair."

Faraq picked up his chair, walked across the room, and sat closer to Myk. He now spoke in a much quieter voice. "Agent McGrath, what we talked about so far is my survival plan. What if we take a different approach? Rather than just survive, why not attack them? I have all the information you need about these people and you possess all the skills to take them out."

Myk felt like a balloon someone had released that now rose higher and higher into the air. He couldn't believe he and Faraq might actually want the same exact thing.

Faraq continued, "If I go back to Europe to restart my life and you go back to the U.S., these animals will attack again. Many lives were lost today, and many more will be lost because of the violence and rioting their plan incited. I will never be able to atone for my mistake helping these degenerates put together the EMP weapon, but perhaps if I assist you in making sure they never harm anyone again, then maybe it will ease the burden I will carry with me for the rest of my life."

As Faraq told Myk his ideas, Myk wore a tiny grin as his heart pounded at the thought of killing Saji and Khatchi. He felt as if he could burst through the cords binding him.

Faraq continued, "I told the men to collect the equipment you had in the back of the van—"

"Where is it?"

"It is locked up in the garage on the other side of the kitchen. One other very important weapon is also in the garage. The EMP device."

"Did you grab my passports? Was my partner, Agent Black, still alive?"

"Yes, we cleaned the whole van out. As far as I know, your partner made it out alive. Agent McGrath, I hope you believe me when I say words cannot express my sorrow for those agents killed in Richmond today. I couldn't prevent their murders, but I swear I will do everything I can to empower you so you can stop this from happening again."

"Faraq, what you have done is between you and your Maker to reconcile. Honestly, over the past twelve hours, I can't count how many times I thought about snapping your neck. But what you have shared with me these past few minutes changes everything. You figured out a way to keep Khatchi away from me, and you spared my life. Ten minutes ago, I was gathering my final thoughts about how grateful I was for my life and how close I was to losing it. Now, I can avenge the deaths of my comrades. Where is Khatchi, anyway?"

"He's here. Well, not right here. He is in a yacht provided by Hakeem. It is anchored off the tip of Cancun a few miles off shore."

Myk asked, "How long? Do you know how long the yacht will

stay near Cancun?"

"No, not exactly. I overheard Khatchi speaking to Hakeem, and it sounded like they want him to stay here for a few weeks until things settled down."

"Okay, good. That gives me some time. Let's get this beheading video going. I'll need some time to figure out how to get to Khatchi before he leaves."

Faraq explained the instructions to Myk, then grabbed three pints of blood he had purchased in town. While he told him what he would do with them, he pulled out a different backdrop to hang on the wall behind Myk.

"This is the same backdrop used in the videos from which we will edit and splice."

For the next fifteen minutes, they worked on certain poses and actions the editor wanted in order to be able to dub in shots from the real beheading videos. Myk put on a shirt that matched the one worn by two other victims in the recordings.

After reviewing everything with Myk, Faraq turned to him. "Agent McGrath, the recording and the acting you will be doing may seem harmless, but have you considered how it will affect your family and peers back home? When the editor finishes the video, it will be violent and gruesome. Khatchi will do everything to make sure this receives maximum exposure."

Myk nodded. "I don't see another way around it. It rips me up to think about their reaction, but if this means giving me the opportunity to fly under the radar while I put some terrorists permanently out of business, then it's something I will gladly do."

Faraq grinned. "Okay, off with your head then."

# Chapter 21

## CIA Central Command

Adelberg remained in the Command Center for 48 hours, making calls and darting to computers. Hakeem's videos had incited massive violence worldwide. Anything American or Jewish became a target. Toward the end of the day, the State Department issued a warning to Americans in other countries to maintain a low profile and seek out a secure location until security could be restored. Ten U.S. Embassies had been attacked; four burned to the ground. The anti-U.S. violence made the attacks on the U.S. embassy in Benghazi pale by comparison.

Pockets of Muslim communities throughout the U.S. had erupted in violence, worst in heavily-populated cities of Michigan and New York. It spread to Los Angeles and Seattle, and because of the White House's delayed response, riot police and SWAT teams had not arrived quickly enough to prevent bloodshed. After the video showed the attack on the White House and the Koran burning, thousands of followers had stormed the streets; the Muslim Brotherhood had planted many group leaders to ensure violence. The mobs looted and vandalized in Michigan, California, Chicago, New York, and Seattle. They torched thousands of cars and houses until the Marines were sent in to restore peace.

In addition to warning Americans in other countries, the White

House also disclosed information about New York's widespread electricity and water problems. Hurricane Sandy could have hit New York ten consecutive times without coming close to the damage the EMP attack caused. The White House told millions to find alternative places to live until power and water could be restored. When the resulting panic seized the city, looting and violence set in, and martial law had to be instituted to restore order. At nightfall, radical Islamists responded to the video by sending thousands of followers into the streets with instructions to burn everything. They set thousands of cars and over twenty small buildings on fire, every building in waterless zones. Nothing could be done except watch the infernos blaze to the ground.

That evening, Agent Stanford showed Adelberg and Bashford the most recent video Hakeem had posted on the internet and Al Jazeera. Adelberg did not want the video shown on the big screens, so they huddled in the small conference room. Agent Kaafer translated as Khatchi appeared on the screen, taking full credit for Agent McGrath's capture and bragging about how the infidels could not keep Khatchi in their jail against Allah's will. Like the recordings of the shootings of the twelve in Washington, D.C., a team had recorded the attack in Richmond. Khatchi boasted about how the immoral infidels stood no chance against Allah's army. The video showed the terrorists zip lining out of the trees and smoke, firing on the agents pinned down in the street. The video then showed the terrorists hauling off an unconscious Agent McGrath.

Bashford drew in a sharp breath. "Myk!"

Khatchi warned that the same fate would befall anyone else who dared to come against Allah's forces. At that point, the video showed McGrath telling the camera his name and that he worked for the CIA. It showed Khatchi beating Myk. Adelberg winced and clenched his jaw.

A black cloth went over Myk's head, then a machete blade appeared behind his neck, gleaming in the light. Agents around Adelberg gasped or cried out as the machete's wielder swung, severing Myk's head in a pinwheel of dark blood. The close-up of Myk's head sent an agent out of the room.

After the video ended, those huddled around the monitor in the small conference room sat motionless. Adelberg felt as though he had fallen off a cliff into a chasm, but his mind buzzed. *Someone needs to break the news to Myk's mother, warn her of the video's violence before she finds out from another source.*

Adelberg could not keep guilt from flooding his entire being. He'd had Khatchi in his grasp when Myk had captured him. Adelberg had struggled with the decision of turning Khatchi over to the Department of Justice, a decision he now regretted. Previous administrations would have left Adelberg alone to do what was best to keep America safe. But now, a few people in Washington only wanted to score political points. The leadership in Washington was drowning in their bad decisions, and there was no lifeline in sight.

He turned and spoke to the other three in the room. "Brodie, black out the windows. I would like complete privacy for what we are about to discuss."

Bashford got up and pushed a few buttons on the digital keypad by the door, and a metal shutter swept across the windows. Adelberg sat down, his eyes still moist. He cleared his throat.

"What I am about to say does not leave this room; is that understood?"

The other three nodded.

"I am taking responsibility for some of what we have seen over the past two days."

Bashford stood up. "Hold on, David. You can't—"

Adelberg held up his hand. "Sit back down, Brodie. Let me finish.

Look, you know we had Khatchi in custody at our military base in Kandahar after Myk captured him last year. As you all know, a few people had a point to prove. None of us wanted to turn him over to Helter at the DOJ, but we had to give them a chance to show us the error of our ways. My gut told me otherwise, and some of you pleaded with me to follow my instincts. Everyone in this room offered to fall on their sword for this. I should have listened to you and followed my instincts. I can never forgive myself for betraying my conscience and country. I hope you can forgive me."

Bashford spoke up again. "David, you can lay this squarely on the lap of those who demanded we turn Khatchi over to them. We have a paper trail that documents our disagreement. They can't spin their way out of this one."

"You may be right, Brodie, but a paper trail won't bring back the dead. It's my job to keep America safe." Adelberg paused for a moment, and then said, "And that includes keeping America safe from the bad policies of its own elected officials. Our careers are of little significance when compared to our country's safety. We had Khatchi in custody. No one here can deny that within a few weeks, we would have had him talking. If I had been man enough to do what I knew was right . . ."

His throat clenched. He looked down and took a long, slow breath. "If I had done the right thing instead of the politically correct thing, Myk McGrath would still be alive."

Silence.

"We can do better. We have to."

# Cancun, Mexico

Myk and Faraq cleaned up the beach house where they had produced the video of Myk's fake beheading. As an added measure for Faraq's future safety, they staged an impromptu recording of Myk killing Faraq. He hesitated at first but acquiesced once Myk demonstrated the effectiveness of the bullet-proof vest Faraq had retrieved from the van in Richmond. They weren't sure if they would ever need the second video, but they agreed they would not have this opportunity again.

Myk chose a penthouse room at the Fiesta Americana to reside while he planned his operation. With his Zeiss high-powered binoculars, he found Khatchi's yacht anchored offshore about a mile south of the tip of Cancun. Myk's resort was located in the heart of all the restaurants and bars in the hotel district. The perfect place to blend in. From the corner penthouse room on the twenty-sixth floor, Myk could see for miles in all directions and monitor the yacht to calculate the weaknesses of Khatchi's security team.

The next day, he rented a small storage unit across the street from the resort to store the weapons and equipment Faraq's men had stolen from his van. The resort shared the surrounding rustic Mexican architecture's flavor and appeal, painted a burnt rust with accenting colors of bright yellows and blues throughout the resort. As Myk eyed the yacht, he reflected on Jen.

*It would be nice to come back someday and spend time with her. That video will mess her up.*

He put his head in his hands and debated whether or not to send her an encrypted message. The blown operation in D.C. still angered him. If he'd had his way, he would have rushed the building and discovered the EMP weapon before they got it down the tunnel. But Bashford told him to sit tight. Here in Cancun, he would be outmanned ten to one but would take those odds every time if he ran the operation. He shook off his thoughts about Jen. He had to get to Khatchi and then work his way up the chain of command to Hakeem to find out the Nazi cohort's identity in the U.S. Hopefully, he could uncover the C.I.A. mole.

Faraq had told Myk that Hakeem had provided the yacht and stocked enough cash for Khatchi to stay there several years. Additionally, if Hakeem had further use for Khatchi, he would be within striking distance to the United States. While Khatchi was preoccupied on another part of the yacht, Faraq had grabbed enough cash to fund Myk's operation. Myk needed to operate undetected, so he destroyed his credit cards. Of course, the resort employees treated Myk, the attractive and polite American, like royalty when he tipped them well.

Myk threw Faraq's file onto the bed and turned up the large plasma television's volume, listening to the latest developments in the U.S. As he listened to the news for the next thirty minutes, the success of the attacks took his breath away and infuriated him. Hakeem's plan depended on the American media buying into the doctored videos to fan the flames of fear and his lies—and it worked to perfection. The media played the distorted terrorist videos verbatim without checking the facts, timing, or sources. With just a few hours of phone calls and fact checking, even a novice reporter would have smelled something amiss. Hakeem had guessed right, and the American media threw jet fuel on a spark that deserved water instead.

Myk watched report after report of the violence and looting in many of the major metropolitan cities. All military bases around the world were on high alert. Those U.S. embassies that hadn't been attacked were abandoned. Parts of Michigan were under siege; guerilla tactics of hiding and destroying property were being used. New York was non-functional; between the loss of power and water and the violence and rioting that escalated at night, the city was deemed unsafe. Myk needed information from Faraq, anything that might help the situation back home. Faraq slept on the boat with

Khatchi and his security team at night, but since he had access to the speedboat, he came to shore twice a day to apprise Myk of the status of Khatchi, the routines of his security detail, and the yacht's layout.

Myk heard a knock at the door and sprang up to answer it. Faraq rushed past him and flung a camcorder on the bed.

Myk asked, "What's wrong?"

"He disgusts me. They follow him in the guise of a religious leader, and yet he pisses all over the morals he professes to follow."

"What are you talking about?"

Faraq picked the camcorder off the bed and held it out to him. "This is what I am talking about. I just finished thirty minutes of recording Khatchi having an orgy with three whores. He just left the door wide open. He was so high on cocaine he didn't even notice me."

"Well, I guess we will just have to make sure the rest of the world finds out exactly the kind of leaders they are going to their graves for, won't we?"

Faraq smiled and relaxed a little.

Tossing the camcorder back on the bed, Myk turned to Faraq. "The situation in the U.S. is getting desperate. I just watched the latest report on what's happening in New York City. Hakeem's plan is taking root. I have to do something. Can you think of anything we could use to the keep this from getting any worse? Names, locations, anything?"

Faraq sat on the edge of the bed and watched the muted news report coming from the wall-mounted plasma television. After a few minutes, he looked out the window. "Jaffa Banzel. I bet he's still there in Washington D.C. He's probably foolish enough to believe nothing could be traced back to him."

"Who?"

Faraq turned to face him. "Jaffa Banzel, the head of the Muslim Brotherhood in D.C. I am surprised your agency didn't have him under surveillance with the amount of communication he has with Hakeem. That's where we stayed the morning we resurfaced from under the old abandoned escape tunnel. The vans took us to his building, where everyone stayed that morning except me. He has two sons, Kam and Masoud, the ones mostly responsible for the attack at the White House."

An image of the flames and smoke rising from the White House window appeared in Myk's mind. He looked down at Faraq, who continued.

"One of the boys won several remote plane competitions. The terrorists also edited the videos there too. After the shootings, the other six recorded everything and brought it back to the Muslim Brotherhood headquarters."

"Where are the C-4 explosives and the EMP weapon now?"

Faraq looked back to the TV. "I don't know. They had a pulley system and carts to get everything out of the tunnel. Everything got loaded into the vans. I guess it got unloaded at the Muslim Brotherhood building where everything else was dropped off."

After a moment of silence, he turned to Myk again. "Agent McGrath, if you are looking to find something that might slow the violence, tell your agency to start with Jaffa Banzel. If Jaffa is as obtuse as I think he is, they'll probably still find him at the Muslim Brotherhood headquarters in D.C."

Myk swiftly pulled a pre-paid phone with international calling capabilities out of his pocket. He had purchased it at the convenience store next to the resort. He punched numbers into the phone, then flipped it to Faraq who caught the phone with one hand.

"That's a prepaid phone that routes through Europe. You will have about fifty seconds to talk before they can start tracing it. I will time you. When you get to forty-two seconds, I'll raise my hand, and you'll need to hang up. I just dialed the number of my boss, Brodie Bashford; you can push 'Send' when we're ready."

Faraq opened his mouth, then closed it. Myk continued, making sure Faraq had no time to protest or refuse.

"As soon as he says hello, say, 'Code in.' Then he will ask you to code in. Say, 'Black storm in the eastern sky.' Do you understand? 'Black storm in the eastern sky.' It's their way of knowing a call is legit. After that, you will have about thirty seconds to tell him about Jaffa Banzel and the possible suspects at the D.C. Muslim Brotherhood headquarters. Let him know there might be video footage if they haven't wiped their computers yet. Remember, I will raise my hand, and you will have to disconnect."

Faraq looked down, hesitated, and then finally hit the green "Send" button. Brodie Bashford answered, his voice crackling in the phone. Faraq gave him all the pertinent information about Jaffa Banzel and the location of the Muslim Brotherhood headquarters, then disconnected the call and let out a deep breath.

"Myk, why didn't you just make the call?"

"Because it's better if they still think I'm dead. I have some unfinished business with Khatchi and Saji that I should have taken care of a year ago."

# Chapter 22

## CIA Central Command

---

Brodie Bashford was in Director Adelberg's office when the call came in from Faraq. After the code was correctly given, Bashford sat down and immediately began scribbling on a scratch piece of paper he had snatched off the desk. When the call went dead, he stared at his notes for a moment and then stood up and shook his head.

Adelberg asked, "What—?"

"Someone may have just given us our first break. That was a phone call from an agent who coded in as 'black storm in the eastern sky.'"

"Refresh my memory on the code, Brodie."

"It has two very specific meanings," Bashford held up two fingers and leaned in as he spoke. "First, 'eastern sky' means whoever just called is deep within a terror organization and, in all probability, surrounded by people who could provide meaningful intelligence. 'Black storm' means the information he just divulged is extremely time sensitive and could become irrelevant if we don't act upon it immediately."

Adelberg's eyebrows shot up. He slammed his hands down on the desk so hard the loose paper clips and other items jumped in the air and off the desk. "That's the best damn news I've heard in a week! Now we're talking. What exactly did he say?"

"He implicated the Director of the Muslim Brotherhood here in D.C., Jaffa Banzel. Apparently, one of Jaffa's sons is an expert in flying model airplanes. The caller said the nineteen stayed at the Muslim Brotherhood headquarters in D.C. the morning they resurfaced from the hidden tunnel, and Jaffa had picked them up from the tunnel. The caller also said Jaffa and his two sons were responsible for the White House bombing. He also said they edited the videos of the shootings at the Muslim Brotherhood location."

"I've heard enough." Adelberg stood and pointed at Bashford. "Screw the Justice Department Brodie; I don't trust that bastard Helter anyway. I'll find someone else who's sympathetic to our cause to issue a search warrant. They aren't going to get off on a technicality, that's for damn sure."

Bashford frowned. "Helter?"

Adelberg's neck had reddened as he spoke, and now as he spoke about the Attorney General Derek Helter, the flush crept higher. "After Myk captured Khatchi, I wanted Khatchi transferred to Guantanamo Bay after they extracted information from him, but Helter wanted Khatchi sent to the U.S. and put on trial. He's never one to shy away from an opportunity to get some face time with the media. But he got his way, under the condition that Khatchi be kept in an undisclosed location."

He looked up at the big screen. *Now that Khatchi's been rescued from Richmond, Helter will have to find another source to get the camera time he craves.* The thought made Adelberg tense, and he turned to look Bashford in the eyes.

"Get the teams assembled! We need to move on this within forty minutes. We're gonna handle these scumbags the way we used to. The gloves are off now. Got it?"

The corner of Bashford's mouth curled. "How could I forget?"

He walked across the hall and got on the phone to assemble his teams for the raids based on the fresh intelligence.

# Muslim Brotherhood Headquarters, Washington D.C.

Jaffa Banzel sat at his kitchen barstool enjoying honey bread and reveling in the CNN and Al Jazeera news. He hadn't even bothered to erase the files as he had been instructed to do. He told himself he would do it later, but instead he replayed and watched the videos. Now, the news drowned out the sound of Jaffa's sons upstairs watching television. Federal agents had to enter the building quickly enough to prevent any destruction of possible evidence by those inside. In one simultaneous move, as if being directed by an orchestra conductor, the building would be overrun by federal agents. Six agents were going to descend the dangling rope lines from silent mode helicopters and crash through the third story windows. Agents on ladders would burst through the second floor windows, while armored vehicles would smash through the garage gate leading to the basement garage.

A series of muffled crashes drew Jaffa's attention away from the news. It had sounded like his sons had dropped a tray full of dishes or broken a vase. Outside, a loud metallic clang made him jump. Then, the front door exploded inward with a boom as twelve agents bull-rushed through it.

Jaffa clumsily stumbled off the stool and ran for the computers. He made it five steps from the stool before the agents tackled him, forcing him face down on the floor and cuffing his hands behind his back. Jaffa flailed and kicked.

"I am an American citizen! I have rights!"

A muscular man with a tattoo of a pair of dangling boxing gloves on his neck got down on one knee in front of Jaffa. His shiny badge read "Sanchez."

"What did you just say, you piece of camel shit?" he shouted.

"I am a citizen! You Americans are all the same, with your whores and materialism. What has started cannot be stopped. Allah is weaving a new thread of morality into the country of infidels!"

Agent Sanchez asked, "Is that right?" Then he stood. "Take the cuffs off this smelly fucker! I'm not listening to another minute of this."

The agents uncuffed Jaffa. As he pulled himself up onto his legs, Sanchez asked, "Now what was it you were saying? I am not quite sure I heard you since your face was smashed against the floor."

Jaffa looked up at the man with the shaved head, and his chest swelled like a bullfrog facing off a snake. "The time has come for you Americans—"

Sanchez immediately jabbed his finger in Jaffa's face and yelled, "The time has come for the world to stop reciprocating your violence with peace. How dare you think you could replace our Constitution with Sharia Law! I wish those who think like you would just climb back into the cave they crawled out of, so I wouldn't have to waste my time putting you animals in the cage you belong in!"

Standing tall, Jaffa curled his lip. "You can't touch me. I have rights."

Sanchez rocked back on his heels and chuckled, then looked over Jaffa's shoulder.

"Hey, did you all see this man make an attempt to hit me?"

An agent behind Jaffa snorted. "Yes we did, sir. He seemed a bit violent."

Sanchez locked his eyes on Jaffa again, and his voice rose again, "When you wake up, you won't find yourself in the penthouse jail like your pal Khatchi. You're gonna wake up in the shithole basement of an old Russian drop house where we will have the proper time to ask you a few more questions."

The veins in his neck throbbed. With each pulse, Jaffa's chest deflated, and his glare turned into the stare of a deer in a truck's headlights. "What are you—"

Sanchez drove a fast, sharp punch into Jaffa's midsection. Before Jaffa could gasp for breath, Sanchez landed a right hook to Jaffa's jaw, then loaded up his powerful southpaw punch and unleashed his left fist to smash into Jaffa's nose, crunching it like a chicken bone.

When Jaffa awoke a few minutes later, a white-hot bolt of splintering pain shot through his jaw and nose. His breath caused another ripple of pain down his ribcage. He opened his eyes to see Kam and Masoud talking to the agents. Masoud glanced at his father and shook his head, then turned and led Sanchez to the computers. Kam led three agents downstairs, and Jaffa winced. In the back of the delivery van parked in basement garage sat the EMP weapon.

# Chapter 23

## Cancun, Mexico

Myk couldn't stand the thought of Jen agonizing over his death, so he found a FedEx store at a mall popular with the tourists and sent her a short encrypted note and a round-trip ticket to Cancun. He wrote that he would explain everything when she arrived, but that she not tell anyone where she was going or whom she was meeting. He would pick her up at the airport in a few days.

For the rest of the day, Myk planned his operation against Khatchi. He wanted to attack Khatchi before Saji and the Khat Man knew what hit them. That's how Myk liked to execute his operations; no reason to overanalyze things—get in and get out. When he left the resort, he wore inconspicuous tourist clothing: shorts, a T-shirt, sunglasses, and a hat.

Myk spent much of his day at a café with free internet, downloading the yacht's specifications. Denmark's famous Helsingor crafted the one-hundred-and-forty-seven-meter luxury yacht, which slept over sixty people, had a heli-pad and every conceivable amenity, and could still reach speeds in excess of thirty knots. Once Myk found the yacht's specifications, he spent the rest of his time memorizing every detail.

When he returned to his resort, Myk walked through the pool area and down to the beach to wait for the boat he had hired to take him out for a scuba dive. He didn't have his diving certificate with him, but it didn't take much cash to convince the guide to take him out anyway. He instructed his guide to take him to a diving location about a mile from Khatchi's yacht. At nightfall, he would be able to get much closer, but he wanted to keep a safe distance and make sure he didn't tip his hand to anyone on the yacht. He intended to stay out of sight on the ride out for the dive, just in case any of Khatchi's security crew spotted him.

Once the boat reached the specific location, Myk came topside dressed in his full scuba gear and shaded his eyes against the bright sun, pausing to enjoy the gentle breeze against the warmth of the rays. After telling the guide he would dive for a few hours, Myk slipped the tight fitting mask over his swollen face and winced as it pressed against discolored, tender spots. Then he plunged backwards over the side of the boat into the translucent blue water.

He dove until he found a massive coral formation and hovered for a moment, admiring the coral's rich colors and the glows and stripes of exotic fish. It was like being in an underwater aquarium surrounded by unimaginably beautifully striped and glowing fish. He swam over to Khatchi's massive yacht, where the gentle ocean waves lapped at its sides. This would be his only scouting expedition of the yacht; the next time he would be in these waters, he would be coming for Khatchi and Saji. The sun's rays pierced through the top of the water, broken when he breached the surface to swim around and observe all four sides of the massive yacht. Everything matched the specifications he'd downloaded, as well as the digital photographs Faraq had provided. He tugged the anchor line to make sure it would hold if he chose to climb it, then observed the security team and the back deck for a few minutes, keenly making mental notes of the area that would be his first point of attack.

When Myk finished, he ducked beneath the water and resurfaced at his guide boat. As they headed back toward the resort, he felt a surge of adrenaline ooze into his body as thoughts of Saji in his grips made him smile.

# Washington D.C.

After waking up on the cold basement floor of an old CIA safe house, Jaffa had a slightly improved attitude. Two CIA agents picked him up off the dirty concrete floor and sat him in a chair beside a table. A female agent with a shoulder sling sat on the other side of the table. Jaffa's face ached, one eye swollen half shut due to his broken nose and the right side of his face bloated from his broken jaw. The waves of pain made him light-headed one moment and turned his stomach the next.

The agent asked, "Jaffa, where's Khatchi hiding? Who's behind the attacks, and where will the next attack happen?"

He slowly shook his head. "I don't know. I need to see a doctor. Please, the pain is unbearable."

"I don't have any time to play games with you. Your operation has killed many people, including a few of our agents. So I'll ask you one more time. You help me, I help you. Once I walk through that door, you're on your own. You will talk, and you will tell us what you know."

Jaffa began to breathe fast, each breath sending a sharp stab in his side and pulling the musty smell of the room into his lungs.

The agent continued, "It's up to you on how much pain you will endure before you tell us. You are being held by four agents who put their country before their careers, and we will do whatever is necessary to prevent more people from dying. We're willing to go to jail if that's what it takes to get you to talk."

Jaffa turned his half-blind, blurred vision to the dark figures in the room. They stood with stony faces, watching Jaffa like wolves closing in on an injured deer.

The agent leaned forward. "For the last time—who's behind this attack, and where will the next one be?"

"I told you I don't know. I had nothing to do with the operations."

"Okay, Jaffa. Have it your way."

The agent scooted her chair away from the table slowly so the chair legs scraped across the floor like fingernails dragging across a chalkboard. Then she stood and walked out of the dark room. Jaffa shook as he folded his arms on the table and put his head down like a first grader during nap time. For the next few minutes, he sobbed into his arms.

"Jaffa, remember me?"

Jaffa winced at the deep voice.

"I am the one responsible for your pain. Do you have any idea how much good evidence you left us on your computers? You're not exactly the brightest bulb on the Christmas tree, are you? Your terrorist brothers snatched up one of our agents from Richmond, and you will tell me where they are. You will also tell me the name of the person behind these attacks and where the next one will happen."

Jaffa lifted his head and squinted. His tormenter had returned to plague him. Agent Sanchez stepped forward out of the darkness.

"The game is over. We already contacted the White House and set up a press conference with your video evidence. The truth is out about the twelve killed in D.C., the Koran burning, and the attack at the White House. Now you will tell me what else we need to know."

As Sanchez strode forward, Jaffa sprang up and cowered into the wall, knocking over his chair. He covered his face with his arms.

"Please don't touch me! I am in so much pain, I beg you."

Sanchez rushed around the table and grabbed Jaffa by the throat with one hand, slamming him into the wall. "Tell me who's behind this and where Khatchi is, or—"

"Stop, please! I know nothing!"

Agent Sanchez squeezed his throat until Jaffa panted and his face turned purple. Then Sanchez used his free hand to grab Jaffa's broken nose between his thumb and forefinger and give it a slight twist. Jaffa's piercing scream rang inside the small room. Sanchez released him and backed away from Jaffa, who crouched and writhed, cupping his bleeding nose.

Towering over Jaffa, Sanchez pointed his finger right in the hyperventilating man's face and yelled, "Listen to me, Ali-fucking-Babba. You can yell and scream all you want. We're in a farmhouse in the middle of nowhere with no one around to hear you."

Sanchez raised his left fist and gritted his teeth, then suddenly paused when he noticed something peculiar. A dark stain ran down the front of Jaffa's pants and dripped from his pant leg, collecting into a puddle of urine on the floor.

Jaffa covered his face and pouted, "Okay, okay. Please don't touch me."

Sanchez yelled. "Who is running the operation and where is Khatchi?"

"South!" The answer spurted from Jaffa's trembling lips.

"What did you say?"

"South. They went south. That's all I know. They had a private jet outside Richmond, and they were going south. I don't know if it was South America or Mexico. I just know they wanted to hide Khatchi for a month or two before sending him back east."

"What else?"

"Hakeem. He's my contact in Saudi Arabia. I don't know his last name, I swear to you. That's it. I know nothing more."

"What about any more attacks with the EMP weapons?"

"I don't know of any more attacks."

"If I find out you're lying to me, you will wish you were dead." Sanchez strode out, and Jaffa sat shivering in his own urine.

Sanchez found Agent Black looking into the room through the one- way glass window. He turned to her and asked, "What do you think? You think he knows anything else?"

She adjusted her shoulder sling from the injury she sustained from the attack in Richmond. "No, I don't think so. I have to admit, though, that was a first. I don't think I've ever seen anyone piss themselves before. I'll call Brodie and let him know what we've got. Nice job, Sanchez; you didn't even have to throw any punches this time! We might actually come out clean on this."

"Trust me; it wasn't easy. You have no idea how hard it was to keep from ripping his head off."

# Chapter 24

## Cancun, Mexico

For years, Myk had nightmares about the sounds, smells, and gut-wrenching pain at the loss of his newlywed wife on the platform of the train station in Madrid. And even though she had died, the person behind the attack still lived. Tonight, Myk would kill Saji Aman.

Myk skimmed through the photos and diagrams of Khatchi's yacht and security detail one last time. He gathered the items he would need for his assault on Khatchi and his team, then hung the "Do Not Disturb" sign on his door as he left. Once out of the lobby, he slung his black, oversized duffle bag over his shoulder; the bag's two shoulder straps allowed him to wear it as a backpack. He waited for a gap in the traffic, then hurried across the street. This section of Cancun remained quiet during the day. After sunset, the streets buzzed with nightclubs and people—tourists from every country, college kids on break, locals peddling their goods, and an army of people selling tours and vacation packages.

Myk and his team had raided the small Pakistani village and captured Khatchi over a year ago. Although the team had succeeded, the plot had already begun. Khatchi's capture only delayed plans already in place. Had they nabbed him a few years earlier, they would have extracted the information from him and possibly prevented the attacks, saving thousands of lives and billions of dollars in property.

Down the street, crowds gathered at the CoCo Bongo Nightclub. The bass thumped as the music flooded out the front doors. Faraq parked the vehicle and waited for Myk across the street at the Grand Hyatt's entrance. Myk spotted the car and jumped into the passenger's seat.

"How long have you been waiting?" he asked.

"Not long. The marina closes in thirty minutes, so I ordered the chum at the bait and tackle shop. He gave me a puzzled look about why we would be doing this at night."

Myk buckled his seat belt. "That's because he doesn't know how we'll use it. Will he have it ready?"

Faraq pulled into the narrow street, dodging the pedestrians crowding it. "Yes, he said it would be no problem and even offered advice. The people here are so eager to please; it is a refreshing attitude to observe."

"That's because they want your money. It's how they make their living. If the merchants provide a good service, people come back and the merchants do well. If not, people take their business elsewhere. It's capitalism in its purest form."

"I suppose you're right. I still think your country is too materialistic though."

"Don't judge the entire country by the actions of a few. We don't condemn the entire Muslim world by the actions of a few jihadists."

"Point taken."

When they arrived at the marina's nearly empty lot, Faraq parked next to the bait and tackle shop and turned the engine off. "Do you have everything? Are you ready?"

Myk looked out across the darkness at the ocean, then turned to Faraq.

"Let's go."

Faraq pulled the boat out of the slip at the marina. A slight breeze from the south slid across Myk's skin, and the full moon's reflection cascaded over the still water. Faraq pushed the throttle handle to full speed and the boat surged forward, skipping across the rolling ocean waves. Myk stood and grabbed the side of the boat. Despite the deadly risk they were taking, the sensation of the salty air whipping through his hair as the boat powered forward still made Myk smile.

It would only take a few minutes to arrive at the drop point Myk had scouted the previous day, but since it was night, Faraq could get much closer to the yacht. He pulled the throttle back, and the boat settled back down into the water as it slowed.

Myk turned to Faraq. "Continue the rest of the way at a wakeless speed." As they drew closer, Myk dressed in his scuba gear and signaled Faraq to kill the engines. "Okay, this should be good enough. Remember, if you can lock Khatchi's room, do so. I don't want him to hear anything when I arrive."

Faraq replied, "If he behaves anything like the past, he will be too busy with his whores downstairs to have a clue. I will try to block the door as a precaution, though."

"Good. I should get to the back of the yacht in about thirty minutes—"

"Agent McGrath, I cannot take part in the killing. As much as they deserve it, I have never killed a man before, and I'm not sure I am capable of it."

"It's okay. I can handle it from here. Just stay clear and get out of the way. You could get hurt or killed if you are anywhere near the fighting."

Faraq nodded. Myk slipped his mask on, his face still sensitive but not as bruised as before, then plunged into the water.

Faraq eased the throttle forward and pointed the boat in the direction of the lights from Khatchi's yacht. As the boat crept forward, Faraq gathered the supplies for the crew that he had told them he would be bringing. Six of the men on board were responsible for recording the killings in Richmond and D.C.

Just like the previous night, Faraq brought the crew back an ice chest full of fresh food and drinks. He hid the chum in the bow of the speed boat and prepared to receive the tow line from one of the crew members aboard the yacht. As he neared the vessel, he cut the engines, grabbed the rope thrown to him, and slid the boat alongside the massive yacht. Once the speedboat was tied off, Faraq handed the awaiting crew the ice chest and stepped aboard.

He turned back around and looked into the dark and out across the tranquil waters and began to get nervous. He desperately hoped things would go well so he could get his life back without having to ever peer over his shoulder again. After listening to Agent McGrath talk about how his first wife had been killed, he had gained an added measure of respect for the American agent. He felt an unexplainable and peculiar connection to him but couldn't quite put his finger on what it was.

From Myk's position underwater, he looked up and saw the yacht's lights shimmering on the surface of the ocean. He slowly broke the surface and took his first look at the yacht aglow against the backdrop of the dark night-sky. He disengaged his oxygen tanks and unharnessed his scuba gear. As he detached the equipment, he let them drop to the ocean floor and then glided through the water to the side of the yacht, where he replaced his fins with slip-proof deck shoes. Snug up against the side of the yacht, he pulled off his mask and snorkel and let them sink into the depths below as well.

As he inched along the side of the yacht, the gentle rolls of the ocean swells pushed him up and down while he approached the back of the boat. He took a deep breath and peered around the back corner of the yacht for the security team. One man stood about fifteen feet away on the back deck, and the other leaned against the railing up one level as he inhaled on his cigarette.

Myk pulled his Beretta 92FS out of the waterproof pouch and screwed the silencer onto the tip of the gun, balancing himself against the side of the yacht as it moved with the gentle waves. Arabic music playing on the yacht's outdoor speakers drowned out the quiet, metallic sound of screwing on the silencer. He held his silenced weapon out of the water with one hand and grabbed a metal rail for balance with his other hand. The man on the back deck spotted Myk glinting in the moonlight, but as he flinched to draw his weapon, Myk squeezed off two headshots, and the man fell forward.

At the sound of the gun's *tap-tap*, the other henchman looked down in time to see the dead man hit the back deck, then the small flash of a spark from Myk's weapon. The overweight Saudi toppled over the railing and fell twelve feet onto the back deck. His flabby body hit the deck with a large thud.

Myk hoped nobody heard the sounds. *Two down, six more to go.* He pulled himself up out of the water and slid onto the back deck like a seal at Sea World sliding across the surface to get a fish from his trainer. Pulling out the waterproof bag he had tied around his leg, he crouched behind the engine hull's fiberglass cover, unzipped the waterproof attaché, and harnessed his weaponry to his body. He dragged both corpses to the back of the boat and rolled them into the water, then climbed the stairs at the back of the yacht.

To prevent the security detail at a higher deck level from gaining the vantage point, Myk needed to first gain control of the top deck and then commence his work of death from the top down. As he reached the top of the stairs, the black boots of one of Khatchi's thugs appeared through an opening in the metal railing. Myk couldn't get a clean shot off from where he crouched in the stairwell, so he holstered his gun and got down on one knee.

Myk sprang from his crouched position and struck the man's throat, crushing his larynx with a loud crunch. The man dropped to his knees. A flurry of gunshots erupted from the opposite end of the yacht, and a sharp stinging pain shot through Myk's left hamstring. He grabbed the man now gasping for air and swung his body around as a shield. He could feel the force of the bullets as they penetrated the body. Then the body went limp, and its weight bore down on him. He threw the corpse to the side and dove behind a large, steel-plated metal chest filled with life jackets as the sound of bullets ricocheted all around him.

His heart pounded, and he glanced down at his leg. It hurt, but he didn't feel anything lodged in the muscle or bone. The bullet must have grazed the side of his leg, maybe even taken out a chunk of flesh—but at least it didn't hit any nerves or bone. As he crouched thinking of what to do next, Myk glanced across at the huge canvas canopy that covered the top deck. The canopy's two back corners were held up by two metal poles that came together at the middle of the canopy, forming a V. If he kicked one of the supporting poles loose, it would collapse the whole canopy, but running to the pole would expose him to the shooter. Still, he had few options and needed to move fast.

Myk fired a few shots at the shooter to provide cover, then sprang to his feet and ran towards the poles. His wounded leg throbbed, and within a second, the shooter shot back. Myk got within ten feet and leaped feet first as if sliding into home plate. He crashed into the support poles, and the canvas canopy collapsed, blinding the shooter on the other side of the canvas.

The shooter fired off four random shots, but Myk slid over the side of the yacht, his legs dangling over the edge as he held onto the railing. He went hand over hand, leaving nothing but his hands in view. The shooter fired several more shots, but Myk made it all the way to the front of the yacht and was now directly behind the shooter.

When he reached the front of the yacht, he swung his injured leg up and rolled back onto the deck. The shooter stood fifteen feet away with his back to Myk, who didn't want to shoot him in the back. Instead, he raised his gun and whistled. The terrorist spun, and Myk hesitated for a split second to enjoy the surprised look on the man's face before he squeezed the trigger. A single round went through the terrorist's head, spraying a film of blood and brains on the canvas canopy draped behind him, where the yellow and red splatter dripped.

He had gained the upper hand by securing the top deck. *Four dead, four to go.* He hoped Faraq barricaded Khatchi in his room; with all the loud shooting, Myk had lost the element of surprise. He pushed the large metal container of life jackets in front of the stairway to obstruct access, then applied medication to his injured leg and tied a bandana around it. From the upper deck, he could see nearly any portion of the deck below because it was almost completely surrounded with large glass windows.

Myk hooked his feet into the bottom rail that ran around the upper deck's perimeter. With his feet securely attached, he hung upside down from the railing like a possum hanging from a branch by his tail. A twinge of pain ran through his shot leg, but as he hung upside down, he spotted two more men at the back of the boat where they waited at the base of the stairs for Myk to come down. He pulled himself back up and ran to the stairwell, his adrenaline drowning out the faint stabs of pain in his leg.

From his pouch, he pulled a small grenade designed for close-range combat, pulled the cap off the detonator, and tossed the grenade to the bottom of the stairwell. After it hit the floor, the panicked voices spoke rapidly in Arabic; a second later the grenade detonated. A light cloud of smoke rose up the stairwell as he hurried down the stairs, landing on every fourth step. Once at the bottom of the stairs, he scanned for movement in the dense, smoky air.

On the ground five feet in front of him came movement through the haze, the outline of one man crawling on his hands and knees. Myk took two steps and kicked the man in the head with his good leg, knocking him out. The action sent a twinge of pain through his injured leg, and his knee almost buckled. As he caught himself and stood up straight, someone groaned behind the stairs. Myk moved toward the sound until he found the other terrorist lying on his back. Myk zip tied his hands and legs and then cuffed him to the staircase, along with the other incapacitated goon.

*Six down, two to go.*

Saji and the remaining terrorist would be bunkered down in the yacht's lower level. Myk could only access the lower level by the stairs, but he didn't have another explosive, and taking the stairs would be suicide. Myk remembered the oversized window while in the water scouting the yacht. He concluded that the possibility of getting a few cuts smashing through the window would be much better than rushing into an ambush.

He ran back up to the top deck to grab the lanyards coiled in piles, tying one end to the safety railing and wrapping the other end around his waist as if rock rappelling. Then, he put a new clip in his gun and lowered himself to the glass window. Once at the lower window, he looped the rope around his forearm several times so he could steady himself with one arm. With his free arm, he pulled out his gun and shot out the glass window, which shattered. Pushing off with his legs, he swung into the opening and unleashed himself from the rope.

Khatchi's suite was located toward the front of the yacht, but first Myk had to deal with Saji and his goon. The remaining terrorist probably waited at the stairway down the hallway and to the left. Myk ran up the hall and ducked into a mechanical room. With the door hinged on the left, he cracked it open to see down the hallway toward the stairs.

A few moments later, shadows moved at the end of the hall. One of the terrorists stalked into view, his weapon drawn. He neared Myk's location. If Myk waited too long, the man might notice the door slightly open. Myk paused, then burst out of the door, his weapon drawn and arm extended. *Tap-tap-tap.* He dropped the terrorist in his spot.

Myk sensed movement behind him and turned just in time to see the gun flash from the remaining terrorist behind him. The man fired two rounds; one grazed Myk's cheek and the other hit him in the middle of his chest. The impact sent him staggering back. He hit the floor with such force that his weapon flew out of his grip. He gasped for air. The Kevlar bulletproof vest had done its job, but the force of the bullet had knocked the breath out of him.

The bearded man approached to finish him off, and cold dread flooded Myk. As the man neared, Myk recognized his face: Saji, who now got a clear look at Myk's face for the first time. Saji's scowl disappeared as his jaw dropped and his eyes widened. He stood over Myk and stared at him, perplexed and pointing his weapon at Myk's head.

"How can this be? I saw the video of Faraq beheading you."

Still gasping, Myk sputtered, "Things are not as they always appear, shithead!"

Myk had waited years for this moment, but this was the complete opposite of how he had imagined things would end with him.

Saji raised his gun. "No matter. It gives me great pleasure to be the one who finally kills you."

Faraq appeared in the hallway behind Saji, holding a fire extinguisher with two hands above his head. He brought both hands down, slamming the extinguisher on the back of Saji's head. As Saji toppled to the floor in an unconscious heap, Myk rolled on top of him, grabbed the zip cuffs from his pocket, and secured Saji.

Every fiber in his being wanted to kill Saji on the spot. *Just snap his neck and be done with it.* But he would wait. He had something better in mind for the man who murdered his wife and hundreds of others.

# Chapter 25

Myk looked up at Faraq, "Thank God! That's twice in one week you've saved my life."

Faraq panted. "I am just glad I got here in time. I did exactly as you said. I blocked the door to Khatchi's room, but then I heard the shots from the top deck, so I found a safe spot. When I heard the explosion on the second deck, I knew you must be getting close. That's when I saw the last two men run to take cover on the lower deck. Saji told me to keep guard and that they were taking both ends of the hall to trap you in the middle if you didn't use the stairs. I knew I had to do something."

Myk smiled. "That was good thinking. Did you say Khatchi is still in the room?"

"Yes, but I haven't heard anyone attempting to get out. The women had a lot of cocaine with them when I dropped them off this afternoon."

"Okay." Myk pointed down the hall. "That's Khatchi's suite down at the other end, right?"

"Yes." Faraq stared at Myk. "Agent McGrath, are you okay? Your face is bleeding pretty badly, and your pant leg is drenched in blood."

Myk wiped a handful of blood from his face and then wiped his hand off on his shirt. "I'm fine. Does Khatchi have any weapons in the room?"

"He has a gun in the nightstand on the right."

"Got it. Where is the first aid kit? I need more medication for my leg." He showed Faraq the back of his shot leg. Blood had soaked through the bandana he had used as a tourniquet, and a steady pulse of pain radiated outward from the wound.

Faraq frowned and looked back up at Myk. "That looks painful. When did that happen?"

"I'm fine. I need to get it sterilized until I can see a doctor tomorrow. The second guy on the top deck shot my leg. I was completely exposed once I came up the stairs. Lucky shot. He had a clear view of me until I found cover. Would you bring the first aid kit down for me?"

"No problem."

Faraq ran upstairs. In the meantime, Myk dragged both bodies to the edge of the stairs so Faraq could help him lift them up to the back deck. When Faraq returned with the huge first aid kit, they opened it to find it stocked with syringes, penicillin, gauze, wraps, and everything else Myk needed. But first they had to take care of immediate business.

It took them thirty minutes to drag the dead bodies off the boat and secure the surviving men. After they lifted Saji's unconscious body into the speedboat, Myk tended to his bullet wound and the laceration on his face. What little anxiety he felt earlier ebbed under the strong swells of anticipation as he prepared for his confrontation with Khatchi.

He turned to Faraq. "It's time. Go get the chum from the speedboat and do exactly as the man at the tackle and bait shop instructed. Take the speedboat out no further than thirty yards from the yacht and disperse the bait. Save the last two buckets for the back of the yacht. We want to draw the sharks as close as possible."

"Okay. Agent McGrath, please don't take Khatchi too lightly. His own men fear him."

"I am well aware of what Khatchi is capable of, but in case you forgot, how many armed terrorists were on this yacht when you arrived tonight?"

Faraq hesitated. "Nine."

"And how many are there now?" When most people underestimated Myk, he often retorted with a tone as cold and sharp as frost. Still, Faraq had earned Myk's trust in the past 48 hours, so Myk's tone did not reach its normal steel.

Faraq grinned. "Okay, you've made your point. I'll go get the chum and speedboat ready."

Myk walked with a slight limp down the hall to Khatchi's suite. When he arrived at the eight-foot double doors, he laughed upon seeing Faraq's improvised method of trapping Khatchi in the suite. *Leave a task for an engineer, and it will always get done right.* Faraq had found two long metal poles from the mechanical room and shoved them through the door handles, then extended the poles beyond the doorjamb. Nobody was getting out.

Myk slid the poles out of door handles and laid them on the floor, then drew his weapon and cracked the door open an inch to peer into the dark room. The only movement came from the ceiling fan. He eased the door open a little more and crept inside the room, relieved that the carpet silenced his steps. He paused. Still no movement. A trace of light emanated from a night light in the bathroom.

As he snuck into the room, his eyes adjusted to the darkness enough to make out the silhouettes on the bed. A pungent smell similar to sour rags mixed with a nasty odor, almost like an outhouse that hadn't been serviced in weeks, flooded his senses. He advanced further into the darkened room and approached the bed. One woman lay on the floor next to the bed, and the other woman looked like she was tied to the bed. Khatchi's body was sprawled out, covering half of the woman.

Myk walked to the spacious closet to make sure no surprises waited for him inside, then checked the master bathroom suite. Afterward, he snuck to the nightstand where Faraq said the weapon would be and felt around inside the drawer until his hand ran across something cool and hard. He took the gun from the nightstand, released the clip, and tossed it toward the door. It hit the carpet with a thud.

No one stirred.

*Okay, time to shed some light on this smelly mass of bodies.* He walked back to the master bathroom and turned on all the lights, then checked the bedroom. Still no movement. With a low growl, he grabbed the gallon-sized ice bucket sitting on the bathroom vanity. The ice had mostly melted, but the water remained cold. He held the ice bucket in one hand and his gun in the other as he walked to the bank of light switches on the wall next to the entrance, set the ice bucket down, and flipped on all the lights. Myk glanced around the suite.

A huge, crystal chandelier hung above the oversized canopy bed, and hand-carved wood moldings and paneling decorated the suite. But when Myk's eyes traveled to the bodies on the bed, his face flushed and he clenched his fists. The woman lay unconscious, naked and tied to the bed. Blood and bruises stained her face and abdomen, as well as her wrists and ankles. Khatchi's hairy body remained slung across the bed.

The other woman lay naked on the floor, face down in her own vomit. Myk picked up the ice bucket and stepped closer to the girl on the floor. He nudged the motionless body with his foot and then got a closer look at her face. Her skin and lips had turned blue-gray, and her eyes stared vacantly into oblivion. On the table beside the bed sat two bags, one empty and the other half full of cocaine.

Myk grabbed his bucket of ice water and tossed it on Khatchi.

The still bodies exploded into action the second the water hit them. Khatchi sprang up, wiping the ice water from his soaked head, then swayed. His eyes wouldn't focus. As Khat Man sat up and tried to focus, his layers of fat folding under him, Myk stood at the foot of the bed and pointed his gun at him, waiting. Finally, Khatchi turned and fastened his attention on Myk, his gaze wavering as if trying to balance on a fence. Then his eyes shot open.

"What?! How—What the hell are you doing here? I saw you beheaded with my own eyes."

Myk tapped the barrel of his gun on Khatchi's foot. "Welcome to the twenty-first century, caveman. If you even flinch, I'll shoot your sorry ass."

Khatchi rolled to his side, then looked down and pulled a sheet over his naked body. Myk immediately put the barrel of his gun on the ball of Khatchi's right foot and pulled the trigger. Khatchi's big toe exploded like a smashed tomato, and he screamed. The hot blood that splattered across the bound girl elicited a shriek from her too.

Myk pointed the gun at Khatchi and yelled, "You don't listen very well do you? You move one more time, fucker, and I'll shoot the other big toe off! Got it?!" He pulled his knife from his side pocket and cut down the girl, who looked up through a swollen, bruised eye at the angry, gun-toting American.

"Gather your things together and go upstairs," Myk said. "The man who brought you here has a first aid kit and will help you. I am sorry for what this animal did to you and your friend."

The naked woman rolled off the bed and grabbed a towel to wrap around her as she gathered her things. Khatchi wailed and rolled around in the bed, clutching his foot as the sheets blossomed with red blooms and streaks. Then, she returned to the side of the bed, cleared her throat, and spat on Khatchi's face.

"Well done," Myk grinned. He turned to Khatchi. "Don't you dare move to wipe that spit off your face! I need to know where the next attack will happen. You know exactly how this works, so don't waste my time. Everybody talks Khatchi . . . everybody."

Khatchi's cries and moans rose and sank as Myk talked, so Myk's volume rose to meet it.

"I don't consider you part of our human race. I'm not sure what species would do what you have done to humanity, so I have no problem inflicting whatever pain necessary. Unlike you, the rest of us don't kill innocent children and women. So, I have absolutely no problem picking you apart piece by piece like a curious boy picks apart a grasshopper. Tell me, Khatchi, where will the next attack take place?"

Khatchi blubbered over his big toe but sputtered a reply. "I've been locked up in your American prison for over a year. How in the hell would I know?"

"Wrong answer, shithead! I'm not wasting another bullet on your sorry ass. I want to feel you writhe with my bare hands! You should have killed me when you had the chance."

Myk lowered his gun, ejected the clip, and threw both toward the front door. "What a joke. You're supposed to be the mighty Khatchi Abu-mon, the most feared terrorist leader in the world, the man who brainwashes young men and trains them to slaughter innocent people. And here you lie in a bed of silk sheets, coked out with hookers. We recorded your exploits in high-def so your followers can see their fearless leader in action."

Khatchi lunged for the nightstand and scrambled to find his gun.

Myk walked resolutely around the corner of the poster bed toward him. "I already took the gun you're looking for. It's in the closet."

Then he raised his right leg up and brought his heel down with

all the force he could muster on Khatchi's mangled foot. Khatchi fell back onto the bed screaming and holding his bloody foot. He rolled to the side, then shot his hand under the pillow and pulled out a large knife. Myk reared back as Khatchi lunged forward, slashing Myk's right arm and chest. As Myk stumbled to the side, Khatchi kicked Myk on the exact spot of his gunshot wound.

The nauseating pain overwhelmed Myk, like a wave that crashed over him and sent him swirling under it. He staggered, then grabbed the brass light on the nightstand, wielding it like a shield against the large knife Khatchi swung at him. Khatchi swiped again, but Myk jumped backwards. As he dodged the large knife, his foot snagged on the dead woman on the floor and he fell on the other side of her. Khatchi hobbled toward him, his arm outstretched and clutching the knife.

As he neared, Myk reached his arm back and heaved the brass light at Khatchi's head. Khatchi ducked out of the way as the light sailed past him and smashed into the wall, but the flinch was all Myk needed. He sprang to his feet and kicked the knife out of Khatchi's hand. Then, he used his other foot to kick Khatchi in the back of knee, causing his leg to buckle and bend sideways in a way knees weren't meant to bend. Khatchi let out a contorted yell and crashed to the floor. Myk immediately leapt toward him and smashed his elbow into Khatchi's face causing his head to snap violently backwards.

Myk climbed on top of Khatchi and spun him around, holding him face down in the dead woman's vomit with Khatchi's arms behind his back. Myk's pulse quickened. He dug his knee into Khatchi's back between his shoulder blades and pulled both arms behind his back at their maximum pressure point.

"Nice try, Khat Man. I would've been so disappointed if you hadn't attempted something, but like I said, everybody talks. How much pain will you make me inflict on you before you change your mind? Of all people, you should know everyone talks. You should also know I love wrestling. Actually, I am pretty good at it. Quite a few people at the NCAA thought the same thing; they made me an All-American for three straight years. Too bad they came up with a sport called cage fighting after I stopped wrestling."

Myk applied a little more torque on Khatchi's arms. "You see, Khatchi, in cage fighting, you can either knock your opponent out or put him in a hold called submission. That's the hold I have you in right now. You're defenseless. If we were in a cage fight, I would be declared the winner, but I've won enough wrestling matches. What I really need is information, and what you need is the use of your limbs. Do you understand where I'm going with this?"

Khatchi gave no response, so Myk pulled harder on his arms. "If you tell me where the next attack will take place, I will let you have the use of your limbs. Otherwise, I will pull each arm out of its socket, one at a time. Got it? So, for the last time, where will the next attack be?"

Khatchi strained, then replied, "I told you I don't know—"

Myk put all his weight into Khatchi's right shoulder and snapped his arm out of its socket. *Crack!* It sounded like someone breaking off the dry branch of a tree. Khatchi's scream hurt Myk's ears. Myk torqued back on his other arm and barked out.

"You worthless fuck! Scream all you want. I have no sympathy for you. You were the muscle behind the Madrid train bombings. You have broken families, destroyed lives, and made children orphans. Since our justice system failed to do its job, I am here on behalf of the lives you've destroyed to eke out a small measure of justice and make sure you never harm anyone again. Tell me where the next attack will be, or I'll pull your other arm out of its socket too!"

Khatchi shook as Myk drove his knee into the man's back and held his other arm behind him. "I told you, I don't know."

Myk pulled the other arm out of its shoulder socket with another loud *snap*, and Khatchi squealed like a speared boar. Then, Myk grabbed Khatchi's limp arms and pulled them backwards. Khatchi's screaming squelched as he let out a wet belching sound and then shot vomit across the carpet.

Wrinkling his nose, Myk turned away from the sickening reek of sour bile and alcohol. But for a moment, he remembered holding his bleeding wife in his arms as she died. Now he made Khatchi's pain energize him. He snorted the stench out of his nose.

"You stupid fuck! You have no idea who you're dealing with and what I'm capable of doing to you." It felt good to let the anger flow through him to the animal he had trapped under him. "My wife was on the docking station in Madrid with thousands of others the day you detonated your bombs. She had her whole life ahead of her, and you took it from her. Tell me where the next attack will take place, or I'll move down to your legs! No amount of pain I could inflict on you could make up for the evil you perpetrated against humanity."

Myk pulled back hard on Khatchi's arms again, but it worried him. Khatchi could pass out or go into shock if he applied too much pressure, but innocent lives were at stake. He had to get the information.

Khatchi gasped. "Okay, okay! They're going to use the EMP weapon on Israel and frame Iran for the attack. He wants to wipe Israel off the map."

Myk released his arms, and the useless limbs flopped to the ground. "That's better. Now tell me when and how."

"They'll dismantle the EMP weapons and reassemble them in Israel."

"When?"

"In three weeks. They're shipping an EMP weapon they used in New York through an electronics cargo container. Please, I need something for the pain!"

Myk got off Khatchi and dragged him across the floor by his mangled foot, then cuffed him to the bedpost. Anger still pulsed through him as visions of his final day on the platform in Madrid flashed into his mind. Impulsively, he kicked Khatchi in his crotch as hard as he could.

"You worthless piece of shit!" Myk's suppressed fury spilled out in his red-faced shouting. "You have no idea how easily I could kill you right here." He picked up the weapons and walked over to the table, then tossed the half-empty bag of cocaine to Khatchi. "Try that. It might help the pain until I get back." Then he tossed Khatchi a towel. "Here. You can use that to wipe the puke off your face, if you can still use your arms." He left Khatchi cuffed to the bed, writhing.

As he slammed the door behind him, a twinge of discomfort made him wonder why he had given Khatchi the cocaine and towel. The man had slaughtered Myk's wife and thousands of innocent people, and here Myk had tossed him something to dull his pain and clean up. Shaking off the thought, he ran up the stairs as fast as his aching leg allowed.

When Myk reached the back deck, Faraq had just finished throwing the chum into the now bloody waters to attract sharks from miles away. Photographers often use chum to lure sharks for pictures. Just to be safe, Myk had asked for twice as much as the guide at the bait and tackle shop had recommended. As Faraq tied off the speedboat, Myk came topside.

"Did everything go okay?" he asked.

"Everything is fine. The girl you sent up seems better after I used the first aid kit on her. I transported her back and forth from the yacht in the past few days, so I think she trusts me. She went to sleep in the room next to the kitchen. I told her we would take her back later tonight. The yacht is a lot nicer than the place she lives."

Myk found the first aid kit and sat down to clean and apply a new bandage to his gunshot wound. As Faraq cleaned, he glanced back up.

"Agent McGrath, I have to admit, I know I was supposed to be safe on the speedboat, but the last five minutes of dropping that chum out for the sharks was terrifying. There are some very large sharks out there now. How did things go with Khatchi?"

"He got lucky. No real surprises, other than the knife. I think I got what I needed." Myk finished treating his leg and looked up across the water. "Don't worry about the sharks. They scare everyone." Then he shook his head. "How in the hell Khatchi got such a following is beyond me. The guy is an empty vessel."

Faraq asked, "What information did you get from him?"

"They disassembled an EMP weapon in New York and plan to assemble it in Israel to draw them into war with Iran. Have you seen the bag I brought with me?"

"Yes, it's right there inside the cabin door." Faraq pointed to Myk's black bag.

Myk hobbled over to the bag. "I have another prepaid mobile phone I bought this morning. I have to call Langley and see if they want me to do anything else with Khatchi."

"Is he alive?"

"Very much so. He's in a lot of pain and probably won't have much use of his arms until I pop his shoulders back into place, but he is alive."

He bent down and rummaged through his bag until he found the phone. He debated who he could trust, then dialed the number for Brodie Bashford's personal cell phone. After a long wait, the connection finally went through. Bashford answered after a few rings.

"Bashford speaking."

"Brodie, it's Myk. Listen, I don't have much time. You will have more questions than I have time to answer."

Bashford's tone and volume skyrocketed. "Is this for real? My God, Myk, is this really you? We saw the video of them beating you and then beheading you. How did you—"

"Brodie, I will explain later. Please just listen. Yes, it's me. I'm fine. I've kept Khatchi under surveillance for the past few days. A little over an hour ago, I took out his security detail and finally had some one-on-one time with him. I had to shoot his big toe off and dislocate both his shoulders, but he told me where the next attack is planned. It's Israel, Brodie. They're gonna wipe out Israel's defense system with an EMP weapon and blame Iran to draw the two nations into war."

Brodie let out a soft noise, but Myk continued before Brodie could interrupt him.

"He told me they disassembled an EMP weapon and are shipping it in an electronics cargo container from New York. That still leaves one EMP weapon unaccounted for, but I can't hurt him anymore or he may go into shock and I might lose him. I need to be able to use him later."

"Great work, Myk. You have no idea what a relief this is to hear your voice—"

"About that. Listen, Brodie, for operational purposes and for a few other reasons I will explain later, do not let anyone know I'm alive. I mean no one. Promise me you will keep a lid on my existence until you hear back from me."

"Sure, Myk, but you have to understand this will put me in a tough position. How will I convince the Israelis the intel is legit?"

"I'm sure you'll think of something. Besides, I think I have a contact I can reach out to. If it will help, I can send you a video of Khatchi."

"Of course, anything will help. Is there anything we can do for you on our end?"

"Actually, there is. I squeezed everything I could out of Khatchi without killing him, but I still need to find out where the other EMP weapon is. I'm sure when he sees what I have planned for Saji, he will tell us everything we need to know. I just want to make sure you don't have any use for this human waste anymore."

"If you think you've gotten everything you can, then I have no use for him. It was a disgrace the DOJ ever let him set foot on our soil in the first place."

"Brodie, one last thing. I need you to take all the restrictions and watches off Faraq's passport. Tell the Israelis they can thank Faraq for the information you'll give them. I will explain later, but you'll just have to trust me on this one, okay?"

"Sure, but it won't be easy to get the DOJ to play ball. Myk, one more thing."

"What?"

"I misspoke when I said I had no use for Khatchi. Would you see if you can get a name out of him? We've got a mole in our agency connected to the attacks. See if Khatchi knows anything. We'll probably have to move higher up the food chain, but it's worth a try."

"Got it." He ended the call.

Faraq stared at him, then said, "Agent McGrath, thank you for that. It's quite unexpected; I'm not sure what to say. Do you think he will really clear my passport?"

"Without a doubt. It's time for me to rid the world of Saji Aman. Make sure you get good video footage of everything Khatchi says.

He should give us valuable information."

Faraq beamed.

Myk gestured toward the open water. "Throw the remaining chum in the water, then grab the five-gallon can of gasoline and douse the speedboat with it. I will help you cut the restraints off Saji when I get back. I want to make sure he has the use of his limbs so he can swim if he wants. Also, put a forty-foot lead line on the speedboat just in case. I'll go get Khatchi."

As Myk made his way down the stairs to the master suite at the other end of the yacht, Khatchi's wails echoed down the hallway. Myk opened the door to the suite, and the stench struck him again. He glared at Khatchi's mucus-smeared face and bloodshot eyes. The terrorist trembled.

"Did you bring me some medication? I need a doctor."

"Shut the hell up! You are still hiding something. We're going up to the back deck so you can see what happens to Saji. After that, I think you'll have a change of heart. There is still one more EMP weapon unaccounted for, and you are going to tell me where the next attack is planned!"

Myk uncuffed him from the bedpost. "One more thing. I want the name of your spy in our government. We know you've got someone on the inside."

He brought Khatchi up to the platform and then cuffed him to the side railing. Faraq lined up the speedboat at the back of the yacht with Saji lying on the floor of the boat.

Myk said, "Throw some water on Saji and wake him up."

Faraq grabbed an empty bucket, dipped it in the ocean, and then tossed the bloody water on Saji. The man shot up, spluttered and coughed for a few seconds, then winced and touched the back of his head. Myk yelled down at him.

"Wake up! I've got your ticket straight to Hell, because that's where you'll spend the rest of eternity. Ready for the ride?"

Saji crawled up off the floor and stumbled toward the yacht. Myk turned to Faraq. "Push the speedboat away. Quickly!"

Faraq shoved the speedboat away as hard as he could. The boat drifted into the open water as the forty-foot tow line that connected it to the yacht grew taut.

Saji yelled out, "What are you doing? I smell gasoline!"

Myk reached into his bag and pulled out an emergency flare stick. He lit the flare, which sprayed sparks. He turned to Khatchi.

"You and Saji set off bombs at the Madrid train stations, killed my wife, and almost killed me. I waited far too long to close this chapter of my life. Unlike my innocent wife, Saji can save himself if he chooses. If he can swim to the yacht, I will cuff him and turn him over to the authorities. We have video footage of you with your whores. There'll be no virgins waiting for you in Paradise, that's for sure."

Then, Myk turned and threw the flare toward the speedboat. It toppled end over end into the night sky, and its reflection shone off the surface of the water as it drifted toward the speedboat. Saji swung up at the flare to try to fend off the airborne flame, but it hit the back of the speedboat. Flames shot up across the boat, turning the waves around it into a brilliant orange mirror and making the back of the yacht glow. At first, Saji curled up in a ball on the floor, but that only lasted a few seconds. As the flames intensified, he looked around for an escape.

Myk yelled, "I remember your face from Madrid. Now your smile will be wiped from my memory forever."

Saji ran forward two steps and then vaulted over the side, sailing into the air. He made it several feet before plunging into the water with a double splash, whose spray misted the spectators on the yacht.

After a moment, Saji broke the surface gasping and then swam toward the yacht as fast as he could. He churned his legs in the water to get away from the burning speedboat.

When Saji got almost five feet in front of the burning vessel, Myk looked at Faraq. "You did throw the rest of the chum in the water, didn't you?"

"Of course."

"Did you see any sharks?"

"I told you, yes. They terrified me when I was alone in that boat feeding them."

"Okay."

Saji swam another ten feet. Myk wondered what contingency plan he needed if Saji actually made it back to the yacht. But his thoughts vanished as a massive gray ribbon flickered under the surface near the boat, a silhouette that made Myk go cold and shudder. The shape disappeared, then thrashed the water behind Saji. Faraq gasped.

The dark fin and the tip of a vertical tail broke the surface. The water distorted the shark's outline, but the firelight flickered patterns across its long, lean body. Each stroke of its tail made the bands of muscle along its hydrodynamic sides ripple.

The enormous shark broke the surface with a frothy splash. Water streamed from its glistening bluish-gray skin, and its black eyes gleamed in the firelight. It opened its gaping mouth, exposing a row of pink gums and triangular teeth. Then, it closed its jaws on Saji's thigh and shook him back and forth like a dog with its favorite toy. An instant later, another shark struck Saji from the front, engulfing his head and shoulders in its jaws. The water churned white, then red. Saji's body disappeared under the water, and clouds of blood darkened the surface.

Myk turned to the pale-faced Khatchi, who watched the underwater feeding frenzy with an open mouth. Myk snapped his fingers several times like a master to his trained dog.

"Hey, shark bait. Look at me. I have more questions for you, and unless you give me honest answers, I will not hesitate to toss you over the side of this yacht. Do you understand?"

Khatchi looked at Myk. "What would you like to know?"

"You told me about the attack on Israel, but where will the other attack take place?"

"Los Angeles."

"Los Angeles is a big city, Khat Man. Where in Los Angeles?"

Khatchi trembled. "The same as New York. They targeted the power generating stations and water supplies that feed into the city."

"When?"

"In a few weeks. It was supposed to happen the same time as the attack on Israel."

Myk replied, "Tell me the name of your man inside the CIA."

"I don't know."

"Bullshit!" Myk rushed over to him, uncuffed him, and grabbed his legs. As he dragged Khatchi toward the side of the yacht, Khatchi yelled and wriggled.

"Please! I know nothing!"

Myk dangled the man over the side of the yacht. "Give me the name of the mole working for you, or I'm feeding you to the sharks!"

Khatchi flailed his feet and yelled, "I swear I don't know his name! He only deals with Hakeem. I was locked up in your prison; I have no idea who he is. Please, don't drop me!"

With a grunt, Myk pulled him back up and cuffed him to the rails. "I hope I don't regret this. Unfortunately, I have other plans for you." Myk turned and searched through his bag, then pulled out his phone, punched in the numbers, and waited for the call back. Then he called Bashford. "Brodie, it's Myk."

"I wasn't expecting to hear back from you so quickly. Is everything okay?"

"Khatchi just gave me the site of the next attack. They're hitting Los Angeles with the EMP weapon. He said they will target the electrical generating stations and the pumping stations for the water supply outside the city. They want to choke Los Angeles from its water and electricity just like they did in New York. He said it's supposed to happen in the next few weeks."

"That's fantastic work, Myk. We'll get working on it right away, and this time we'll have our people waiting for them. We will post agents at every electrical generating station."

Myk replied, "I don't think he knew the name of the mole. I tried, but I really don't think he was in the loop."

An anonymous call flashed across his screen. "Brodie, sorry, something has come up. I have to disconnect the call." Myk switched over to the incoming call and answered, "Hello."

"Agent McGrath, I can't tell you how thrilled I was to get your text message. We saw the video and thought you were dead. Tell me, what's happening?"

"First, you were right; the CIA has an infiltrator, but that's not why I contacted you. Tonight, I took control of a private yacht harboring Khatchi Abu-Mon and eight others who were part of his entourage, and I obtained critical information from him. Their group plans to attack Israel with an EMP weapon being shipped in a cargo container from New York. He didn't have any specifics, but he said something about framing the Iranians."

"Agent McGrath, that's a tremendous find. I knew you wouldn't disappoint."

"Thanks. I would really like to know how you knew a spy penetrated the agency, though."

Mordechai replied, "When we get the situation under control, we'll have more time to talk about it. What do you plan to do next? How did you go from being a headless hostage to capturing Khatchi? That's quite impressive."

"Good fortune, I suppose. I don't have any details worked out yet, but I am going after Hakeem Ferron. I think he's the one behind the attacks. I squeezed everything I can from Khatchi, so Hakeem is the next logical step. But what you said to me back at Langley has really been on my mind; how did you know my father and mother so well?"

"I will answer those questions at another place and time. I'm not sure Director Adelberg shared it with anyone, but we informed him we had photos from a surveillance team in Karachi that identified a Nazi who fell off our radar decades ago. He met with Saji. I think they intend to do a lot of damage to Israel or Jews abroad. I have to get moving on this information, Agent McGrath. The State of Israel thanks you for this invaluable piece of intelligence."

Myk asked, "There's one more thing I think you can answer."

"What is that?"

"Why does my mother have so much animosity towards CIA Director Adelberg?"

Mordechai remained silent for a few moments, then replied, "You're right; I do know. But I assume she hasn't told you for a reason, so it might be best to get it from her. If she doesn't answer, then I'll share it with you sometime in the future. We'll talk later."

The connection went dead. Myk glanced at the blank screen and then walked to the other side of the yacht and leaned against the side rails, staring out at the full moon's reflection. He thought about everything that had taken place and the difficult task ahead. As he gazed into the moonlit ocean, the quiet waves lapping at the yacht and his own slow breathing surrounded him. He turned back to Faraq.

"Cut the line to the speed boat. Let's pull up the anchor; we need to get the girl back to shore. Do you know anything about her friend?"

Faraq replied, "She has no family. Apparently, she was an orphan."

Myk shook his head. "I'm sorry to hear that. I'm sure Khatchi wouldn't mind if we give her some of his cash. Take ninety thousand dollars and set up a bank account for her when you take her back to shore. The world is a much better place tonight now that Saji is dead."

"I couldn't agree more."

Since Myk had persuaded Khatchi to be more forthcoming, Myk peppered him with questions while Faraq recorded the entire forty-minute exchange. Khatchi gave up detailed information about who funded the operations, where to find Hakeem, and anything else Myk asked. Satisfied that he had enough information to plan his next move, Myk tossed a small package of pills to Faraq.

"Give him four of these. It should put him to sleep for a day and knock the edge off of the pain. Once he's out, I'll pop his shoulders back into their sockets. I'll need him somewhat coherent when we get to Saudi Arabia." Myk looked back at Khatchi, then shook his head and looked down at Faraq's feet. "You have no idea how hard it is for me not to just toss his sorry ass in the water with those sharks. If this plan doesn't work, I will regret not seeing that piece of shit eaten alive."

They pulled up the anchors. When they finished cleaning up the boat, Myk fired up the yacht's engines and oriented the yacht toward Cancun's shimmering lights off in the distance. He left the engines at half speed as they cruised across the calm waters.

# Chapter 26

After tying the yacht off at the slip in the harbor, Myk didn't arrive back at his resort until three in the morning. Faraq spent the night on the yacht, and the two of them agreed to meet at the resort the next morning to finalize Myk's plans.

As Myk rolled out of bed, his whole body screamed from the night before, and he groaned. Putting pressure on his injured leg sent waves of pain and nausea through him and made him light-headed. A mirror hanging near the closet revealed the massive bruising on his chest and the welts from the bullets hitting his Kevlar vest. Faraq had helped him sterilize his lacerations and other wounds while on the yacht, but he still needed a doctor to check his leg to make sure the wound didn't get infected. Now, Myk could focus on dismantling Hakeem's nest of terrorists and putting him out of business forever.

Other than his aches and pains, Myk awoke from his deep sleep with an overwhelming sense of relief and inner peace. Saji, the creature responsible for the terrorist attack in Madrid that killed Myk's wife, now rested in pieces in the bellies of sharks. Khatchi slept subdued and under his control. The previous night's events had quenched the smoldering, all-consuming rage, and Myk wanted to move on. But a few things still unsettled him, like the mole in the agency and what Mordechai knew about his parents.

The first task at hand would be to get to Hakeem. It wouldn't be long before Hakeem grew suspicious and attempted to contact Khatchi. Myk needed to get to Hakeem before he discovered the truth and tried to disappear. With the video of his beheading floating around, Myk could not surface anywhere without endangering Faraq.

After showering, Myk went downstairs to eat a light breakfast before Faraq arrived. When he got back up to his room, he turned on the television to get a quick update on the situation back in the U.S. The state of affairs in New York improved by the day, now that Americans realized they had been attacked again. They helped one another and squelched the spread of fear and violence. Myk recalled that when the terrorists' bombs went off at the Boston Marathon, video footage showed many brave Americans running back towards the blasts to help complete strangers. Flight 93, the only plane not to hit its target on 9/11, was brought down by courageous Americans who sacrificed their lives. The hijackers had intended to crash the plane into the White House.

Reporters hoped power would be restored to the city months sooner than they had anticipated. As it turned out, the Chinese had all of the equipment needed to replace the generating stations, so the governments arranged a deal, and now six ocean liner barges traveled en route with everything necessary to rebuild the stations.

With another hour to kill before Faraq arrived, Myk glanced at some of his files on the desk hanging halfway out of his pack. He walked over and grabbed the thick binder, Faraq's file. He felt compelled to skim through the file again, so he spent a few minutes perusing through the records. Because Faraq's father was from Palestine, Myk had spent most of his time reading about that when Adelberg gave him the file. And because the attacks happened so quickly, Myk didn't have time to analyze Faraq's complete file.

He turned to the pages at the end of the report for the first time. It struck him as very odd that Faraq's Jewish mother had married a Palestinian. He looked at the birthplace of Faraq's mother: Czechoslovakia, which spurred his curiosity. He scanned down the page to the category "City/Town."

Lidice, Czechoslovakia.

Myk froze. *There's no way.* He flipped the page and found the names of Faraq's grandparents: Josef and Anna Wiesel.

"What the hell?!" He sat motionless and stared at the paper. "How could this be?"

After a moment, he flipped back and forth through his file, checking birthdates, names, and siblings. He kept returning to the page with Faraq's mother's birthplace and his grandparents' names: Josef and Anna Wiesel, born in Lidice, Czechoslovakia. The only sibling listed was Hannah Wiesel, Myk's mother.

Myk pushed his emotions down, but his eyes watered. Josef and Anna Wiesel were Myk's grandparents. His and Faraq's mothers were the twin sisters.

"You've got to be kidding me."

He stared at the page and shook his head. His heart pounded harder now than it did the previous night. Closing the binder, he set it back on the desk and gathered his thoughts as he looked out at the vast blue ocean and waited for his cousin Faraq, a cousin he had never known existed until now. Then he remembered the strange feeling he had when he had run into Faraq at the Holocaust Museum in D.C. He shook his head. "No wonder I couldn't get a good read on him."

When Faraq arrived, Myk let him in and then sat in the

comfortable reading chair next to the sliding glass balcony door. He gestured toward the chair at the desk, and Faraq sat.

"Agent McGrath, is everything okay? You look very pale and your eyes are bloodshot. I think it might be from blood loss. We should find a doctor to look at your leg injury."

"I'm fine. We'll find a doctor in a few minutes, but first I need to ask you a few questions."

"Is something wrong?"

"No, no. I just came across some information I wasn't aware of, so I'm hoping you can help shed some light on a few things."

"Sure. What would you like to know?"

"Tell me again about your mother and her family."

"I told you, she didn't have any family. What little family she had disowned her when she married my Palestinian father."

Myk pointed to his notebook on the desk. "I received a file with information about you and your family when I was back in Washington, D.C. I spent the little time I had to research you and your father. Tell me about your mother's side of the family."

"Okay. I guess it's a little sad. My mother doesn't talk about it. The only thing she told me is she has no family still living other than her sister. Apparently, they had a fight before she gave birth to me. She always told me it had something to do with my father being Palestinian, but I think it might have something to do with my uncle who was killed."

Myk sat up. "Why do you think that?"

"I don't know. She doesn't think I know anything about him, but she and her twin sister stopped talking around the time my uncle was killed, not when my mother married my father. Anyway, I've never met anyone on her side of the family, and she refuses to talk about her sister. After these many years, I believe she still has tender feelings about what happened. She tried to reconcile with her sister after she married my father but gave up after ten years."

"Any idea why her sister had such bitter feelings toward her?"

Faraq sat for a moment, then said, "I don't know. I guess you would have to ask her sister. But perhaps since my mothers' family endured so much persecution, maybe her sister felt she was turning her back on her heritage that had suffered so much for her to live."

Myk gestured with empty hands. "Sorry, none of that information is in your file. Would you mind elaborating?"

"Agent McGrath, I don't understand what this has to do with anything."

"Just humor me; I only have a few more questions."

"Okay. Well, my mother and her twin sister were orphans. Their parents were murdered by the Germans, and my grandfather's business partner raised the sisters."

Myk found himself breathless as Faraq told the same story he had related to Jen a few weeks ago in Canada. It was strange hearing his family history from someone else's perspective. He cleared his throat. "Faraq." He paused while he figured out the best way to phrase his words. "Listen, I'm not quite sure how to say this. But your mother and my mother . . . uh . . . well, they're sisters. I'm still in shock about it myself, but after listening to you recount the story of your mother and her sister, there's no doubt in my mind. Our mothers are the twin sisters."

Faraq's face flushed as he squinted at Myk. "Agent McGrath, you have to be kidding me. What is the purpose of this discussion? What are you really after?"

Myk held his hand up. "Stop. I know this is an unimaginable circumstance. I just learned the information this morning while looking through your file. Nevertheless . . . we are cousins."

Faraq put his face into his hands. "My God. You're not joking, are you?"

"No. My mother's maiden name is Hannah Wiesel, and her twin sister's name was Rachel. Your mother. Right?"

"Yes, but—"

"My mother told me her parents were sent to the Ravensbruck concentration camp during the war when she and her sister were just infants. A few years ago, I found out she'd lied to me. Our grandparents, along with the entire town of Lidice, died in a massacre. When Reinhard Heydrich was killed, Hitler plowed the whole town under: farms, lakes, buildings, houses, trees, everything. He even had the town name removed from all German maps."

Faraq stood and ran his fingers through his hair as he paced about the room. His eyebrows furrowed, and his eyes grew moist. He paused for a moment and then said, "This is unbelievable. I knew there was something about you." He stared at Myk as he tilted his head to the side. "I should fill you in on a few other details about our grandfather you may not know. Agent McGrath, do you know who killed Reinhard Heydrich?"

"No. I found out the Czechs had a lot of animosity toward the Germans but could not stop them. A group of Brits ambushed Heydrich's envoy and then disappeared. Somehow, Lidice came up in Hitler's crosshairs."

Faraq turned to face him and leaned against the window, crossing his arms. "A few years ago, I spent some time with the man who raised our mothers. His name is Aaron Zomosky. He passed away nine months later. He became very emotional when he told me about raising the twin girls, which he called '*his privilege*.'"

"I wish I could have met him."

"The Czechs hated the Nazis. Pockets of anti-Fascist resistance fighters popped up everywhere. Hitler couldn't control the resistance movement, so he sent in Reinhard Heydrich. One of the first things Heydrich did was imprison five thousand anti-Fascist freedom fighters. The Nazis controlled the courts, so they had no problem executing all five thousand without a trial. Heydrich even ordered that extra scaffolding be built to perform more executions."

Myk sat up as Faraq continued, "From that point on, Heydrich became known as the Hangman. Mr. Zomosky told me Heydrich executed many of his friends. Our grandfather and his business partner, Aaron Zomosky, launched a plot to kill Heydrich—"

"Wait a minute. Are you telling me it was our grandfather's idea to assassinate Heydrich?"

"That's exactly what I'm saying. The British codenamed the operation 'The Anthropoid.' Two of our grandfathers' friends, Jan Kubis and Joseph Gabcik, had joined the British forces a few years earlier. Our grandfather and Aaron Zomosky coordinated Heydrich's assassination with the Brits."

The new information's scope and significance riveted Myk.

Faraq glanced out the window as he spoke. "British Intelligence needed local help to watch Heydrich's movement so they could plan the attack. They formulated a plan, and a few months later, Gabcik and Kubis parachuted near Prague, where our grandfather and his business partner helped them in the attack. On May 28th, 1942, they ambushed SS Reinhard Heydrich on his way to his office a few miles outside Prague and assassinated him."

Looking back to Myk, Faraq smirked. "Agent McGrath, you should've seen the look on Zomosky's face as he recounted the story to me, so proud of standing up to the Nazis. He told me he was sorry about our grandfather Josef, and he expressed his love for the twins. I didn't have the heart to tell him they don't speak."

Myk's chest swelled upon hearing these stories about his grandfather, and yet his thoughts returned to his mother and her secrets. "That's going to change! There's been too much tragedy in this family, which my stubborn mother shouldn't have compounded. Too many people have sacrificed for those twins not to talk to each other. When we finish with Hakeem, I will reunite your mother with her sister."

"But my mother tried many times to contact her."

"Look; my mother thinks I'm dead. If she saw the video of my beheading, she's probably devastated. When she finds out her nephew, who came from the marriage she so vehemently opposed, saved her son's life, I guarantee she'll have a change of heart."

Myk and Faraq talked for hours. Myk wanted to know everything about Zomosky, and Faraq asked about Myk's mother. But unlike Faraq, who answered every question, Myk could not answer many questions about his own mother.

# Chapter 27

––––––––––– /// –––––––––––

Myk looked up at the monitor to check the status of Jen's plane, due to land any time. As anxious as he was to get to Saudi Arabia, he knew he needed a little time to heal before taking on Hakeem and his security team. In addition to taking out Hakeem, perhaps he would unearth the mole.

The airport bustled with tourists, tour guides, and time share vacation sales people barking out in broken English and holding up signs about the available free offers in exchange for a few minutes of a potential customer's time. Myk spent a good portion of the day at the doctor's office getting his wounds treated, including his leg. He brought his passport, told the doctor his gun had misfired, and paid cash. The doctor seemed happy to have an American pay cash, and Myk doubted he cared much about the truth—particularly about the odd angle of the bullet wound.

He planned to call Bashford and go over the plans of his pending action in Saudi Arabia. He needed more equipment for his operation against Hakeem, and Bashford could get the necessary weapons to Saudi Arabia for him.

Faraq sat with him in the airport and asked, "Agent McGrath, how did you meet her?"

"You have to quit calling me Agent McGrath. It's awkward

hearing you call me that now that I know we're cousins."

He smiled. "Sorry. It will take some getting used to."

"She worked with a developer who had listed a property I was interested in. She showed me around the property and the relationship developed slowly. She is very attractive and intelligent, and she I think she found it refreshing that I didn't pursue her at first."

"Isn't it risky to fly her down to Cancun when you have unfinished business? I assume the CIA wouldn't be too pleased to know you flew your girlfriend here."

Myk paused while he decided whether or not to let Faraq in on something the agency didn't know. "Well, she's not really my girlfriend. Since the agency strongly discourages their field agents to marry, Jen and I were secretly wed in Costa Rica last year. You're the only person who knows this, Faraq. I've gone to great lengths to conceal it after what happened to my first wife."

Faraq smiled. "I understand. Your secret is safe with me. I can't wait to meet her."

Myk stood up. "You won't have to wait any longer; that's her."

He pointed to Jen, who walked down the long crowded corridor toward them. Myk couldn't figure out why she looked even more beautiful every time he saw her. Perhaps, unlike married couples who saw each other every day, they were always apart, so each time he saw her felt like seeing her anew. Whatever the reason, the sight of her strolling toward them sent a quiver through Myk, making him breathe faster. She stood a few inches short of six feet but had more curves than most tall women. Her thick, light brown hair fell just below her slender shoulders, and her deep blue eyes sparkled with life. But what pierced Myk every time was her smile, always genuine.

Jen hadn't spotted him yet. He wasn't sure how she would react to his appearance; he hadn't shaved for almost two weeks and had a few stitches from the lacerations. As she neared, she still hadn't spotted him. He raised his hand high and waved at her.

"Jen, over here."

She recognized him and ran toward him. They embraced for several minutes, and Myk felt her warm body trembling under his arms. He put his hand behind her neck and gave her a long, passionate kiss. As he cupped her face with both hands, her hot tears spilled over them.

She looked up at him. "I thought I lost you. You have no idea how long that plane ride seemed, and now here you are standing in front of me."

He embraced her again, whispering into her ear, "The past is gone; it ended last night. I dealt with the men responsible for Dana's death."

She stepped back and looked at him with glistening eyes. "Is that what these cuts on your face are from? Saying goodbye to your past?"

He kissed her again. "Thank you so much for coming. I love you."

She tilted her head and raised one eyebrow. "Your demons really are gone, aren't they?" Then she squeezed his hand.

He squeezed back. "I have a lot to tell you. We only have a day. There's still a lot left to do, but I'm giving myself a day to heal up before I leave." He grabbed her luggage and took a few steps, then stopped. "I am so sorry. I almost forgot to introduce you. Jen, this is my cousin from my mother's side of the family, Faraq Majed."

She gave him a puzzled look. "Cousin? I thought you said you didn't have any family on your mother's side."

"Well, that's what I thought at the time. I'll fill you in on the ride to the resort."

Faraq extended his hand to shake hers, but she brushed it aside and hugged him. "Faraq, what a pleasant surprise to meet you. Has anyone told you that you two look alike? Especially now that Myk is sporting this scruffy beard." She tugged Myk's half-grown beard.

"Ouch!"

She swatted his behind. "Oh, come on tough guy. It looks like you've been through a lot rougher treatment than that!"

Myk and Faraq made eye contact, and Myk grinned. *You have no idea.*

---

Faraq loaded Jen's luggage into the back of the rented SUV. He drove while Myk sat up front so he could turn and talk to Jen while they spoke. They exited the airport and began the thirty-minute drive to the resort.

"Okay, Myk," Jen said. "What's with all the secrecy? Our country thinks you're dead. Why was it so important that I not tell anyone where I was going and who I was meeting? Why did you tell me you had no family on your mother's side?"

Faraq looked up into the rearview mirror at Jen.

Myk replied, "I'm not sure where to begin. First, what I told you a few weeks ago was true. At the time, I had no idea my mother had a nephew. Actually, I'm not sure she even knows. As it turns out . . ." He paused. "Providence brought Faraq and me together."

Faraq made eye contact with him. Myk turned back to Jen. "I will have to fill you in on the details later. As for the secrecy, some malevolent people would likely torture and kill Faraq if they found out I was alive. In fact, these same people would kill his family as well."

She leaned forward and put her hand on Faraq's shoulder. "I'm so sorry."

Myk continued. "The same people responsible for the attacks and turmoil this past week are connected to those who would come after Faraq. In a nutshell, Jen, we need to find them before they figure out we're on to them. We have to get to them before they disappear."

She asked, "What do they have against Faraq?"

Faraq spoke up, "Agent McGr—I mean, Myk, please let me respond."

"By all means."

Glancing in the rear view mirror, Faraq spoke. "I will give you the *Reader's Digest* version. I hope this makes sense because I'm still trying to come to terms with it myself."

She leaned forward as he spoke.

"Did Myk tell you the circumstances under which our mothers were raised?"

"Yes. It was extraordinary."

Faraq explained how they had discovered they were cousins, while Myk answered some of her other questions. But as they told their stories, Myk still wondered what had caused the decades of silence between the sisters.

After Faraq pulled into the resort and parked in the temporary space next to the elaborate front entry, they brought the luggage up to the lobby and spent the next twenty minutes down at the beach and pool area taking pictures. As Jen looked through the lens at the two cousins, she laughed at how much they looked alike now that Myk hadn't shaved. Before she and Myk went up to the room, she hugged Faraq again. Faraq left for the yacht, and Myk grabbed her luggage and took the elevator up to his penthouse room.

When the elevator doors shut, Myk couldn't wait a moment longer. He put one hand behind her neck while his other hand went up the back of her silky blouse, touching her soft, bare skin like a man in the desert bringing water to his lips. The two kissed until the elevator dinged when it reached the 26th floor. They stumbled out, and before the elevator doors closed behind them, he shoved his hand back in so he could get the luggage.

As he fumbled to get the electronic key into the door lock, she ran her hands up and down his body and kissed his neck.

"Damn it!" He put the plastic key into the lock upside down and the light turned red.

She whispered into his ear, "What's wrong, Myk? Are you a little distracted?"

He rolled his eyes and then turned the key around and swiped it again. The light turned green, the door burst open, and they spilled into the master suite. She paid no attention to the luxurious surroundings or the intensely blue ocean view beyond the glass windows. Piece by piece, clothing hit the floor.

Jen pulled his shirt over his head and touched the healing gash across his chest. Then, ripping off her shirt and bra, she crawled on top of him. He slid his mouth along her neck, kissing his way up to her ears until goose bumps covered her skin. But when she jerked at his pants, they caught the bandage on his leg. He yelped.

"Careful, baby."

With an apologetic smile, she worked his pants off and threw them to the floor. They made out for another few minutes before the last piece of clothing hit the floor. He threw her tropical silk skirt over the side of the bed, then brought his tanned hand up to caress her skin as they nestled together. She rocked forward into his kisses, the mouth of the man she had thought was dead just two days ago. She pulled him closer, and as she reached her hand down on him, a foreign voice came from the other room.

"Señor McCain? Señor McCain, would you like—"

Myk had checked into the resort using the name Matt McCain.

The maid turned around and covered her mouth as she ran back toward the front door. "My apologies! I am so sorry."

The two lovers sat still as the front door slammed. Jen, who had covered herself up with the sheets, turned to Myk. "Didn't you shut the door after you came in?"

"No. I pulled the luggage through the front door, and I thought you got it."

They burst into laughter.

"I can't believe the conversation going on downstairs right now between that maid and her coworkers," she said.

After a moment, Myk asked, "Now where were we?"

She stroked his torso. "Why don't you go check the door, and when you get back, I'll show you where we left off, Señor McCain."

He rolled out of bed naked, limped to the door, and hung the "Do Not Disturb" sign on the door handle. Then, he closed and locked the door. As he walked back to the bedroom, she admired his physique, then pointed. "Are you okay? It looks like those must have hurt."

He hopped into the bed, rolled next to her, and said, "I'll be fine." She ran her fingers through his thick brown hair and kissed his forehead. He looked into her eyes and asked, "What did you say about showing me where we left off?"

She grabbed his muscular body and pulled him on top of her.

---

When Myk woke the next morning, he opened his eyes just in time to see Jen's unclothed backside as she walked into the bathroom and shut the door. He put his head back down on the pillow and looked at the clock, then reasoned to himself that he would enjoy the rare moment of relaxing in bed. He pondered momentarily on the peace he experienced, a feeling brought on by being in Jen's presence and getting to know his long-lost cousin.

Letting go of the past and embracing hope in a bright future brought a sense of calm. The future still held the dark cloud of Hakeem over the life of his newfound cousin, but he hoped to discover the untold story of his mother and her sister. The thought of what lie ahead sent a refreshing surge of adrenaline through his body.

When Jen turned on the shower, Myk got out of bed, pulled the phone from his bag, and dialed Bashford.

"Brodie Bashford speaking."

"Brodie, it's Myk. How are things going with the Israelis?"

"They had no problem running with the intel we provided. I just spoke with them an hour ago, and they believe they may have already identified the containers coming from New York with the EMP weapons. They were extremely grateful for the tip. Based on the damage the EMP weapons inflicted here in the U.S., the information you extracted probably prevented a catastrophe from occurring in Israel."

"You can thank Faraq as well. Did you get his name off the watch list?"

"Yes. I had to pull a few strings, so I trust your judgment on this one. I still don't understand."

"I'll give you the details later. When this is all over, we'll have a lot to thank him for."

"I believe you. We were just watching the video clips you sent. It's nice to know Saji met his demise; the sharks were a nice touch."

Myk smiled. "Well, you'll be happy to know I gave him a choice. He could either burn to death like many of his innocent victims or take his chances with the sharks."

"I'm glad he chose the sharks. As it turned out, we didn't need the evidence for the Israelis. However, the intel you recorded from Khatchi was extremely useful. We have bank names, the top funding sources, and other great intel, Myk. We can do a lot of damage with it if we play our cards right."

"Brodie, I have to see this thing through to the end. I can't sit back and trust that the authorities in Saudi Arabia will make things right. We have to strike now. I need your help getting the equipment required for an operation in Saudi Arabia. Faraq thinks he can get me close to Hakeem, but I need weapons, and we have to convince the Saudi Intelligence to look the other way for a day or two while I work."

"Myk, if you go in there and get caught, you'll cause severe damage to our Saudi relations, which are already tenuous as it is."

"I know. I thought this through. They won't want us to take care of their dirty laundry on their own turf, just like we wouldn't let anyone come into our country and clean up our mess."

"But we might have a couple of things working in our favor," Brodie said.

"What's that?"

"First, when we spoke to the Chief of Saudi Intelligence last week and grilled him about the terrorists coming out of his country, he sounded embarrassed that they slipped by him. He got duped by his own people, so I think he might take this as an opportunity to save face. I will make a few phone calls, but I bet he would let you slip into the country as long as it doesn't come back to haunt him."

Myk nodded to himself. Cooperation between nations made operations much easier.

"Second, we found out Hakeem is not exactly one of Prince Ali Ferron's favorite sons. The Prince does a lot of business with the U.S., and when he finds out Hakeem was responsible for these attacks, I don't think he'll come running to Hakeem's defense."

"So what are you saying?"

"If you can sneak into Saudi Arabia and keep the mission low profile and out of the DOJ's earshot, it might work. What passports do you have?"

"I have a Brazilian passport I used a few times and a way to get into the country without anyone knowing."

"Okay, that works for me. You understand you will have to go off the grid, right? If you get caught, this can't be traced back to the Agency."

"Of course. But listen, Brodie. I need as much intelligence as you guys can get on Hakeem's complex and his security detail. I want to see what I'm walking into."

"Of course. The weaponry will be waiting for you when you get there. As soon as I hang up, I'll get a team working on the intelligence you'll need. You will have it before you leave."

"Okay. Thanks, Brodie. Hey, be careful. I don't want the mole to get wind of this."

"I have a few people in mind I know I can trust."

"Okay." Myk hung up and jumped back into bed just as Jen stepped out of the bathroom. She gave him a coy smirk, then let her white towel drop to the floor.

The next day, Myk and Jen sat in the Cancun airport waiting for her flight, which would depart within the hour. She turned to him.

"Are you sure you don't want me to tell your mom you're alive?"

He grabbed her hand. "I'm sure; nobody can know. I think we have a mole in the agency, so I can't take any chances. I will be back in a week or so. After we're done in Saudi Arabia, I will go see my aunt and convince her to come back to Florida with me."

"Okay. I'm a little nervous about being with her before you arrive. What should I—"

"You won't need to say anything. Being there is enough."

Myk still smiled from the day he spent with Jen. They had taken the yacht out and gone snorkeling for half a day. She swam with a school of playful dolphins. Faraq stayed on shore, so Myk and Jen took full advantage of having the luxurious yacht all to themselves. They spent the rest of their time walking along the beach and relaxing in the penthouse suite, their evenings filled with wine and sunsets.

Myk returned to the yacht where Faraq waited. While Myk had spent time with Jen, Faraq had hired a local yacht repairman to fix the yacht's damage so nobody asked questions when they pulled the yacht into Hakeem's slip in Saudi Arabia. They loaded it with the weapons taken from the back of the van during the Richmond attack, as well as the EMP weapon. Hakeem had left more than two million dollars in cash on the boat for Khatchi to fund his next operations, so Myk hired a reputable sea captain in Cancun to navigate the yacht to Saudi Arabia, its original port of call. Using Hakeem's yacht would be the best way to enter Saudi Arabia unnoticed.

To keep the hired captain from asking questions about Khatchi, Myk told him they had a sick passenger downstairs and prohibited the captain from entering the lower level. Then, to make it worth his trouble, they paid him triple the going rate, which the captain accepted without hesitation or questions. Before they set off, Myk and Faraq sedated Khatchi and locked him in a downstairs bedroom.

# Chapter 28

## Ras Al Khafji, Saudi Arabia

The three days at sea gave Myk and Faraq time to review the operation. Deputy Director Brodie Bashford had sent detailed information about Hakeem and his property to Myk. The yacht traveled up the Persian Gulf at a wakeless speed toward the Ras Al Khafji harbor about forty miles from Hakeem's massive estate. Hakeem owned a spacious luxury home on thirty acres of desert land just south of Khafji, perched on a bluff that overlooked the Persian Gulf. He had his own Jack Nicholas designed nine-hole golf course that surrounded his house. The course had waterfalls and ponds stocked with fish on every other hole, as well as its own private beach and a resort-style swimming pool with a negative edge looking out to the sea. Hakeem's twenty-two thousand square foot house was the smallest of Prince Ali Ferron's sons' homes, and Hakeem was also the youngest of the Prince's four sons.

Prince Ali Ferron had been an Assistant Vice President of the Arabian Oil Company when one of his teams discovered the Khafji Oil Field and the Hout Oil Field in 1960. The Ferron family shared rights with another family in Saudi Arabia and a few families in Kuwait. After Saddam's forces invaded Kuwait, they overtook Khafji on January 29th, 1991. Two days later, coalition forces drove them right back out during a little-known battle named The Battle of

Khafji. The city didn't come into existence until the discovery of the oil fields.

The captain masterfully maneuvered the massive yacht into its slip at the Ras Al Khafji dock. As he motored the vessel into its place, the service technicians on the dock tied off the craft onto the massive hold downs secured to the dock. Faraq told the service crew not to disturb a friend of the Prince onboard who did not feel well, but said they could clean the ship in another day or two when the friend felt better. Faraq gave them a generous tip, and the service crew nodded and smiled as they walked back up the dock.

Downstairs, Myk attempted to wake up Khatchi and get him in such condition that he would speak to Hakeem. To do so, he gave Khatchi an energy drink. When Faraq came back downstairs, Myk sat Khatchi up in the chair.

"Okay, Khatchi. As much as I would have loved to have fed you to the sharks, I am keeping up my end of the deal. Now it's your turn to call Hakeem. Tell him what you told me on the back of the yacht, that he's a spoon-fed daddy's boy too afraid to get his hands dirty. Tell him you're taking his yacht and money and will call the shots from now on."

He pulled out his suppressed weapon and placed the barrel of the gun to Khatchi's temple. "Understand? Faraq will interpret to make sure you don't say anything stupid. Got it?"

Khatchi nodded, his pupils still dilated from the heavy sedation and drugs.

Myk said, "Okay, dial Hakeem's number."

Khatchi dialed the number. After a few rings, Hakeem answered, "Hello."

"Hakeem, this is Khatchi," he slurred.

Hakeem's voice grew sharp. "Why haven't you answered my calls? Is everything okay?"

Myk nudged Khatchi's head with the tip of his gun. Khatchi looked up at the gun and then said, "Hakeem, Saji and I have lost what little respect we had for you. A real leader must be willing to get into the trenches with those who follow him; you have never gotten your hands dirty."

A loud noise on the other end made Khatchi jerk his ear away from the phone, but now he spoke louder and with more conviction than before. Myk snorted as he suppressed a chuckle, and the corner of his lips twitched.

"I am not even sure you know how to fire a weapon." Khatchi now held the earpiece away and spoke into the mouthpiece, his eyes glazed but fixed on the phone. "I am taking over the operations. I am taking the yacht and your money. Don't bother looking for me, or I will cut your head off just like I did that American."

Hakeem screamed over the phone, his voice tinny. "What the hell are you talking about, you ungrateful piece of shit?! If it weren't for me, you'd still be rotting in an American jail. It was my plan to steal the technology from the Chinese and assemble the EMP weapons! We finally have superior technology against the Americans because of me. I'm the one who has the contact within the American government!"

Myk nudged Khatchi with his gun, took the phone from him, and disconnected the call. Then he turned to Faraq. "Did you record that nice little confession?"

Faraq looked down at his recorder. "Yep, got it all."

Pulling a cord out of the phone's port, Myk wrapped it around the recorder and then handed it to Faraq. "Lock this up with our other video recordings from the back of the yacht. It will open the eyes of a lot of people in our country and throughout the Middle East. After you store them, go up to the parking lot."

Faraq nodded as Myk spoke. "I received a message from Brodie that the weapons I requested are in a van at the harbor parking lot, a white van with the logo of the Arabian Yacht Servicing, Ltd. A briefcase in the back has surveillance photographs of Hakeem's estate and an inventory of the weapons. Punch in the door lock code '97842' and bring me the case."

Faraq stood. "Okay. I'll be back in a few minutes."

"Oh, I almost forgot. See if you can find the marina service crew that helped us on the dock. We will need help loading the EMP weapon into the cargo van. Tell them it's a crate with heavy scuba equipment or something. They might have a forklift they could use to help us."

"Okay, Myk. I'll see who I can find when I get up there."

He stepped off the back of the yacht, shielded his eyes from the blinding sunlight, and put on his sunglasses. A moment later, he strode down the long dock leading up to the marina and the parking lot area.

They would need to wait a few more hours for sunset before they started Myk's plan. The drive to Hakeem's complex would take a little over thirty minutes. After Faraq returned with the briefcase, they went over the plans one more time and then loaded the EMP weapon into the back of the van with the marina service crew's help. Before they left, they reviewed the download again that Myk had received from the CIA showing the layout of Hakeem's complex and detailed information on his security detail.

A few miles from the entrance to Hakeem's compound, Myk asked Faraq, "Are you ready?"

"I think so. He's not expecting me, though. What should I do if he doesn't let me in?"

"Trust me, he will. After Khatchi's call, he'll be looking for any connection. You'll have to do a convincing job at the gate and then later on in the house. If I can pull off a persuasive performance on the fake beheading video, then you can definitely get Hakeem to let you in."

Myk peered through the front window. "I better get down into the cargo hole. We're getting close. Don't forget you have two hidden cameras on you. Just try to face them in the right directions. Hakeem will give us some valuable information."

Myk unbuckled his seat belt and stepped into the back of the cargo van, which contained two custom-made concaves in the floor specially made for hiding human cargo. He sat down and slid the door shut over the top of him. Khatchi slept next to Myk, loaded up with morphine. They just needed him to stay quiet until the right time.

Faraq pulled the van off the main highway and onto the half-mile road leading to Hakeem's mansion. The road that led from the guard house was lined with mature trees on each side of the road that created a canopy, and at night, the canopy created the illusion of a lushly vegetated tunnel. Hakeem's resort style pool overlooked the sea below and had a huge waterfall with a secret grotto and loveseat behind the waterfall. The fifteen-car garage had Hakeem's latest auction winnings, including some vintage 1940s automobiles.

In the floor, Myk shifted and rolled a bit, while his shoulders and back vibrated against the bottom of the concave. The sensation reminded him of riding a roller coaster, and despite the situation's seriousness, a little quiver of giddiness rippled through his gut.

As Faraq slowed next to the guard house, he lowered his window. Myk watched from the peephole in his hidden compartment. There were two guards inside; the more robust guard with a thick bushy mustache approached the cargo van.

A guard asked Faraq, "Can I help you?"

"I need to see Hakeem."

"Is he expecting you?" The guard looked at his clipboard with his flashlight. "I don't have anyone on the approved list for tonight."

"It's urgent. He's not expecting me. Please, tell him Faraq Majed is at the gate."

"Just a moment. I will call up to the house."

Gravel crunched under the guard's boots, then something beeped as the guard punched numbers into a video monitor on the exterior wall of the guard house. After a short wait, Hakeem's face appeared on the monitor and he spoke to the security guard. Faraq tried to listen.

The guard spoke again. "Hakeem, I am sorry to trouble you this evening, but a man here at the front gate says it's urgent that he see you. He said his name is Faraq."

"What! Let me speak to him!"

The security guard turned and motioned with his hands towards Faraq to get out of the van and join him at the video monitor. Faraq unbuckled his seat belt and stepped out of the van. As he neared the monitor, Hakeem's face on the screen almost made him cringe, but he had to act as normal as possible.

"Faraq, is that you? What's going on? What are you doing here?"

Faraq was nervous, but he took a slow, deep breath. "Yes, Hakeem. It's me."

"How did you get here? You're supposed to—"

"Khatchi hired a captain in Cancun and paid him to navigate the yacht here. I snuck off the first chance I got to come warn you—"

"What do you mean, warn me? I thought he was in Cancun."

With the guard distracted, Myk slid the door to the concave compartment open, then eased the back door open. He lowered himself to the ground without a sound, crouched behind the rear wheel, and drew his gun.

"Khatchi is acting crazy, Hakeem. I think I overheard him talking to his team about a plot to kill you. They would have killed me if I stayed. Please, let me in. I have no place else to go."

"Let him through."

More gravel crunched, then the van shifted as Faraq got back in and shut the door. He started the ignition and pulled away from the guard house. As the van rolled forward and left Myk in a cloud of exhaust, the ornate wrought iron security gate crept open, giving Faraq access to the illuminated driveway to Hakeem's estate. The guards had their backs to Myk.

Myk sprang up and extended both arms, a Taser in each hand. He fired both Tasers, and both men dropped to the ground and convulsed wildly, their jaws clenched and saliva sliding down their cheeks. Within thirty seconds, Myk cuffed the first one in plastic zips and moved to the next guard. Afterward, he dragged both bodies into the bathroom of the guard house and locked the door.

Faraq had parked on the side of the long driveway, just on the other side of the gate. Myk jumped in the van and slipped back into the cargo compartment as Faraq drove through the canopy of trees to the front of Hakeem's stone-clad, French Provincial-style mansion. He circled the van around the twenty-foot-tall fountain and parked. As hundreds of gallons of water tumbled from the top of the hand-carved stone fountain, twelve cherubic angels sprayed streams back up.

Two guards stood outside the twelve-foot spiraled iron front door. Faraq stepped out of the van and walked up to the entrance while Myk watched from the hidden peephole. One guard gave Faraq a quick pat down, then opened the front door and pointed him in the direction where he could locate Hakeem. The other guard approached the van. Myk lay still, but dread gnawed at his stomach at the thought of Khatchi making a noise in the compartment next to him. He glanced over in the dark at the shape of Khatchi, dimly lit by what light filtered in through the peephole. The man's thick, wet breathing filled the compartment, but nothing more.

The van door opened, and the vehicle moved and bounced as Hakeem's large bodyguard stepped inside. Myk held his breath and tightened his grip on the silenced weapon. Beside him, Khatchi let out a small sigh and Myk tensed, but the guard's clanking masked the noise. *Damn it, is he waking up?*

A few moments later, the van moved again as the guard stepped out and closed the door. Myk checked the peephole; the guard walked back to his post at the front door. When both gunmen had returned to their positions, Myk slipped out the rear door again. Crouched behind the van, he strapped the high-powered sniper rifle with night vision over his shoulder and crept around the front corner of the house. Then, he ran another twenty yards into the darkness and onto the golf course that surrounded the estate, stopping to crouch in the shadows like a stalking jaguar.

He raised his rifle. Through his scope, Myk spotted two gunmen posted at the upstairs balconies on the front and back of the house. From the download he received from the agency, a vantage point lay thirty yards out on the putting green along the side of the house. He could pick off both guards without moving from his position.

Stretching out on the grass, he looked through the scope of his rifle again and waited a little over five minutes for both men to come into his view at the same time. The gunman on the back balcony lit a cigarette and leaned over the stone balustrade railing, peering into the darkness in Myk's direction. Myk adjusted his scope slowly so it didn't put off any reflection and tip off the guard. He checked his scope again as the other guard walked into perfect position. Putting his index finger on the trigger, he sat motionless. The gunman stepped into position.

Myk squeezed the trigger and dropped the guard in his tracks. Then he pivoted the rifle around and found his second target still smoking his cigarette as it glowed red when the guard inhaled. Myk hesitated because the man leaned against the balustrades, which meant noise from the impact if he fell. He prepared for the worst and then squeezed the trigger twice. *Tap-tap.* Sure enough, the guard toppled over the balustrade railing and smashed onto the secondary short clay roof, cracking the tile. Then, he rolled off the roof and fell fifteen feet to the hard pavers below with a loud thud, where he lay in a contorted pile, limbs bent.

Springing up, Myk sprinted in the dark across the grass and onto the fairway next to the house. As he ran, he focused on getting around the side of the house, which blocked his view of the front door. As he cleared the side of the house, he pulled out his suppressed pistol. One gunman stood at his post at the front door and another with his weapon drawn was walking around the side of the house to investigate the noise.

Myk put three rounds into the man, each loud pop spraying blood across the elegant stone inlayed on the house. The gunman spun around and struck the house, then slid down the stone, leaving a trail of blood as he dropped onto the European pavestones. Darting behind the elevated grassy fairway hill, Myk watched the other gunman stationed at the front door. As Myk unscrewed the suppressor on the end of his gun, the guard radioed for help.

If the information sent by Langley was correct, only two of Hakeem's security guards remained, one at the front door and one inside the house. Myk needed to make enough noise outside to draw out the bodyguard inside with Hakeem. He put the suppressor in his pocket, then stood and sprinted from the concealed darkness of the golf course towards the guard.

He unloaded the entire clip at the man and the surrounding

door. The glass-vibrating blasts of bullets ricocheting off the heavy iron clad door reverberated inside the house. With all the guards taken care of on the outside, he waited to draw Hakeem's personal bodyguard outside, loading a new clip and firing at the security cameras in the process.

After he took out the security cameras, Myk holstered his revolver and took cover behind the front wheel of the cargo van. The hidden container of the van rattled as Khatchi rolled around. Myk took the sniper rifle from his back, laid it across the van's small hood, and aimed at the front door while he waited for the gunman to appear in the crosshairs of his scope.

A shadowy figure moved behind the front door's stained glass. Myk lined up his scope between the spindles of the iron front door and waited for his target to move into his line of fire. When movement flickered from the backlit lighting behind the stained glass, Myk fired his weapon. After two shots, the stained glass shattered, and Hakeem's bodyguard ducked for cover. Myk squeezed off eight consecutive rounds, three of which ricocheted off the iron spindles of the twelve-foot door. The other five rounds dropped the man. Myk ran up to the door and, finding the man crawling along the floor, kicked the gun out of his hand and dragged him out of the way.

As Myk walked back to the van to get Khatchi, he hoped everything inside the house had gone well with Faraq and Hakeem. He stepped inside the van and opened the hidden container where Khatchi lay.

Khatchi stared up at Myk with glazed eyes and saliva dripping out of the corner of his gagged mouth. "Okay, Khatchi, I told you I wouldn't leave you for the sharks back in Cancun. This is where we part ways and you are on your own."

Khatchi's eyes rolled, his pupils still dilated. Spit soaked the gag in his mouth, and some dripped from his lips and chin. Myk grabbed his syringe and injected Khatchi with a dose of adrenaline, hoping the terrorist could walk without falling down from the cocktail of drugs flowing through his veins.

Pulling Khatchi up and out of the compartment, Myk helped the dazed terrorist out of the van, then pulled the gag out of his mouth. "Sit down for a minute."

Khatchi sat on a step and groaned, his eyes half closed. He looked down at Myk taping a gun to his hand with clear packing tape.

"What's going on? Why are you taping a gun to my hand?"

"You are at Hakeem's. There's been an attack, and a lot of men have been killed. I'm taping this gun to your hand for your own protection, since you're still under the influence of so many drugs and I don't want you to drop the gun." Myk glanced back at the front door. "I don't know if Hakeem is still alive. You'll have to go in the house and yell for him. I have to get out of here before the Saudi Intelligence agents arrive; you're on your own, Khatchi."

As he rose from his crouch, Myk slapped his blood-speckled hand on Khatchi's shoulder like one comrade to another. The soft impact made Khatchi wobble where he sat, and he looked up into Myk's hard stare. "If I ever see you again, Khatchi, I will kill you."

Khatchi closed his eyes for a moment and swayed. Myk helped him stand up and steered him toward the front door. From there, Khatchi swaggered into the house like a drunken man with a blood alcohol content ten times the legal limit. Myk pulled out his weapon and followed behind at a safe distance.

While Myk had put Hakeem's men out of commission outside, Faraq worked on getting Hakeem to believe Khatchi was coming with his men to kill him. Hakeem completely bought it. When Faraq arrived inside the house and met with Hakeem, he told him he had barely escaped the yacht alive. He told him he thought Khatchi had planned on coming to the compound the next day, but when the gunfire erupted, Faraq went into full pretend panic mode. He was in the kitchen with Mineesha, Hakeem, and his body guard when the first shots were heard at the front door. Faraq turned to Hakeem with a look of complete terror on his face and exclaimed, "He's here! Khatchi and his men, they are going to kill us."

Hakeem replied, "Settle down, Faraq. I have seven highly skilled armed guards on the property. You have no reason for concern." Hakeem walked confidently over to his security monitor to check on the various cameras throughout his estate. The first camera he checked was the guardhouse. He noticed both men were missing. He looked on the monitor to check for signs of violence or a struggle, but there was nothing, just an empty guard house.

He checked the cameras at the front door and saw the van and what looked like one of his guards lying on the ground near the side of the house. Then he heard it; there was no mistaking it. Shots fired at the front door. Hakeem turned to his body guard nervously and said, "Go check it out. I can't get a response from the front gate or anybody else."

Right on cue, Faraq yelled, "It's him. He's going to kill us all!" Hakeem's goon pulled his weapon from his holster and ran towards the front door. A few minutes later, the sounds of the glass from the front door exploding from Myk's gunfire echoed throughout the house.

Faraq looked at Hakeem's pale face and asked, "Hakeem, do you have a gun? We need to protect ourselves."

Hakeem quickly retrieved a gun from behind the door of the

pantry. There was a long silence. Faraq, Hakeem and Mineesha were still in the kitchen when they heard Khatchi's unmistakable voice.

"Hakeem, where are you?"

Glass crunched under Khatchi's feet as he walked through the front entry. He yelled again.

Faraq whispered to Hakeem, "It's him. It's Khatchi."

Hakeem turned toward Faraq and put his index finger toward his lips. Then Hakeem raised his weapon and peered down the hallway. Hakeem had seen from his security cameras that his entire security detail had been killed. Hakeem peered around the corner and saw Khatchi getting closer.

He raised his weapon, took aim for Khatchi's head, and pulled the trigger. He missed badly and fired another shot that hit Khatchi in the shoulder. He squeezed off two more rounds. Hakeem had never actually shot anyone before; a living, breathing attacker is much more difficult to hit than a stationary target at the shooting range. The next two shots hit Khatchi in the abdomen and then in the leg, dropping him to the ground. Khatchi arched his neck and gasped, his breathing ragged. Deep red blood spread across the polished travertine floor.

As Hakeem got closer to Khatchi, he noticed something peculiar: the shiny, clear substance on Khatchi's gun hand. Hakeem stood over Khatchi, whose gun was taped to his hand with clear packing tape. Khatchi was trying to say something.

Hakeem bent over to try to hear better. Blood oozed out of Khatchi's nose and mouth. Hakeem moved closer as he listened to Khatchi whisper, "They know about you. Faraq didn't kill the . . ." Then his chest fell and did not rise again.

Hakeem yelled at the corpse, "Faraq didn't . . . what? What about Faraq?"

Without making a noise, Myk suddenly appeared from behind

the hall doorway and crammed the barrel of his gun in the back of Hakeem's neck. "What Khatchi was trying to tell you before you shot him to death is Faraq didn't kill the American."

Hakeem looked up to see Myk McGrath staring down at him, smiling. "Drop the gun, fat-ass, or your life ends right here. By the way, that was some mighty fine marksmanship you displayed there. It only took you five shots at close range to hit your target!"

Hakeem dropped his weapon, which clacked loudly as it bounced against the hard travertine floor.

"Where's Faraq?"

"Myk, I'm right here."

Myk kicked Hakeem's gun and watched it slide across the floor to Faraq, then looked back at Hakeem who grinned from ear to ear. Before Myk could react, cold metal pressed against his neck, and he flinched. A soft female voice with a heavy Arab accent came from behind him.

"Release the weapon, Agent McGrath, or I'll pull the trigger."

*Mineesha.*

Myk let his weapon fall to the floor. His shoulders fell.

Hakeem rose from Khatchi's corpse and turned to look Myk squarely in the face.

"It appears your luck has run out, Agent McGrath."

Hakeem raised his fist and punched the right side of Myk's face. His massive, diamond-studded ring ripped open Myk's right cheek, and blood gushed from the wound. Hakeem smiled.

"I don't know how you kept your head attached to your shoulders after I last saw you strapped to a chair in Cancun. I guess it had something to do with Faraq. But I will deal with him and his family after I am done with you. Any last words?"

Myk stood tall. "Yeah. You still owe me my Diet Coke and

peanuts from the plane ride, you fat piece of shit!"

Hakeem stepped back and looked at Mineesha. "Shoot him now." Myk closed his eyes. He had expected hundreds of memories to flood his mind as he took his last breath, but only one image rushed to the forefront: Jen's soft blue eyes staring at him in the dim light of a Cancun sunrise.

The revolver's loud bang stabbed through his head, so loud the hair on his arms quivered. Then a ringing pierced in his ears. The cold barrel on his neck disappeared. He looked up to see Faraq's arm extended, smoke rising from the gun barrel. Myk spun around in time to see Mineesha crumple to the floor with a single hole through her temple.

He crouched down and took her gun, then turned and pointed it at Hakeem with his left hand. Balling his right hand, he punched Hakeem in the bridge of his nose. It crunched like eggshell, and blood flooded out of Hakeem's nose. He let out a cry and bent in half, cupping his gushing nose.

Myk pointed the gun at Hakeem's forehead. "Looks like you're the one whose luck has run out." He then turned to Faraq. "I thought you said you couldn't kill anyone?"

Faraq smiled. "There are exceptions to everything. Besides, you're family."

Hakeem's brows furrowed.

Myk grinned. "Well done! Did you record it? Did you get a good view of him killing Khatchi?"

Faraq still shook, but he replied, "Most definitely." He then turned his head away and said, "You are finished, Hakeem!"

Hakeem turned to look at Faraq. "What's going on? Have you conspired with this infidel?"

Myk stepped behind Hakeem, squared up, and punched him as

hard as he could in the back of his head, dropping the terrorist to the floor. He yelled down at the unconscious man, "You worthless piece of shit! We'll turn your comfy little terrorism world upside down. Do have any idea how many people would die for the opportunity get a piece of you?"

Hakeem groaned and moved. Myk leaned back and kicked him in the groin as hard as he had ever kicked anyone, and Hakeem's groan burst into a scream. His lips moved as he curled into a ball, blood oozing from his broken nose and his eyes swelling.

The blood from Myk's gash dripped onto Hakeem. "What's wrong, Hakeem? Having a tough time speaking with your balls kicked up into your throat?"

A few seconds passed. After gurgling and moaning, Hakeem lifted his eyes to Faraq and barely muttered out his words. "How could you do this, Faraq? You betrayed all Muslims."

Faraq stepped over Hakeem and stood directly in front of him so he could make eye contact with him while he spoke. "You betrayed them. You deceived others to bring about your plans. You took the lives of thousands of innocent people. You will not be missed, and you are so far past reality you can't even comprehend the truth."

Myk pulled out his zip cuffs and tied off Hakeem. As he secured the terrorist, Hakeem's pants pocket vibrated and lit. Myk jumped, then pulled out the phone and tossed it to Faraq.

"Answer it."

Faraq pushed the green button. "Hello." No answer.

"Hello, who is this?"

Myk stared up, breathing hard. The line went dead, and Faraq looked at the screen.

"The call came from the U.S., do you recognize the area code?"

He handed the phone to Myk, who looked at the phone. Then, Myk stepped on Hakeem's throat.

"The call was from the D.C. area. Who's your inside man, Hakeem?"

Hakeem's voice contorted from the pressure of Myk's foot. "I don't know. I only talked to him over the phone. Saji met him face to face."

"Bullshit!" Myk kicked the back of his head. "You'll tell me who he is sooner or later."

# Chapter 29

## Riyadh, Saudi Arabia

———————————— /// ————————————

Myk and Faraq drove all night from Hakeem's complex to Riyadh, the financial capital of the Middle East and parked the cargo van with the EMP weapon in a parking garage a few miles away from the Saudi Stock Exchange. They loaded Hakeem up with the same drugs they had used to sedate Khatchi. With Hakeem's entire security team taken out, it took very little pressure from Myk before Hakeem began babbling about contact names in different countries, silent partners who wanted to fund operations, and the religious zealots who goaded the young and hopeless into sacrificing their lives.

But Myk still couldn't get any details on the mole in the government. He did, however, have Hakeem's cell phone and the number from his associate in the U.S. The man Hakeem described sounded like a very old German, not exactly the fitting image of anyone employed at Langley. Before leaving Hakeem's estate, Myk transferred all the intel he had obtained back to Langley but kept Hakeem's cell phone to himself.

After Myk squeezed everything he could from Hakeem, he stuffed the terrorist into the hidden container in the back of the van. Then, he waited for the peak of the business day to destroy the Saudi Stock Exchange. Faraq turned the EMP weapon on to make sure everything worked. Myk started the van and pulled out of the parking garage and onto King Faud Road, driving toward the Saudi Stock Exchange a few miles away. As he got within a block of their first target, he looked for parking spaces. Someone pulled out of a space the perfect distance from the Saudi Stock Exchange; Myk flipped his blinker and waited for the car to pull out.

He turned to Faraq. "This is it. Are you ready?"

"Yes. Make sure we turn everything off."

"Of course."

Myk pulled into the parking space while Faraq looked over the EMP weapon. Cars filled the streets from the lunch hour, and the sidewalks were flooded with Saudi businessmen, many dressed in the flowing ankle-length white thobes with the ghutras adorning their heads. A few were dressed in traditional dark business suits.

Faraq looked up at Myk. "Okay, open the back doors and I will fire it off. Remember, any running cars within three blocks will stall out, so you'll have to maneuver around them when we leave."

"Got it."

Myk hopped out of the van, rushed to the back double doors, and swung them open. As soon as he cleared out of the way, Faraq fired the EMP weapon. A light blue wave, faint in the bright daylight of the thriving Saudi desert city, shot out. Myk's hair stood on end. Seconds later, everything with an electronic circuit was destroyed.

Across the street at the Saudi Stock Exchange, a panicked crowd of people flooded out of the building. Saudi businessmen using their phones stared at the blank screens, bewildered. Cars stalled in the middle of the road, and the multitude of pedestrians stood still and tried to figure out what just hit them. Pandemonium set in.

Myk closed the double doors, ran to the driver's side, and started the engine. The traffic lights had died, so he drove right through the dysfunctional intersections. The weapon's impact gave Myk second thoughts about destroying it. Two miles later, he pulled in front of their next targets: the Al Rajhi Banking and Investment Bank and the Al Jazeera Bank. Over the past three years, more terrorist funding had been traced back to these two banks than any other institutions; both Khatchi and Hakeem confirmed this. Myk grinned.

*Time to start a war between the banks who funded the terrorists and their violent cohorts.*

He pulled the van into the parking structure across the street from the banks and drove up the ramp to the second tier, then backed the van up so the EMP weapon faced the two targets. Both banks lay across the street from each another, so they only needed to fire the EMP weapon once. The massive skyscrapers stood as a symbol of Saudi wealth. The buildings were adorned with imported hand-carved marble with gold inlays throughout, kept immaculate by the constant cleaning and polishing of crews that worked every hour of the day.

Myk got out and opened the back doors, and Faraq fired the weapon, frying everything within a square mile. The hard concrete structure of the parking garage produced an unanticipated heavy wave of static that left Faraq and Myk momentarily staring at each other. It would be months before the banks would operate again.

Myk closed the doors and hopped back in the driver's seat. After he fired the weapon, Faraq dismantled the most critical components so it could not be duplicated by the Saudis when Myk gave them the location of the van with the weapon and Hakeem still inside. By leaving Hakeem and the EMP weapon next to the banks, Myk hoped it would be a long time before they ever funneled their money to these unconscionable killers again. He put together a small explosive that would destroy the EMP weapon but not the van. Myk wanted the Saudi police to recognize Hakeem Ferron, the terrorist responsible for the attack in downtown Riyadh that afternoon.

Pulling Hakeem out of the hidden cargo container, Myk dragged him to the driver's seat. Hakeem groaned and slumped over the steering wheel, resting halfway on the driver's side window. After Myk put the explosive device on top of the EMP, he gave Hakeem another injection to knock him out, then stepped out of the van and joined Faraq. They walked toward the rental car they had left in the parking garage earlier that morning and got into the car. As they passed the cargo van, Myk turned to Faraq.

"I think it's time to close this chapter in your life. You will never be bothered by Hakeem or his people again."

He held the detonator up for Faraq to see and pushed the button. A small explosion lifted the van's back wheels about a foot. Seconds later, a small fire and thick smoke poured out of the shattered windows. Myk punched in the number for the Saudi Secret Police and gave them Hakeem's location and name. He told them the weapon might still be in the van.

Faraq drove the rental car out of the parking garage and attempted to weave through the cars the EMP weapon had rendered useless. Unlike the location at the Saudi Stock exchange, the crowds in front of the banks had flooded into the streets, making their exit much slower than anticipated. Several people glared at Myk and Faraq as they drove the only functional car through the streets. A few slapped on their windows and asked if they knew what happened.

After a few blocks, Faraq maneuvered out of the congestion and onto a main highway where he could finally accelerate. They drove for two hours toward the Persian Gulf, where Hakeem's yacht and the sea captain from Cancun waited. They encountered no trouble on the drive to the harbor, so if they could get out of the Persian Gulf and into the open water, they would be home free. They boarded the yacht without any questions from the authorities.

The last hurdle was the harbor police. If they decided to question Myk and Faraq, the yacht could make it to open water before any real trouble began. Fortunately, they motored the vessel out of the harbor without incident, then sailed from the Persian Gulf out to the bay of the Arabian Sea. Once in the clear, Myk powered up his satellite phone and texted Jen.

*"Safe. No injuries. Will be in England in a few days to meet my aunt. Wish you were here; it's beautiful. I love you. See you in Florida. M"*

---

They navigated the magnificent yacht from the Arabian Sea along the coast of Africa and stopped in Cape Town at a restaurant overlooking the Atlantic Ocean. Myk had convinced Faraq he couldn't pass it up. Their sea captain anchored the boat a half mile off shore while Myk and Faraq took a dinghy into the beach. The LeGrande Café was situated right on the beach, which made it easy to pull their dinghy up onto the sand and walk to the family-owned café.

Live music on African steel drums filled the air, as well as the aroma of the four brick ovens that used the local mesquite wood to flavor the food. The place bustled with energy as people stood shoulder to shoulder around the bar conversing with each other. But the local wine's unique bite stuck in Myk's memory, and he couldn't wait to share the tastes as he celebrated with his newfound cousin. As he sat in the café looking out at the kite surfers and enjoying the ambiance, Myk relaxed, perhaps from the wine or maybe the realization that he had caused a major rift in the terrorist world. After a few hours, they motored the dinghy back out to sea and boarded the yacht.

After their stop at the LeGrande Café, Myk learned more about

Faraq's family, fascinated by some of the idiosyncrasies he thought were unique to his mother, only to find out Faraq's mother shared the same tendencies. They shared with each other the quirks of their upbringing from twin sisters and gained a great deal of respect for each other's accomplishments as they talked on the yacht's top deck. Faraq impressed Myk with his in-depth knowledge of electromagnetism and physics, and Faraq couldn't believe Myk's mother made him attend three survival camps before the age of sixteen.

While Myk's friends had gone to normal Boy Scout summer camps, his mother stuck him in grueling survival camps. But when Myk returned to school and talked about summer break with his friends, they all envied his stories. He told them how he learned to catch animals with a snare, camouflage himself, and stay downwind from a large elk so he could get close enough to kill it with a bow and arrow. He captivated them as he told them he had to cut the elk up himself. For some reason, they just weren't quite as enthusiastic about their experiences of basket weaving and knot tying merit badges from their camps.

After Cape Town, they stopped in Lisbon, Spain, and then made their final stop in England. They paid the captain out of the cash left by Hakeem and told him to take the yacht back to Cancun after Myk met with Mordechai and flew back to the U.S. Until then, he was instructed to take a day or two off and enjoy England's sights. And if no one showed up to claim the yacht in the next two years, he could keep it. Until then, they left him responsible for maintaining it.

# Chapter 30

## London, England

Myk had heard stories about his aunt since he was a child, yet he had never met her. He had been on his way to meet her with his first wife when the bomb had exploded in the train station in Madrid. But now he would finally meet his Aunt Rachel. When he first arrived at the home of Faraq's parents, Myk still couldn't piece together what had torn apart the bond between her and his mother. During the hour-long taxi ride to Aunt Rachel's house, Faraq called to make sure she was home and tell her he brought a surprise.

The taxi pulled into the driveway. Myk paid the driver, slung his duffle bag of clothes over his shoulder, and walked up the stone walkway to the house. Faraq tried the locked door handle, then rang the doorbell and waited with Myk. Hard shoes clacked against the ceramic tile on the other side of the door as they neared, then the deadbolt's tumbler unlocked the door, and the red colored wooden entry door swung open.

Myk gazed at his Aunt Rachel. She resembled his mother—certainly the same bright eyes—but looked younger and seemed to have more energy. She focused on Faraq, hugged him, and then turned to Myk.

"And who is this?"

Faraq replied, "This is my surprise."

She looked at Myk with a polite smile and no recognition. How could there be? The last time she'd seen him, he'd been an infant. She looked back at Faraq and raised her eyebrows.

"It's Myk, Mom. Aunt Hannah's son."

She stood perfectly still for a few seconds. Myk thought she might not have heard what Faraq said. Then it hit her. Rachael's jaw dropped, she turned pale, and then she gasped as she staggered against the wall, bringing both hands to her mouth. As she stared at Myk, tears flowed freely down her face. Then she lowered her hands and Myk stared into her beautiful watery eyes.

"Mykial, is that you?"

Myk's heart melted, and he immediately outstretched his arms to hug her. "Yes, Aunt Rachel. It's me . . . Myk."

Myk stooped and gave her a loving embrace. She raised on her tiptoes and kissed his cheeks and hugged him tight. When she released him, she cupped his face.

"What is this? What are these welts on your face, Mykial? Are you in trouble?"

He had never been called "Mykial" before; his mother told him it was an old Jewish Czech name. His aunt loved him. He could feel it. He could see it. "I slipped on the yacht's deck. It's nothing."

She paused, then asked, "Is everything okay with your mother? Please tell me Hannah is alive and well."

Aunt Rachael clasped his hand and stroked the back of it with her other hand. He had never seen this much affection from his mother. "The last time I checked, she was doing just fine."

"Oh, what a relief. Come and sit down and tell me all about Hannah. I want to hear all about her." she held his hand as she led him down a short hallway to her living room. When they sat, she continued to clasp his hand, like a mother cleaving to her returning son from the war.

"Aunt Rachael, Faraq and I have spoken at length for the past few days, and I would like to take you with me to Florida tomorrow to see Hannah. I already bought tickets for all of us."

Her eyes narrowed as she pursed her lips. There was a brief moment of silence. "I don't know, Myk."

"It's time, Aunt Rachael. It's time."

She stroked the back of his hand. Tears welled in the corners of her eyes again when she looked at Myk. "You're right, Myk. It's time." Myk wanted to get home and let his mother know he was alive, but he wanted to reunite her with her sister even more. Their flight left in the morning. Still, his Aunt Rachel refused to share any specifics about the divide with his mother, telling him he should sort it out when they got to the U.S. Myk then turned his thoughts to his meeting with Mordechai in a few hours. He hoped that Mordechai would be able to enlighten him on his family history. He looked forward to finally meeting the man.

Myk had arranged to meet Mordechai within the private confines of Hakeem's yacht, which Myk had left moored at the Yacht and Boat Club an hour's drive from his aunt's house. A thick haze of misty air hovered over the creaking dock as he waited for Mordechai to arrive. Despite being the middle of the day, the clouds and wet fog cast such darkness that it seemed more like dusk. Myk wondered about the wisdom of meeting such a man in private without any backup, but in every phone conversation he'd had with Mordechai, Myk got a good read on him. Besides, he couldn't pass up the opportunity to pick the brain of someone who professed to contain so much knowledge about the intricate workings of the clandestine world and, more importantly, about Myk's unknown family history.

Through the foggy, damp air, the outline of a large figure turned down the dock and headed toward the yacht. He wore a long, dark overcoat that almost touched the ground as he walked with a slight limp on his left side. As he neared, Myk ran out to help him up the steps. Mordechai instantly reminded him of an older John Wayne, only with a much larger upper body. Myk reached out to grasp his hand, and as he did so, respect overcame him. Mordechai possessed a certain aura about him.

Mordechai groaned from the strain of the steps. "Why, thank you, young man. Believe it or not, there was a time when I was just as nimble and agile as you are. My name is Mordechai Rinzler, and it is a pleasure to finally meet you."

"Mordechai, it is nice to meet you as well."

They walked together along the deck as Mordechai started things on the lighter side. "This is quite the vessel, Agent McGrath. The CIA must compensate its agents much better than Mossad."

Myk laughed. "To the victor go the spoils, right? Actually, I'm sending it back to Cancun."

"And is that quote from the British or the Americans?"

"American, of course. Senator Marcy used it in 1831 in defending Andrew Jackson in his heated Presidential campaign against President John Quincy Adams."

Mordechai slapped him on the back and laughed again. "I had no idea."

Myk opened the door for him. "I'm glad you came. Thank you. As you can probably imagine, I have a lot of questions."

"No, Agent McGrath. It is I that should thank you. The State of Israel owes you a debt of gratitude. Our enemies conspired quite a clever plan to bring us into a war with Iran. I'm afraid without your efforts to uncover the truth, their plans may have come to fruition."

As the two walked into the yacht's front room, Myk asked, "Sorry for being so blunt, but who are you?"

Mordechai chuckled in a deep baritone rumble. "Of course. No need for apologies, though; we have a lot to talk about. I have been involved with Israeli Intelligence my entire life. And as you can see, that has been quite a long time!" Myk grinned as Mordechai continued. "As you may have figured out, I was the Director of Mossad for twelve years, and I still look after Israel's safety—and will do so until they lay me in my grave. However, with you, Agent Myk, I have taken a personal interest."

Myk tilted his head. "How so?"

"I always made it my policy to refrain from making personal opinions on the parental decisions of others. In your case, however, I believe your mother did you a disservice by keeping you in the dark for so long while she raised you—"

"You mean while she trained me."

Mordechai smiled. "Actually, you are one hell of an agent because of her. Why she chose to shield you from the past is between you and her. Unfortunately, that leaves me with the painful and solemn duty to divulge some necessary facts about your family. I hope shedding some light on your mother's past will help bring clarity to you about the present."

"I am afraid Faraq beat you to the punch. He already told me about my grandfather's involvement in Heydrich's assassination and the massacre at Lidice."

"I see. Well, that's just the tip of the iceberg, Agent McGrath. As a side note, it was wonderful to hear how you and your cousin discovered one another. I believe the hand of Providence was at work. But I am afraid that before I go any further, I must offer you my deepest apologies for your father's death. He was a great man whom you never had the privilege of knowing. Regretfully, my first order of business is to let you know I am the one responsible for his death."

Myk stared at Mordechai, who held up his hand. "Please, please, hear me out. When I contacted you for the first time a few weeks ago to warn you of the spy in your agency, I told you I knew I could trust you because I knew your mother and father."

"Yes. I remember."

"At the time, you told me your father died in an automobile accident. Has your mother shared any other details with you about his death?"

Myk thought for a second, then replied, "No. She won't talk about it." He ran a hand through his brown hair. "It's been a source of tension between us. Of course, it didn't help that I thought her husband was my real father for the first eighteen years of my life. So you can imagine my shock and confusion when I found out my biological father died before I was even born."

Mordechai shook his head. "Like I said, I am not quite sure why your mother chose to keep those things from you, but I think she was determined to conceal from you that she had been a Mossad agent."

Myk's eyes widened. "Really?!" He paused. "A Mossad agent, eh? Of course, now it makes sense."

"She was a member of my team. Your parents were part of a secret organization called the Nazi Hunters, and they were damn good agents."

Waves of astonishment washed over Myk, but along with them came refreshing clarity that drowned out his lingering frustration. He leaned forward as Mordechai talked. "The night your father died, I was supposed to be his backup, but I got distracted and, in my weakness, let my guard down. It is a moment I will forever regret."

"So what happened?"

"I left my post . . . and that's when it happened."

"What?"

"Your father and another agent were in a car parked on Kensington Gore Street, a block away from a suspect we had under surveillance in London. One of our informants must have blown our cover, because I had only left my post for about ten minutes when I heard the gunfire. Your father managed to get off a few shots and wound the attacker, but his own wounds were fatal."

Mordechai looked down and shook his head, then the corners of his lips twitched in a wry smile. "The assailant made the mistake of fleeing the scene and running north, directly into the path of our first agent to arrive. Had he chosen to go south, he would have gotten away. When he came within ten feet of our oncoming agent, he was dropped in his tracks with one bullet between his eyes. The agent who shot your father's assassin was none other than your mother."

Myk's entire understanding of his mother fell apart. He knew nothing about her. He braced his fingertips against his temples and shook his head.

Mordechai stared through the large window at the movement of the fog and the boats that bobbed up and down along the dock. "When I heard the first shots of the ambush, I ran back to the window and saw your mother Hannah fire her single shot. Then she stepped around the body of the man she had just shot as if it were excrement on the ground and ran to your father's car. We removed his body and the other agent and returned to Israel before the police arrived. She and I spoke at length on the flight back, but that's the last time I ever spoke to or saw your mother."

"It doesn't make sense; why did she disown her sister for all these years and blame his death on her?"

"It was your Aunt Rachel who came to my door that evening when I should have been at my post. We had fallen in love. It was my birthday, and she had brought me a pastry from the bakery across the street."

"The bakery on Kensington Gore?"

"Yes. Why do you ask?"

"Every year around Hanukkah, we received a package of baked goods from that bakery."

"I see. You're connecting the dots. Well, as you know, surveillance work can get monotonous. I let my guard down for just that moment, and that's when they struck. Only your mother knew about our relationship, and she had warned Rachel to remove herself from the operation. That must be why she stopped speaking to her sister. She was pregnant with you and blames her sister for your father's death."

Myk shook his head. "Why didn't Aunt Rachel take a leave of absence?"

"Actually, a better question would be why didn't I remove Rachel from the team. After all, it was my operation. We talked about it, and she begged to stay on since we had finally found the Nazi we were looking for, Dieter Wisliceny. Dieter's father was the commander in charge of the slaughter at Lidice. As a boy, Dieter may have even fired several shots at those lined up on the side of the barn that day."

An image of a Nazi commander showing his impressionable young boy how to murder innocent people appeared in Myk's head. He glowered and curled his lip in disgust. Mordechai looked up at Myk, then continued.

"As the Nazis' defeat neared, Dieter's father helped the Nazis hide the wealth stolen from the Holocaust. We had Dieter under surveillance the night your father was murdered. After the incident, he disappeared. The only consolation was that your mother had killed his son Erik. Every birthday reminds me of your father's death. And that is why, Agent McGrath, I have taken such an interest in you."

Myk sat up. "Wow. I guess that explains a few things. Did you ever find Dieter Wisliceny again?"

"No. Actually, I think that was the straw that finally broke the camel's back, so to speak, for your mother."

"How so?"

"We had gotten so close to Dieter I think the whole incident spooked him. That's when he brokered a deal with the CIA in exchange for diplomatic immunity and was put into the witness protection program."

Myk's voice hardened. "You're shitting me. How could they make a deal with a Nazi?"

"It's simple, actually. He ratted out a whole list of other Nazis. His list led to the largest number of Nazi war criminals ever captured."

Myk stood and rubbed the back of his head. "Damn."

"There's more, Agent McGrath."

Myk furrowed his eyebrows. "More? Okay, go on."

"The name of the CIA supervisor who managed the deal with Dieter was a young agent named David Adelberg."

Myk groaned. "I guess that's why my mother calls him a traitor every time I bring his name up. It never made sense until now, but then again, these last ten minutes have opened up a new reality for me that will take a while to process. Actually, quite a bit about my mother didn't add up until now."

Mordechai reached across and gripped Myk's arm. His eyes glistened as he spoke in a soft voice. "Myk, words cannot convey how sorry I am for depriving you of a lifetime of experiences with your father."

Myk placed his other hand on Mordechai's shoulder. "Look, if he didn't get killed on that operation, he may have been killed on some other mission. It's hard for me to have feelings for a man I never knew. Besides, thank God it wasn't my mother who died that day, or I wouldn't be here. I don't need to tell you. It's part of the business; it comes with the territory."

Mordechai nodded as Myk continued, "I've got another important question, though. When you first contacted me, you said there was a mole in our agency. What information do you have?"

"Unfortunately, only enough to let you know you needed to be careful who you trusted and what information you divulged."

Myk replied, "Ever since your call, I have been very careful. Only a few people even know I'm alive. What intelligence can you share with me?"

Mordechai shifted in his seat. "We contacted Director Adelberg to warn him an attack was being planned on U.S. soil. We based part of our intel on a meeting we uncovered in Karachi, Pakistan. One of the attendees at the meeting was an old Nazi confined to wheelchair. The Nazi had gathered with half a dozen members of an al-Qaeda network loyal to Saji Aman."

"I know. Director Adelberg told us they had gotten a tip from Mossad."

"True, but Mossad wasn't exactly forthcoming about everything."

"How so?"

"The CIA doesn't know that the man in the wheelchair had dropped off Mossad's radar several decades earlier. They didn't want to lose him again, so they gave the CIA a different name. The man in the wheelchair was Dieter Wisliceny. He had finally reared his head out of whatever hole he'd been hiding in, so we gave him a different name. I don't really give a damn how old or decrepit Dieter is now. I have unfinished business with that Nazi bastard—"

Myk leaned across the table. "I want him, Mordechai! Let me help. Most people think I'm dead anyway, so I can operate under the radar. What can I do?"

"I anticipated this reaction. Unfortunately, we reached another dead end. We traced communication to Florida, but that's it. We are confident he has a source inside Langley, because some communication originated there. That's why I warned you."

Myk reached into his pocket and pulled out Hakeem's cell phone. "Maybe this will help. This was Hakeem's. He received a call from the U.S. while I was with him, so hopefully your agents can find something." He handed the phone to Mordechai. "So why do you think we received the package of treats from the bakery in London every year at Hanukkah?"

Mordechai smiled. "Your mother and her sister had become friends with the young woman who owned the bakery during the weeks we had Dieter under surveillance. She was the first one to console your mother and the only person who ever knew about the incident. We cleaned up and returned to Israel within hours." Mordechai paused. "Why did you leave the Israeli Army? They had never seen anything like you. You would have shot up the ranks like a star."

Myk thought for a moment. He had never discussed why he left, not even when his mother had pressed him. "After Madrid, I guess I just wanted to make a difference."

"But you could have made a difference with Israel."

"Look, no offense to Israel, but I felt I could do more with the assets of the U.S. intelligence. As long as terrorists kill innocent people, I'll be around to kill the terrorists. I've carved out my own niche in the food chain just to prey on terrorists. They'll always have to look over their shoulder for guys like me."

As the sky went from turquoise to a fiery red and then to a cool indigo, Myk shared what he knew about his Aunt Rachael, and Mordechai shared everything he could about Myk's father.

The following day as Myk waited in the airport with his aunt and cousin, his phone vibrated. It was Mordechai.

"Myk, we traced the call from the phone you gave us. The call originated out of Langley from an Agent Luke Stanford. Do you know him?"

Myk scoffed. "Damn. Yes, I know him. He's what the Agency calls a targeter, one of our best. The CIA assigns them to dig up as much information as they can on high-profile terrorists. He was Khatchi's targeter."

"He's dirty, Myk."

A few seconds of silence stretched out until Mordechai broke the silence. "Are you still there?"

"Sorry, I was just making a connection. Now it makes sense. Stanford must have set up the ambush when we went in to grab Khatchi last year."

"If Stanford is the CIA mole, then he's our only connection to Dieter Wisliceny. I can't lose Dieter again, Myk. I don't care how old he is. If I find him, I'm taking him back to Israel with or without your government's permission."

"I'll call Director Adelberg and have him detained."

"No. Agent Stanford can't know he's been outed. I need you to leave that phone call to me."

An announcement came on over the overhead terminal speakers that his flight was ready to board.

"I've got to board my flight. Are you sure you don't want me to call?"

"Absolutely. Catch your flight, and we'll talk when you land."

---

Minutes after Mordechai's conversation with Myk, Director David Adelberg's phone vibrated. He finished his conversation with an agent and answered his phone on the second ring. "Hello."

"David, it's Mordechai."

"Of course. Do you have any more information?"

Mordechai cleared his throat. "Yes, I have some very alarming intelligence. Unfortunately, I am in the precarious position of whether or not I should share the information with you."

"Well, I'm assuming you've made that decision, since you already made the call. What do you want in exchange?"

"Trust."

Adelberg walked into an empty room off from the Command Center and closed the door behind him. "Okay. I'm listening."

"I need the name and location of Dieter Wisliceny when he entered into your witness protection program."

Adelberg nodded. "When you first contacted me about the Nazi meeting in Karachi, I had a feeling it might have been him, so I put out a search for him. Unfortunately, he's covered his tracks. He went off the grid over five years ago. I would give you his name, but what good would it do at this point?"

"That was expected. David, I can flush him out, but to do that, I have to trust you with the information. The last time I did that, Dieter disappeared forever into the abyss of your witness protection program. As you would expect, many Israelis never forgot that. If I give you the information, I need your word you'll let me take him back to Israel. Do we have an agreement?"

Without hesitation, Adelberg said, "Of course. What do you need?"

"I can link Dieter directly to someone in your agency. If I give you the agent's name, I need your word you won't arrest him. He's our only link to the Nazi. I need you to leak the information that Agent Myk McGrath is alive and made a connection between Hakeem and Dieter. It should spook the agent enough that he'll try a warn Dieter. If he takes the bait, he will lead us right to Dieter. Deal?"

"Absolutely. What's the agent's name?"

After hesitating, Mordechai replied, "Luke Stanford. Agent McGrath gave us Hakeem's phone, and our Mossad team traced the call from Agent Stanford." The room spun a bit around Adelberg as he processed the information. Luke Stanford. He put a hand to his forehead.

"David," Mordechai continued. "I have no idea what his motivation is; everyone's got a price, I guess. I suspect it's something deeper, though. He wanted to see Israel's destruction."

# Chapter 31

## Miami International Airport

As the flight attendant announced that they were making their final approach, Myk glanced at his Aunt Rachael. Her hands shook, and her lip quivered as she stared out the window. He took her hand.

"Are you okay?"

A tear rolled down her cheek as she turned to him. "The last time I was in your country, you were just a baby. Your mother stopped communicating with me years ago. We moved on with our lives, and I'm just not sure this will turn out as you had hoped." She glanced out the window, then back at Myk. "Are you sure you shouldn't have told her we were coming? I mean . . . seeing you alive will be a lot for her to handle. But then for her to see me after all these years . . . it just might be too much for her to handle. I don't want her to think I'm taking advantage of the situation."

Myk shook his head and leaned close to her. "My mother was wrong to keep you from us all these years. You have nothing to be nervous about. I have been looking forward to this moment ever since I met Faraq. Everything will be just fine, I promise."

The plane touched down and taxied to the terminal. When it stopped, Myk stood and got his items out of the overhead compartment, then stretched his legs. After waiting for those in front of them to exit, they stepped off the plane and walked through the doorway into the expansive, crowded airport.

Before Myk could get his bearings, four FBI agents rushed in and slammed Faraq to the ground. Cameras flashed around them like a paparazzi circus. Myk reached into his pocket and pulled out his CIA identification, then ran to the senior agent on the scene and flashed his ID.

"What the hell is going on here?! I am escorting this man. Who ordered this arrest?"

The FBI agent looked at his CIA identification. "Agent McGrath, we were given orders to arrest Faraq Majed the minute he got off the plane. I was only told that he's supposedly the mastermind behind the recent attacks."

Myk's face flushed, and the veins in his neck swelled. "I am telling you right now you've got the wrong man. You will embarrass yourself and your agency if you don't release him right now. Who ordered this?"

"The order came down directly from the Department of Justice."

"Who? Who at the DOJ ordered this?!"

"It came all the way from the top, the AG Derek Helter."

Myk shook his head. "Where in the hell did all the media come from?"

"It wasn't us, that's for sure, so it must have been the DOJ."

Myk caught up with Faraq as agents led him through the terminal handcuffed with reporters and photographers following the entire way. "Faraq, I will find out what's going on here. Trust me, someone made a serious mistake. Don't worry. I'll get you out of this."

Rachael ran to Myk and grabbed his arm. "Myk, what's happening? Why are they treating Faraq that way?"

"I am not sure. I'm afraid to tell you what I think might be happening, so I'll make a few phone calls and let you know. But Faraq will be joining us when you see your sister again."

He took his aunt to one of the airport restaurants and told her to enjoy a good meal and to watch a little American television. He would be back shortly with news on Faraq. After finding a vacant gate, he called Brodie Bashford, who answered after a few rings.

"Brodie Bashford speaking."

"Brodie, it's Myk. We just got off the airplane in Miami, and the FBI completely bull-rushed Faraq and arrested him the minute he got off the plane. I thought you cleared his name off the No Fly List? What the hell's going on? This place was buzzing with reporters, too!"

"We did clear his name to fly, Myk. We've been watching the whole thing unfold on the news right in front of us. I can't remember the last time I saw Director Adelberg so mad. We're on our way to the Department of Justice right now. I just hope he doesn't blow a gasket."

Myk's voice rose. "I hope he does blow a gasket! Someone will pay for this. Faraq is innocent, Brodie. If it wasn't for his help, you wouldn't have gotten Jaffa Banzel or stopped the plot in Los Angeles or Israel or anything."

"I know, I know. Myk, I have to call you back; we're on our way up to the DOJ right now."

# Chapter 32

## Department of Justice, Washington D.C.

///

Director Adelberg and Brodie Bashford took the elevator to the top floor of the Attorney General's office. Adelberg's face no longer remained beet red, but he still breathed hard and stared at the digital elevator numbers tick away as though willing it to move faster. He gripped a manila envelope in his hands.

When the President nominated Derek Helter as Attorney General, the decision had sparked a major battle between the Justice Department and the CIA. There had been a rift between the two ever since. Prior to his appointment as Attorney General, Derek Helter's firm had represented numerous enemy combatants held at the Guantanamo Bay detention facility. Almost all of the combatants his firm represented who were released, later blew themselves up in Iraq, killing many innocent Iraqis and Americans. The CIA kept tabs; eight American soldiers and forty-two innocent Iraqis had been killed by terrorists represented by Helter's firm. Adelberg held Helter responsible for those deaths.

Adelberg caught terrorists, and Helter got them released. Helter, whom the media considered a darling, got a free pass, so few Americans knew of his contempt for the previous American foreign policy. It only took two months before Adelberg refused to call Helter by his proper title and instead referred to him as "The Hater."

Stepping off the elevator, Adelberg walked directly to the desk of the assistant for the AG.

"Take me to Helter."

The assistant frowned, then called Helter. After he hung up, the assistant turned to Adelberg. "I'm sorry, sir. Attorney General Helter is on a very important conference call and won't be free for at least another hour."

"I see." Adelberg put both hands flat on the desk, leaned forward, and said almost in a whisper, "You tell him I scheduled a press conference in thirty minutes downstairs on the front steps. Tell him I have information I would like to share with the press about Hugo Mendez."

He leaned back and folded his arms. Helter's assistant relayed the information, then put the phone down. "The Attorney General will see you now."

Adelberg smiled as he walked to the large set of double doors and shoved them open. Helter sat at his desk, fixing his gaze on a file in his hands, when Adelberg and Bashford walked in. He looked up with a half-lidded gaze and the faint trace of a sneer.

"Director Adelberg, what brings you in?"

"Wipe that pompous look off your face, you piece of shit! You know damn well why I'm here. Why are you using Faraq as your picture boy?"

"Jaffa Banzel implicated Faraq as a key player in these terrorist attacks. You should've thought twice before having your thug Agent Sanchez rough him up. He already pressed charges and named names. You can tell Agent Sanchez he won't have a job tomorrow." Helter scowled at the men. "Director Adelberg, you should get a little more control over the loose cannons running around your agency. Our country should set the example of civility. If it weren't for antics like this from your agents, our country wouldn't find itself at odds with terrorists in the first place."

Adelberg chuckled as he furrowed his eyebrows and squinted at Helter. "Did you come up with that all by yourself, or does it come from that great Ivy League education of yours? C'mon, you're smarter than this. That form of reasoning defies common sense. You should know Jaffa Banzel tried to attack Agent Sanchez after we obtained a perfectly legal search warrant. We have two witnesses, so your allegations will never stick, and you know it. He tried to attack my agent and got his ass kicked." He held up two fingers. "Second, and probably more important, suppose Jaffa did get a broken nose. Are you going to sit there and tell me the lives of thousands of Americans aren't worth the broken nose of a fucking terrorist?"

Helter sat forward. "If you haven't noticed, Director Adelberg, there's a new sheriff in town, and I have a better way of doing things than my predecessors."

Adelberg folded his arms. "Aha. I see. How's the administration's new olive branch policy with the terrorists working out so far? If you didn't notice, your new friends just attacked us again."

Helter stared. Adelberg continued, "I'll tell you how it's working out, you ignorant, complacent jackass. They laugh at your weakness and infiltrate weak minds with their dogma while you talk nice to them!"

"I am not releasing Faraq."

Adelberg leaned forward on the desk. "The hell you're not. With Faraq's help, Myk McGrath almost singlehandedly broke up Hakeem's terrorist ring, and they probably gave the Saudis a few things to think about for the next several years before they ever fund any al-Qaeda cells again."

Helter narrowed his eyes. "Are you saying your agency had something to do with the violence in Saudi Arabia last week?"

"I said nothing of the sort. Listen, Derek." He threw the manila envelope on Helter's desk. "I'm tired of wasting my breath on your sorry ass. Here's the deal. I scheduled a news conference to take place on the front steps in a few minutes . . . with or without you. The news conference can go two ways. I can share the details of the pictures in front of you. Take a look. I think you might enjoy them."

As Helter thumbed through the pictures, his face paled.

Adelberg continued, "Or you can tell the press you are personally responsible for the huge mistake and that Faraq has already been released. It's your call. I'll be waiting downstairs with the press for your answer."

He gave Helter a half smile as he turned with Brodie Bashford and walked to the door. Just before they stepped out of the office, Adelberg turned back. "You'll be happy to know that Khatchi got justice served to him. Sorry you didn't get that camera time you wanted on that one . . . but there are plenty of cameras waiting for you downstairs."

Helter raised his hand off the desk and flipped them both off. Adelberg slapped Bashford on the back as they walked out. He couldn't contain his ear-to-ear grin.

# Chapter 33

## Florida

---

Myk looked at his phone as it lit up. It was a text message from Bashford. A few seconds later, his phone vibrated.

"This is Myk."

"Hey, Myk. Good news. I just texted you the FBI location where they are holding Faraq. You can go pick him up."

"Damn. That was quick. What happened?"

"The DOJ got their nose bent out of shape when they lost their high-profile trial of Khatchi. Anyway, The Hater copped an attitude with David, who shared a few photographs he'd been saving for such an occasion. Fifteen minutes later, Helter told the national media he'd made a mistake. Myk, I wish you could've been there to see Helter in front of the cameras! I thought his head would explode! I don't think I've ever seen David smile so much."

Myk laughed. "I wish I could have been there too! So what was in the photos?"

"I can't give you specifics, but I'm pretty sure it had something to do with Helter receiving money for presidential pardons a few years ago. The money came from an unnamed member of a certain drug cartel."

"Interesting. Brodie, one more thing. Did they recover the EMP weapon in L.A.?"

"No. That's the one bit of bad news we have. Someone must have tipped them off because the weapon never showed up. It's still out there."

---

Myk flipped his turn signal on as he exited the I-95 for Boca Raton. His mother lived a few minutes away in a newly renovated condominium that fronted the beach and had direct access to the ocean from the back patio. Faraq sat in the back seat of the rental car while Rachel sat in the front passenger's seat.

Confused by what he'd learned about AG Derek Helter, Faraq leaned forward and asked Myk, "Why do so many people in your government feel it is necessary to cater to those who hate your country so much?"

Myk paused for a minute while he tried to figure out the best way to answer. He glanced in the rear view mirror. "It would take a few hours to give you the proper answer your question deserves. But if I had to summarize it, I would say two of the United States' greatest presidents, Abraham Lincoln and Ronald Reagan, called our country 'the last best hope for mankind.'"

Faraq looked away as Myk gave him a moment to reflect on the statement, then continued. "Most people would agree the United States has done more to raise the standard of living and elevate mankind to a higher plane in its very short history than any other nation. That being said, our country has made mistakes as well. So, to answer your question, a small number of people with a very loud voice have made it their life's ambition to use some of our country's mistakes to justify tearing it down. They focus on our faults instead of all the good we have done."

Faraq nodded. "Makes sense, I guess."

Myk pulled into the driveway of his mother's condominium and parked. He turned to his aunt, whose eyes had already filled with tears. "Are you ready?"

She wiped her eyes with the back of her hand. "Yes. I want you to know I really missed her all these years. Now that we're sitting outside her house, my mind is flooded with memories of her; she was my best friend for so long."

Myk's own throat tightened as he looked at her. He put his hand on hers. "I'm sure she missed you too. Let's go inside."

The three got out of the car and walked to the front door. He texted Jen, who had arrived the night before. She opened the front door with a smile, and Myk kissed her. "Where is she?"

Jen's smiled faded. "She's sitting down at the beach."

"Is she okay?"

"Not really. It's been a rough few weeks, and she's frustrated with the agency because they won't give her more details. She can't figure out what to do about a funeral for you."

The thought of his mother sitting alone on the beach mourning her dead son compounded his tight throat, and tears stung his eyes. He looked down, then shook his head. "Now I really feel bad. But it was for her own protection." Myk turned to his aunt. "Aunt Rachel, this is the girl I told you about. This is Jenifer Webster."

Jen hugged Rachel. "It's a pleasure to finally meet you."

Myk turned to them. "Why don't you follow me outside? I think it might be best if you wait on the back patio while I go down to the beach and talk to her. Give me a few minutes with her, and then I'll signal for you to come down when the time is right."

Rachel dabbed her eyes with a tissue. Myk hugged her. "C'mon. This moment has been too long in the waiting."

They followed him out to the back patio and waited while Myk and Jen walked down to the beach where his mother Hannah sat in her beach chair, staring out at the waves crashing on the beach. When Myk came within ten feet of her, she turned her head halfway to the side, then adjusted herself in the beach chair so she could turn her head all the way around.

She froze. Then, she stood to face Myk. As she brought both hands up to her face, she sobbed and fell to her knees in the soft, dry sand. Between the tears and sniffing, she said over and over again, "Thank you, God. Thank you. Thank you."

He knelt down in the sand beside her and wrapped his arms around her. Amid her sobs, she said, "I knew you were alive. I just knew God wouldn't take another from me. How are you here?"

"Mom, you can actually thank your sister." He paused. "Her son, Faraq, saved my life."

She looked up, her face wet. "What?" She paused. "What are you saying?"

"Your nephew. He saved my life. I brought him with me so you can thank him yourself. And Rachel is here too. They're waiting up on the back patio."

He stood and pointed to Rachel and Faraq. Then he motioned them to come down and join him. Rachel and Faraq clambered down through the sand as Hannah stood and attempted to wipe the stream of tears from her face.

"Oh my God. I can't believe it's her! What's happening? Can she ever forgive me? Look at her . . . oh, how I missed her!"

Tears flowed anew as Hannah stretched out her hands to Rachel, seventy feet away. Rachel looked up at her sister's outstretched hands and ran through the thick white sand. The two sisters held each other in a tight embrace as they swayed back and forth and sobbed uncontrollably.

"I am so sorry, Rachel. Please forgive me. I missed you so much." They cupped one another's face in their hands as their foreheads met while they laughed and cried together.

When tears filled Myk's own eyes and his nose burned, he took a few steps back and turned toward the ocean as the glimmering sun sank and then paused at the ocean's edge. As the waves rolled to shore, he tried to regain his composure. After a few minutes, Jen's soft hand slipped into his. They stood before the ocean's gentle waves slapping the beach as his mother talked and laughed with her sister behind them.

# Chapter 34

Part of him wanted the moment to last forever. Nothing touched his peace—Saji, Hakeem, Khatchi. Nothing disturbed the calm that came with the swell of happiness in his chest, Jen's soothing touch, or the slow rush of the waves. How could he bring the demon of distant memories roaring back to the present? He might just let Mordechai move on without him. After all, hadn't Myk's mother been guilty of hiding an arsenal of bombshell secrets herself?

The internal debate didn't last long. Myk decided to wait a few hours before he told her a ghost from her past, Dieter Wisliceny, had finally been caught. Agents had taken him to a secure location an hour's drive north. The Nazi war criminal had overseen the entire town of Lidice eradicated from the map; he had pulled the trigger as just a young boy, and murdered innocent Jews. He had caused the death of Myk's father, recently funded the attack that had caused the largest massacre of Jewish people on American soil, and nearly brought Israel to the brink of war with Iran. After they had all walked back up to the beach house, Myk spoke to his mother alone on the back patio.

"Mom, Dieter Wisliceny was caught."

She didn't even ask him how he knew who Dieter Wisliceny was. She didn't scowl or cry. Instead, she asked, "Where are they holding him?"

"Mordechai is holding him in a facility an hour away."

Hannah blinked. "Can I see him?"

After a phone call to clear it, he agreed. Mordechai could even use her as an additional witness to verify Dieter's identity.

---

The drive to meet Mordechai was the longest hour of Myk's life. Hannah stared out the window. Just a few hours earlier, she had wept tears of joy after reuniting with her sister, but now she sat frozen, lost in memories.

Myk broke the silence. "Why, Mom? Why didn't you share any of this with me?"

She stared out the window.

"Is there anything else? What else are you keeping from me?"

She adjusted herself in the seat and looked at Myk with glistening eyes. She hesitated, then turned back and looked out the window. Myk drove in silence. She cleared her throat as she stared into space, then said in a quiet voice, "Your father had a younger brother. He may still be alive." She paused, then continued, "I am sorry, Myk. Things are very complicated, as you will soon find out. I did what I thought was best."

"Why the secrets, Mom?"

She replied with one word, a Hebrew word. "*Shomer.*"

Myk squinted at the road ahead. The word meant "protector."

"Protector? Am I supposed to know what you mean by that?"

Hannah shook her head and sighed. "I hoped we would never have this conversation." She paused and took a deep breath. "This family has sacrificed too many men for Israel. I didn't want to lose you too, Myk."

"So you took it upon yourself to keep it from me? Don't you think that would be something I would like to know?"

"No. You are my son. My father, grandfather, and great-grandfather all died too young. I know you, Myk. You would've felt some sort of honor to follow in their footsteps. Israel can fend for herself now. This is one secret I wish I could have taken to my grave." Within minutes, they arrived at a gated community of large plantation-style custom homes scattered on two- and three-acre lots. As he approached the gate, two CIA agents waved him through. He drove past fifteen spacious homes with impeccably manicured green lawns and landscapes—and CIA and FBI agents securing the community's perimeter. Myk parked in front of Dieter Wisliceny's home.

"We're here. I want to learn more about this when we finish with Dieter. Who are these 'protectors' anyway?"

Hannah glanced up at the house. "When we have time, I'll share what I know. They originate from the stonemasons of King Solomon's Temple in Jerusalem."

He looked at his mom but said nothing. His head swam with questions. Then, with a sigh, he turned back to the house. Six other vehicles parked out front, and nine agents remained posted at different locations. As he and his mother walked along the drive toward the front entry, they passed not CIA or FBI agents but Mossad agents. Mordechai and his team had the place in complete lockdown. He and Director Adelberg had agreed that Mossad agents would carry out the mission while the U.S. agents secured the community's perimeter. The front door remained open but before entering, Myk turned to his mother.

"Are you sure you want to do this?"

She nodded, then stepped through the door, almost pushing him out of the way as if on a mission. Once inside, they approached a Mossad agent standing at the top of a long flight of stairs leading down to the basement.

Hannah asked the agent in Hebrew, "Where is he?"

The agent tilted his head and motioned down to the basement. Myk's mother strode forward and descended the stairs, leaving Myk to scramble after her down two flights of glass stairs. The bottom opened up into a spacious entertainment room with a wet bar and a massive wine room behind it. Myk and his mother walked through the room and to a door in the back, which led to a large theatre where four men awaited them: Mordechai, Adelberg, an old man in a wheelchair, and another man handcuffed to the billiard table in the middle of the room.

Hannah barked out fluid Hebrew to Mordechai. Before he finished responding, Myk said, "In English, please!"

Mordechai pointed to Adelberg. "She wants to know what the 'traitor' is doing here. Director Adelberg and I have come to an agreement that will allow us to take the Nazi back to Israel."

From the other side of the room, the old man in the wheelchair asked in a heavy German accent, "Who's the Jewish whore?"

The hairs on the back of Myk's neck stood up as he suppressed his urge to rush the decrepit old man and rip his head off.

Mordechai responded, "Hannah is here as a witness to identify you, Dieter. I am taking you back to Israel. You escaped us forty years ago, but Israel will have its justice."

Dieter spat out a forced laugh. "Not before I killed hundreds more Jews at that wretched Jewish wedding in New York a few weeks ago. And I damn near got Israel to start a war with Iran. Too bad. That would have been the end of Israel for good!"

Mordechai asked, "Hannah, I have to be sure. For the record, is that him?"

She glared across the room, her light eyes bright and sharp as ice. "I don't know. Maybe I should get a better look."

She made her way around the billiard table toward Dieter. When she got within a few feet of his wheel chair, she recoiled and slapped his face with an open hand so hard she lost her balance. His saliva splattered on the window across the room, and a bright red handprint appeared on his old wrinkled face. Then, she spat into his eyes and looked back to Mordechai.

"Yes, that wretched piece of flesh is Dieter Wisliceny." As she walked back to Myk, she passed Luke Stanford, who remained handcuffed to the billiard table.

"Who's he?"

Mordechai answered, "His name is Luke Stanford, Dieter's insider who infiltrated the CIA." He paused, then added in a more somber tone, "And . . . we just found out he is Dieter's grandson."

Myk's stomach instantly dropped. Hannah spun toward Adelberg. "My God, David. Look what you've done. You made a deal with the devil, and now he spilt Jewish blood on your own soil. May God forgive you, because I won't! How could you allow his grandson to work in your agency? Could you possibly be that incompetent?"

Adelberg stood motionless and then said, "I will investigate it."

As Dieter wiped the gooey spit from his eyes, he grinned. "Now I remember you. You're the pregnant wife of the Jew we killed in the streets of London decades ago. I never had the chance to properly thank you. If it hadn't been for your team getting so close to me, I may not have been able to spend so many years without a worry here in the United States under their witness protection program."

Hannah squinted at him. "One missing caveat, Dieter. A life without your only son. Take comfort in knowing the last thing your son saw was my face before I put the bullet between his eyes."

Dieter adjusted himself in his wheel chair. It appeared he hadn't known she was the one responsible for his son's death. Unconvincingly, he replied, "A worthy sacrifice for the cause. Besides, my grandson has proven quite capable."

Agent Stanford jerked on his cuffed hands and yelled back at him, "Shut up, you babbling fool! They have nothing on me yet."

Dieter continued, "We came so close again. You worthless Jews. How is life always looking over your back?"

"You ignorant piece of shit!" Hannah snapped back. "You couldn't be further from the truth. You and your way of thinking will be eradicated, not Israel or her people. The Jewish people pressed on and weaved our way into the fabric of almost every society, while those who fight against her come and go. You can take that fact to your grave!"

As she walked to Myk, she put her arm around his waist while still talking to Dieter. "When I stepped over your dead son in the streets of London that day, my son kicked within me. This is him." She pulled Myk tight up against her. "You can thank him for stopping your futile idea of killing more Jews."

She pulled his weapon from his holster. Myk reached for the gun. "Mom—"

"Quiet, Myk." She pointed the gun at Dieter. The tone in her voice sharpened. "Your father brought you to Lidice that day in June of 1942. After he ordered his men to slaughter the innocent people of the town, he gave a gun to you—just a boy—so he could train you in the Nazi ways. You animals murdered my parents that day, a mother and father I could only learn about from stories."

Mordechai said, "Hannah, leave the past. Put the gun down. He's not worth it. We'll take him back to Israel."

"Maybe." She replied. Then she swung her arm around and fired two shots. The blast deafened Myk for a moment with blinding pain in his ears, and he ducked out of reflex.

"Mom, what the hell have you done?!"

Agent Luke Stanford folded over the table to which his hands remained cuffed, curling over his bleeding abdomen.

Hannah turned to Dieter and waved the smoking gun at him. "You won't live without some measure of suffering. Look at your last glimmer of hope as he dies. You'll take this memory to your grave. You and your grandson do not deserve any additional breath of life without pain."

Myk pulled his cell phone out to call for an ambulance. His mother turned to him and pointed her gun at Dieter. "Disconnect the call, Myk. I'm sorry, son. I know it is against your nature to watch a man suffer, but these Nazi bastards are no men. Put the phone back in your pocket, or Dieter doesn't make the trip to Israel. If I wanted Agent Stanford dead, I would have shot him in the head. Dieter can suffer while he sits and watches his grandson take his last breath."

She straightened her arm and aimed at Dieter. Myk ended the call and put his cell phone back into his pocket. Hannah then turned to Luke Stanford, who wheezed and coughed up blood as more spilled across the edge of the table to drizzle on the floor.

"You sick son of bitch. What kind of person massacres innocent people at a wedding of all places? There is no Hell deep enough for your kind."

Mordechai piped in with his soothing baritone voice. "Hannah. There's been enough killing, justified or not. Let me have the gun."

"Not until he passes." She motioned toward Stanford.

Adelberg turned to her. "What have you done?"

She stared hard at Adelberg. "That bleeding waste of a human is responsible for the deaths of thousands of people this past month. Every breath he takes is one too many. I will not allow him the media coverage his trial would have most certainly attracted; it would have turned into a circus. That's not going to happen! Not to mention the other sick bastards out there who would have idolized him. This ends here, in the quiet basement of a home purchased with the blood of the Holocaust. He does not deserve the American justice system."

Glancing at Dieter, she snorted. "And as for Dieter, I will keep my promise I made as a Mossad agent over forty years ago: to return him to Israel alive, if possible. But if he's spending the rest of his days in Israel, he'll do it with the memory of this day and the image of his only bloodline dying in front him." She gritted her teeth as her stare pierced his eyes. "I hope this memory of the Jewish woman who wiped out your entire lineage torments you forever. Your son and grandson are dead because of you. Can your feeble old mind comprehend that fact, Dieter? You killed your posterity the day you killed my husband. If that episode hadn't occurred, your son and grandson would still be alive. You linked them together forever."

Stanford's head thumped motionless onto the floor. She peered over the billiard table; he had stopped breathing. Then she effortlessly flipped the gun around, like she had been handling guns her entire life, and handed it back to Myk.

Through the painful ringing in Myk's ears, the sound of a jet reverberated through the partially opened window. All three men looked around in a stupor, and memories of Myk's childhood and adolescence flooded him: learning to shoot at such a young age, the memorization games, the ability to read facial expressions, the survival camps instead of scout camps. She always trained him, always taught him about a culture or language. Most of his questions had vanished.

Mordechai spoke first. "David, this was not my intention. I'm afraid we have created a bit of a mess here. I hope you will stick to our agreement; I need to take him back to Israel."

"Of course," Adelberg replied. "But now I have to explain a dead body and a homicide. How can I, in good conscience, put Hannah into our legal system at her age, especially after what she's been through?"

Hannah, who spoke in a much more congenial tone, said, "David, let the judicial process run its course. My only concern is God's judgment. What I did here is between Him and me. I don't know if it makes any difference, but my conscience is clear."

Adelberg looked at Mordechai. "Could you sneak her back to Israel with your entourage?"

"Absolutely. But it's not up to me. Hannah, do you want to return to Israel with me?"

"Of course. Do I have to stay in Israel, or can I live with my sister in London?"

Mordechai replied, "First, we need to get you out of the country. What you do after that is your own business."

"All right then, I will leave with Mordechai. Are you okay with it, Myk?"

With a grin, he replied, "Beats the hell out of visiting you in prison."

Mordechai turned to Adelberg. "David, I'm sorry for the mess, but you know better than I that the sooner we leave, the better."

"I know. Take Dieter and Hannah with your team, and I will touch base with you in a few days." He reached into his pocket and threw his keys to Myk. "Take the cuffs off Agent Stanford. Leave your gun in his hand; this looks like a suicide to me. I want you to leave along with the rest of the Mossad team. I will take care of things here, so don't concern yourself with any of this. When all of you clear the front gate, I will call the outside CIA agents back to the house."

Myk said goodbye to his mother. He would arrange to send whatever belongings she wanted with her sister when she returned to London. The three black sports utility vehicles carrying the Mossad agents, his mother, and Mordechai drove past Myk as he got into his vehicle.

He drove slowly through the tree-lined community, turned onto the main road, and merged onto the highway. As he accelerated to catch up to the caravan of vehicles carrying his mother, two motorcycles screamed past him. They had to be going at least one-hundred and forty miles per hour.

He pushed the gas pedal to the floor and reached for his cell phone. Unless he could reach Mordechai, his mother and the others would soon be dead. A situation like this had played out in Iran years before in which Iran's top nuclear physicist had been killed in his car while driving home. A man on a motorcycle had pulled alongside him and attached a magnetic bomb to his vehicle.

Myk dialed the number while he tried to coax his rental car to go faster, but to no avail. The motorcycles turned into dots on the horizon. Seconds later, an orange fireball and a massive balloon of smoke exploded up ahead. A cold wave washed through Myk, dropping through the bottom of his stomach like a ball of ice. His breath caught in his throat.

He arrived at the scene a few minutes later to find one of the black SUVs blown to pieces, body parts and bits of the vehicle strewn about all over the highway and on the side of the road. Agents from the other vehicles had already put flares on the highway to redirect traffic. His mother and Mordechai stood off to the side near an untouched vehicle.

Myk's shoulders slumped as he sighed and pulled off. Hopping out, he ran to them. "Mordechai, I tried to warn you when the cycles sped past me, but they were going too fast. What happened?"

Mordechai shook his head. "They knew exactly which vehicle he was in, Myk. Someone really didn't want us to take the Nazi back to Israel. We tried to distance ourselves from the vehicle with the bomb. I am sorry, Myk. We can't stick around to see how this concludes. We can't be seen anywhere near this. We'll talk later."

He and Myk's mother got back into the vehicle. As they pulled away, the sirens from the first responders rose in the distance. Myk debated whether or not he should leave as well, but he decided to stick around. His phone vibrated, and when he looked at the caller ID, it read "private caller." He answered.

"This is Myk."

After a long pause, the caller spoke. "Agent McGrath, that attack is a warning to you. The Nazi is dead, and you have served your country well by containing the recent terrorist attack, but there is nothing left for you on this one. Move on. We know your mother is going to Israel, and we know about your secret marriage."

Myk ducked his head over the phone. "What the hell did you--"

"Agent McGrath, you have no idea who you're dealing with. Let things be, or people you know will pay the price for your stubbornness. You've been warned." The call went dead.

Myk ran his fingers through his hair as the sirens neared, and after a few moments, he decided he couldn't do much to help the local authorities. This would end up a federal matter anyway, so he decided to get to a place where he could clear his head and decide whether or not to heed the caller's advice.

As he pulled back onto the highway, it dawned on him that this was the first time he had been alone since Cancun. He reflected on how every seemingly insignificant event in his childhood led to this moment.

*Coincidence?*

The idea of plowing through that train of thought exhausted him, and he dropped it for now. Still, he grinned. The caller told him he had no idea who he was dealing with, but if the caller hadn't hung up so soon, Myk would have told him the same thing.

*You have no idea who you're dealing with.*

# Fact

On September 29th, 2011, undercover FBI agents arrested 26-year-old Rezwan Ferdaus, a U.S. citizen from Ashland, Massachusetts. Rezwan planned to use a model aircraft filled with C-4 plastic explosives against the Pentagon. Rezwan has a physics degree from Northeastern University in Boston.

# Fact

As a consequence of the assassination of SS Obergruppenführer Reinhard Heydrich outside of Prague, Adolf Hitler ordered the massacre of the town of Lidice. No adult males survived. On June 9th, 1942, every building was blown up and leveled to the ground. Lakes were filled in, streams were diverted, and farms and trees were flattened. Lidice was removed from all German maps.

# Fact

In 2001, the United States Congress authorized the formation of the United States EMP Commission. Its formal name is the Commission to Assess the Threat to the United States from Electromagnetic Pulse (EMP) Attack. An EMP damages electrical and electronic circuits by inducing voltages and currents that the circuits cannot withstand. On July 15, 1996, President Bill Clinton issued executive order No. 13010, which identified infrastructures critical to the nation's survival: telecommunications, electrical power systems, oil and gas storage, transportation, banking and finance, water supply systems, and emergency services. Unfortunately, a 2004 congressional report singled out these critical infrastructures as being vulnerable to EMP attack—and remain so today.

## Fact

In November 1941, Haj Amin Al-Husseini, a radical Islamist, met Adolf Hitler for the first time. The Nazis granted him political asylum and paid him a monthly salary of 20,000 Reichsmark for organizing Muslims in the Balkans and North Africa. Ernst Verduin, a Jewish Dutchman who survived Auschwitz 3 (The SS tattooed the number 150811 in his arm), testified that he saw Al-Husseini with approximately fifty men "wearing strange clothes and golden belts" accompanied by high-ranking SS at Auschwitz. The SS stopped Verduin when he tried to get a closer look. When he asked the guard who these men with strange clothes were, the guard told him Haj Amin Al-Husseini and his men were there to see the final solution being carried out so they could do the same to the Jews in Palestine.

## Fact

Attorney General Eric Holder was a senior partner in the prestigious law firm Covington & Burling. His firm secured victories for several Gitmo enemy combatants in the U.S. Court of Appeals. One of the detainees the firm fought to release later blew himself up in Mosul, Iraq, killing 13 soldiers and seriously wounding 42 others.

## Fact

Reinhard Heydrich was indeed called "the Hangman." One of the first things Heydrich did was imprison and execute five thousand anti-Fascist freedom fighters without a trial. He ordered that extra scaffolding be built to perform even more executions. The British operation called "The Anthropoid" was executed by Jan Kubis and Joseph Gabcik, who were dropped by parachute near Prague. On May 28th, 1942, they ambushed SS Reinhard Heydrich on his way to his office a few miles outside of Prague.

## Fact

Three days before the election on the morning of March 11, 2004, ten bombs exploded on four separate locations on the Cercanias commuter trains in Madrid, Spain. The terrorist attack occurred during the peak of the morning rush hour; 191 people were killed and 1,800 were wounded.

# Acknowledgements

Years ago it was my privilege to visit Holocaust Museum in Washington, D.C. While I wanted to linger and reflect, I had younger children who wanted to move on. While the world moves on, hopefully there will always be those of us who take a few moments to linger and reflect. We must never forget.

While I was in Shanghai my heart sank when I heard the news of the terrorist attack at the Boston Marathon. I had friends who ran the Boston Marathon that day. Fortunately they crossed the finish line much earlier. Many of my ideas for Defector in our Midst came from real events. I would not have been able to create Defector in our Midst without the help of numerous people. Thank you, Jeanette, for your patience and love. Heather and Lacy, thank you for your insight and time and hard work. Without you, this final product would not have been possible. Mitch, thanks for your help and great ideas. You were the inspiration for Myk's time in the Israeli Army. Thanks to Ken and Margaret Fitzgerald and Trish Walker who, despite a very rough first draft, encouraged me to carry on. Special thanks to Jeremiah, J. Brady, and her mom. Thanks to L. Bartnek and S. Braun and R. Wilson and to Jed. Thanks again to John Arnett. Thank you Devon. Thank you to the men and women who serve our country to keep watch over us against those who wish to do us harm.